P9-BZA-149

"ENGROSSING...
VIVID...COLORFUL....
I RECOMMEND IT."
—Steven Brust, bestselling
author of JHEREG
and PHOENIX

TRIAL BY SWORD!

Only twice before had I held a sword in my hands; I still didn't much like the feel of it. I couldn't think straight. None of this made sense. This wasn't how an acrobat was supposed to die, cut down by a swordsman, with a sword in his hands. Of old age, perhaps, or killed by a jealous husband or father, or by a fall from a trapeze, or a broken neck when doing a high dive-and-roll wrong.

Dun Lidjun and I squared off, him circling first to the right, then the left, me just holding the challenge sword out in front of me, hoping to block him . . .

D'SHAI

JOEL ROSENBERG

ACE BOOKS, NEW YORK

This one is for Mark J. McGarry:
writer, reporter, editor, copyeditor,
smartass, friend

This book is an Ace original edition,
and has never been previously published.

D'SHAI

An Ace Book / published by arrangement with
the author

PRINTING HISTORY
Ace edition / February 1991

ISBN: 0-441-15751-3

Ace Books are published by The Berkley Publishing Group,
200 Madison Avenue, New York, New York 10016.
The name "ACE" and the "A" logo
are trademarks belonging to Charter Communications, Inc.

Acknowledgments

I'm grateful for the help I've gotten with this one from Bruce Bethke, David Dyer-Bennet, Emma Bull, Peg Kerr Ihinger, Harry F. Leonard, Victor Raymond, and, particularly, Pamela Dean. Particular thanks to Beth Friedman, for the last-minute proofreading.

Special thanks to my agent, Eleanor Wood (she knows why) and to both Beth Fleisher and Susan Allison, for the sort of patience that Job would envy.

—J. R.

PROLOGUE

Way of the Runner

BEGIN WITH A secret: balance is the Way of the Runner.

Attention to balance is all; the rest will fall into place. Balance is not just the Way of the Runner; it is the way of D'Shai.

It was time to be going.

"I thank you, Innkeeper of Oled," Duerni Draven said, taking an oblong coin from his pouch. The thin coin was of dull copper, patinaed with age; he laid it on the smooth wood in payment.

Old Adan, the keeper of the Scion's Inn, who had spent part of the previous hour sharing gossip with Duerni Draven, fell silent. It was a commonplace to chat with a customer; it was another thing entirely to leave oneself open to an accusation that one had interfered with a runner.

Duerni Draven stood easily, his weight balanced as he hefted the half-empty tankard of bitter ale. He swallowed quickly, "eating like a runner," before he exited through the dust curtains and into the golden morning.

He had taken food and ale, and now it was time to be on his way before the spirits of the ale prevented him from raising kazuh. Once he had raised kazuh, nothing but his own will or his death could drop it; balance is the Way of the Runner.

The others of the fifty-two kazuhin had their own Ways; none could understand his. It wasn't speed, although that was the face a kazuh runner turned to the public.

A lie: speed is the Way of the Runner.

The truth, and the runner's secret: the balance created the speed. Speed was the effect, not the cause.

Balance is the Way of the Runner.

Duerni Draven, seventh of his line, knelt on the cold dirt, facing morningwise, letting the rising sun's red warmth wash over him in gentle benediction.

His twin packets of dispatches were, like his purse, already bound tightly to the belt around his waist, and tied firmly to his thighs. Other than the twisted cotton lotai about his loins, the belt was to be his only garment.

He stripped off his tunic, rose to one knee to unfasten his right sandal, then his left, then took the three steps forward, leaving his tunic and sandals behind him, ritually leaving everything except his duty, and his running, and his Running, behind him. Tense muscles already loosening in anticipation, he bent forward in the first of the Nine Stretches that would protect his tendons and muscles during his running.

The first hour of the day was the hour of the cock, and the first stretch was of the hamstring that existed to soften the impact of the balls of his feet—

The clattering of a horse's hooves interrupted his meditations. He turned to see a great white beast thundering through the town, passing him on the edge of the road. The red stripe diagonally across the rider's snow-white tunic told Duerni Draven that the horseman was one of the minor nobles of Lord Nerona's court, out for a morning canter. And while not even Lord Nerona himself would dare to interfere with a runner in the performance of his duties, there was no penalty for distracting him. A different matter entirely.

Duerni Draven returned to his meditations. There were nine, each named for an hour of the day.

Sometimes it was hard to concentrate, to push the world aside; he found himself noticing the clattering of hooves off in the distance, and the wind on his body, and the sun in his hair.

"Powers that Be," he said, quietly, in the Runner's Prayer, "a kazuh runner faces you. Let me raise kazuh, and be on my way, for I have duties to perform." The words were important, of course, but the attitude, the Way, was all.

He rose in the meditation of the first and second hours, the hours of the cock and of the hare: stretch the hamstrings, like a cock rising to announce the first hour of the day, and like a hare kicking out its leg before bounding into flight.

Meditation of the third hour, the hour of the horse: he tossed his head on his long neck, loosening the muscles that balanced his head.

Meditation of the fourth hour, the hour of the ox: leaning forward as though pulling a plow, he tightened and then eased the strong shoulders, the shoulders that would support his pumping arms.

Fifth and sixth meditations, the octopus and snake: whirl the arms, from the wrists to the shoulders, first gently, loosely, bonelessly, then swiftly, sharply, like a striking snake. Seventh and eighth, the bear and lion: squatting, spraddle-legged, he moved his body from one side to the other, stretching the muscles of the thighs, the pillars that supported the moving body, then leaped up, springing high into the air, like a cat bringing down a bird.

Ninth and last, for the hour of the dragon, the hour before dawn: like a dragon breathing frost, he expanded and contracted the chest, the temple that held the breath and balance of the Runner.

Breath was everything in the running, although as nothing in the Running.

Duerni Draven set off in a slow walk, leaving meditations, like his outer clothing, behind him. He knew that the innkeeper would launder and oil his linen and leather, making them clean and ready for Duerni Draven's next time in the Oled—

He stopped himself. He was letting his mind wander, and his mind must not be allowed to wander. Gently, he nudged his thoughts back to his running. The technique came first: keep the walk deliberately slow for the first league, ignoring the muscles that protested the languorous pace.

He walked: slowly, carefully, precisely. Form was everything. Step. Step. Step. His feet wanted to jog, to run, to fly, but he kept his pace slow.

Step. Step. Step.

After the first league, he let himself break into a brisk walk, and then took that to a light jog, concentrating on the land-and-roll of his feet, letting the heel take up the shock.

The road was cold and dirty, but empty of pebbles; pebbles, wheels, and Bhorlani were forbidden on D'Shaian roads, by order of the Scion of the Sky Himself. Lined by watching elms, the road clove straight through the golden fields toward the dark forest ahead. There it would twist and turn; here it was simple and direct.

His jog became a trot, his breath beginning to catch in his lungs. Still, he was running from the outside, not raising kazuh.

Never mind, he thought. *Never mind, nevermind, never the mind.*

The balance, not the mind. Balance is the Way

of the Runner: he sought to land easily, letting his body flow forward, not lurching as his speed increased, his pistoning arms and legs pumping as fast as the *thrum-thrum-thrum* of his heart.

Stepstepstepstepstepstepstepstepstepstep.

No matter. All was a matter of balance; he would hold himself in a sprint until he raised kazuh or died. Or both, in the Runner's Death.

Gradually, his stagger from balance to balance became a flow, always in equilibrium, each step a continuation of the previous one, no longer discrete.

Still, his lungs burned with distant fire, each moment became more painful than the last, but Duerni Draven did not concentrate on speed. Speed is nothing but an effect of balance, of form, of the flow of arms and legs, of the deep breath and the full release, of the inhaling and the ex—

And then, flaring together in mind and body like sudden fire from stirred ashes, the familiar miracle happened: Duerni Draven raised kazuh.

The needs of his body became distant and vague; not nonexistent, merely irrelevant.

His arms and legs seemingly slowed, moving with an exquisite, delicate languor, but the rest of the universe had slowed even more; from the corner of his eye, Duerni Draven glimpsed a redbird hanging in the air, its wings flapping lazily as it climbed into the day.

But it was unimportant; its glossy black and

fiery crimson faded, as did the blue of the sky, the cool green and warm brown of the watching elms, the black-spotted yellow of the daisies lining the wheat fields, until they all were pallid ghosts of themselves. Smells, too, went vague and distant. They, too, were unimportant.

Birds, trees, roads, fields, arms, legs, lungs— they were insignificant.

The Running was not important; the Running was all.

He Ran, and at the center of the Running, and at the center of Duerni Draven, there was a quiet peace, untouched by the movement of arms and legs, buoyed up by the slow intake and release of the unimportant air.

Duerni Draven Ran.

And when he passed the cantering horse and rider, only a small part of him could smile; there was, as always, not enough for it to reach his face.

He reached Den Oroshtai in the hour of the snake, the dirt still pounding beneath his feet.

Hours of Running were behind him, as was the forest, as were leagues of the fields and paddles surrounding Den Oroshtai. His Running was almost at an end. Ahead, the guard station of the lower town loomed, gray and vague at the limits of his perception.

The danger was always to bypass his destination, to continue Running.

It was the Runner's Death, the way Duerni

Draven's father had died, and his father, and his, all the way back to the beginning of the line. The Runner's Death: to Run across the land until the last threads of flesh and bone broke, leaving the spirit to race across D'Shai forever.

Oh, that would be a wonderful thing. That was always a temptation, to leave blood and bone behind.

But no. Not now.

Duerni Draven's time was not yet, so he dropped kazuh, and let the world come back.

He staggered up to the guard station, each step an agony of bruised muscles and battered bones. He became aware that he was panting, his breath ragged and painful, almost sobbing like a proud but beaten child. His heart pounded, although the pounding was already beginning to slow as he dropped into a walk. His naked body was covered with sweat and with dirt as he tottered to the guardpost, and the waistband of his lotai was painfully dank against his belly. Out of breath, he knelt at the guardpost, handing over the package of dispatches to the waiting guard captain, who examined the contents before handing it off to a rider.

"Runner, do you need anything?" the guard captain asked, his silver voice holding the purity and clarity that sounds always did when they became significant again.

"Water . . . Captain," he gasped out. "For drink. And for washing." Then rest, then food, and then more rest. The local keeper of the Scion's Inn would have linen and leather.

"Show him, Hervel." The chunky guard reached out a hand to help him, then drew it back.

A runner walks by himself.

As he was led away toward the local tavern, the guard captain grunted. "I don't suppose that he'd have almost killed himself running if he'd known all he had were some broadsides about an acrobatic troupe."

Duerni Draven chuckled. They didn't understand, they couldn't understand. The dispatches didn't matter; Lord Toshtai didn't matter; birds and fields and fire didn't matter.

Balance is the Way of the Runner.

1
No Splendor, Some Ceremony

BEGIN AT THE beginning, Gray Khuzud would always tell me. Proceed, with all the grace you can muster—and I know that's not much, but try, try, Kami Khuzud, you must try—until you reach the end.

Then stop, clean up after yourself, and put the props away.

So, obedient to command, I begin with the arrival of the troupe of Gray Khuzud in Den Oroshtai.

"They come;

"The Troupe of Gray Khuzud ar-rives," the soldiers at the battlements sang, their lovely four-part harmony growing stronger as we wound our way through the dusk, up the darkening road, toward the castle.

Lord Toshtai always insisted that his troops be of good voice, and while the war had worn some of his good intentions away at the edges, we were far away from those frayed edges, in Den Oroshtai. Firm, glassy young tenors mixed with heady baritones, bold bass voices supporting the structure of song.

"Wonders will be seen,

"We are sure.

"What wonders they will be,

"Will be re-vealed,

"In the hour of the snake."

They broke into a game of musical catch—a fugue, I think it's called—on that last phrase, which slowly faded.

"Not quite yet," Gray Khuzud said, "but let us prepare." He dropped his pack to the ground and loosened his tunic, and then bound it peasant fashion about his waist.

We all did the same, unworried about the possibility of theft. While stealing is in theory not permitted anywhere in D'Shai, it is D'Shai, after all—but Lord Toshtai's face was never turned from theft.

I shivered as the cold evening wind breathed against my chest; I had worked up a sweat as we climbed. I flexed my shoulders and hands, trying to work out the kinks.

Gray Khuzud hurried up the line, gesturing both tumblers and anchors into place, shaming careless Fhilt into better posture with a frown, favoring Large Egda with a quick, affectionate pat, tucking here and polishing there. There was a hint of nervousness in his fastidiousness, perhaps. Or perhaps not; I never really understood my father, and certainly there was nothing unusual in his taking pains on the troupe's entrance.

Finally, he arrived at the head of the line, and stopped in front of me. "Eldest Son Acrobat," he said, formally, as our names are always pronounced formally: Old Shai is formal for everything but names.

"Gray Khuzud," I responded, bowing properly, my eyes fixed on his. Gray Khuzud, of course, was always a mix of formal and casual, as was his name. There was no Old Shai translation of the first part of his name—it was not the light gray of the predawn, Erevair, nor the dirty gray of the late winter snows, Belen. He was never Gray Acrobat, never Erevair Khuzud, never Belen Khuzud: he was Gray Khuzud, always and only.

Gray as a rat, he was a fine figure of a man, even in his fifties, the muscles still firm beneath his broad chest, his belly flat and rippled like a washboard, the treetrunks of his legs solid as ever. The years had lined and creased his face until it looked and shone like old leather, and what was left of his hair was bound behind him in a long thin pigtail.

His powerful shoulders and arms were of flat, hard muscle, far stronger than they looked, but the hand that rested on my shoulder was a horror of horny ugliness. All our hands were. If you spent much of your life dangling and swinging from rings and ropes, your hands would be, too.

He was my father, and I loved him.

* * *

Stately jimsum trees bowing over us, the Troupe
of Gray Khuzud arrived at the castle in Den
Oroshtai without splendor, but with much ceremony.

Den Oroshtai is laid out like many of the
smaller lord's cities guarding the way to Seat of
the Scion: the keep is set on a hill above the village, a trail screwing its way up the side through
the thorny ironweed and astringent jimsum, past
the treeskin houses that are all the town-bound
peasants can afford, past the wooden homes of
the hill-dwelling middle class and the bourgeoisie, past the brick permitted the relatively minor
lords and ladies and the stone allowed the com-
paratively major lords and ladies, up toward
where the keep sits, its walls, towers and granaries dominating more than the view.

Springstream was a pretty time to be arriving
in Den Oroshtai: the savorfruit trees were just
into their first flower, buds popping scented
silken streamers into the air and turning the trail
misty and vague. Silk burst into momentary
flame at the touch of my torches, a fine ash set-
tling on my face and shoulders.

I jumped, startled, as the night high above the
castle burst into a silent explosion of light.

The soundless fireball faded, and the giant
translucent figure of a man loomed over the castle: fat and scraggle-bearded, a plain rope belt

holding his stained robes together. Behind him dim, wavering bottles and shelves and tools hung in the dark, battling with the stars for visibility.

"I see Narantir's dressing for the occasion," Fhilt muttered.

"Hush," Gray Khuzud said. "He's announcing us."

The image bowed deeply as it faded, and was immediately replaced by that of a massive black bear, its arms spread wide, its mouth open to reveal yellowing teeth.

A golden lion, its mane too rigid and immobile to be real, leaped upon the back of the bear.

"I've seen better lions," Enki Duzun whispered. "Narantir probably carved the model himself."

"With an axe, I'd wager," Fhilt said.

"From pine, it would seem," I said. "And not very good pine, at that—I saw a knothole."

The bear disappeared, leaving the lion to prance woodenly until a frosty breath turned it to ice, then shattered the ice into a shower of blue sparks.

We didn't see the dragon, of course. I don't know enough about mahrir, wizard-magic, to know why, but even the representation of dragons involves dangers that make wizards hesitant to manipulate their images. It was one thing for Narantir to take some carvings or paintings in his study, and magnify and transform their images using some magical principle or other—but there

is magic in dragons that it's better not to be
around.

The breath of the dragon gave way to an image
of a cock crowing silently, its red wattles rippling; the cock gave way to a fat hare.

"I bet you he's got a real chicken and rabbit,"
I said.

Enki Duzun nodded.

A waxy-looking horse kicked the hare into invisibility, only to be shouldered away and into
nothingness by an old ox, its steel horncaps
rusted through in spots, its back sagging with almost impossible weariness.

"He probably bought that carving," Enki Duzun said. "It's too good."

The ox faded to a sketchy octopus, and the octopus was replaced by a green garden-snake, its
scales gleaming with reflected fire.

"I think he put his candle too near the snake,"
Enki Duzun said.

"Probably." Fhilt turned to Gray Khuzud. "It is
the hour of the snake."

Gray Khuzud gripped my shoulder. "Lead us,"
he said. My father was never much for wasted
words.

We were road-weary, but we were the Troupe of
Gray Khuzud, and I kept my head high as I led
the troupe through the gates of Den Oroshtai,
past rows of soldiers singing at attention.

It seemed larger than it was, but leading the

troupe into the castle was really only a small part—which suited me just fine; I had other things on my mind. And it was hard enough just to be Kami Khuzud, Eldest Son Acrobat, and to be as inept as I was.

Am.

As Gray Khuzud says, clumsiness is not the Way of the Acrobat.

But while I was not the tumbler or ropewalker that I should have been, juggling was something that I could do reasonably well, and that looked harder than it was, at least at my level.

Juggling is the first of the arts that make up the Way, which is why a juggler always leads the Troupe of Gray Khuzud into town.

For me, juggling had always been a simulation of kazuh, rather than kazuh itself: I would just get the mind out of the way, and let the muscles do what they knew best.

The mind was always the problem in juggling, anyway—it kept telling me that each hand was handling four or five flares at once, instead of only one. That is the secret of juggling: just handle one thing at a time, and don't worry about what comes next.

Not a bad way to run your life, but much of the Way of the Acrobat is a good way to run your life, no? Acrobat or not, it's good to keep yourself and your props clean; it's wise to think about what you're doing and practice it often; it's sound to listen to the more experienced with the proper mixture of respect and doubt; it's sensible to learn to handle fire and steel with firmness, safety, and respect.

Flame hissed through the early evening air as I twirled and spun and flung the flares through the simplest shower:

—right flare up;

—catch the hilt of the flare descending toward the right hand;

—and then left flare up;

—then catch the descending flare in the left hand before switching over.

A circular juggle is much more difficult; the shower was simple, but like so much that was simple, apparently complex. There is a game of points of light that wizards play, with only three simple rules, which generates almost impossible crystalline structures of light and movement.

The smooth-worn hilts of the flares slapped reassuringly into my hands, just as they should; I wouldn't even have looked if looking weren't part of the act.

A juggler must have a mind like the moon, but a face like water: it should reflect the faces of the audience, and the audience gaped in amazement at the flames spinning through the dusk. A better juggler could have raised kazuh, focused only on the juggling itself. Me, I kept the flares showering, but watched the crowd from the corner of my eye. It's more fun that way, and everybody was enjoying it, as far as I could see.

Except for one.

Fat Narantir, his massive belly barely held in by the rope holding his robes together, scowled. Magicians don't like zuhrir, of which kazuh is the expression, and either Narantir wasn't sensitive enough to detect the fact that I was only using skill, or he wasn't trying.

Or maybe it was just that magicians are famous as lechers, and that NaRee was becoming prettier by the year. Perhaps fat Narantir had his eye on NaRee, and wished his hands on her as well.

I looked for her, and ached for her. But she wasn't there.

"Hei, hei," I called out. Behind me, my sister, Enki Duzun, clapped her hands twice, and then, in perfect rhythm, flung another flaming wand over my shoulder.

It slapped into my horny palm, and the crowd gasped, and then hissed their applause. I bowed my thanks—a hard move; *you* try to bow gracefully while showering five burning wands—as though I'd done something wonderful.

I've always been unusually sensitive to the flare of others' kazuh. It's no great gift—you can usually *see* it; you don't have to feel it—but it is sometimes a comfort.

This time it was Enki Duzun, of course, who had done it, raising kazuh enough to be sure that she could throw the wand exactly right, precisely correctly. I could barely feel her kazuh simmering, then subsiding. I was mildly surprised; Enki Duzun relied on her skill much more often than her kazuh.

I broke from the shower into a circle—much harder; but, as I say, I'm not a bad juggler—and then back into a shower, so that I could bow in the direction of Narantir.

The audience hissed their applause, two young girls chewing spring daisies, spitting the petals out in front of the troupe.

I thought I caught a glimpse of NaRee between two of the nobles' palanquins near the rear of the crowd—members of our beloved ruling class are as fond of acrobats as are the lower classes. But I could have been mistaken, and the next time I looked, there was nobody there.

The sand cold under my feet, I juggled my way into the center of the square. Beneath the immobile torches guarding the walls of Den Oroshtai, my flaming wands tumbled through the night air, until my shoulders became so tired that I knew I could keep up the juggling only by raising kazuh.

Which I knew I could not do, not yet, so I finished with a flourish, then one by one planted the wands in the sand of the square, diving over them and cartwheeling off into the dark.

Invisibility is part of the act, and the way to become unseen is first to get the crowd's attention, and then to focus all *your* attention on the next act. The crowd's focus will follow yours.

Paying attention to the next act wasn't hard—Fhilt's and Enki Duzun's entrance was spectacular.

Ropes, pads, and guy wires tight about their waists, the two Eresthai brothers (while they had been with the troupe for ten years, I still couldn't reliably remember which of the over-muscled men was Eno and which was Josei) had taken up their positions behind me, stretching the ropes tight between them, then planting double-ended spikes all around them in a seemingly random pattern with quick, jerky wrist-flicks.

The spikes were plated in rippling gold and black—showy in the flickering torchlight. Spikes and knives don't quite generate the same kind of drama and tension that height can, but they are an acceptable substitute during the troupe's entrance. The only other choice would be to send the Eresthais in a day or so early, and have them set up our equipment. But that's contrary to the way Gray Khuzud sees the Way: when the troupe arrives, it should all arrive.

Fhilt, always straightforward, did it straight-forwardly: he ran toward Large Egda, who cupped his massive hands, tossing Fhilt into the air. He landed catlike on the rope, then bowed, turning his bow into a forward roll, springing from the shoulder of the far Eresthai brother, and then

21

landing in the dirt, ending with another deep bow.

Now it was my sister's turn. Enki Duzun began with a tumbling run, her thin legs pumping, then springing her into a series of handwheels that ended with a leap in the air that launched her headlong toward Large Egda, who bent to catch her feet in his massive hands, then flip her head-over-heels toward the low rope.

She landed squarely, but then teetered on the edge of disaster.

And then she fell, and the crowd gasped with one voice as she caught the rope with one hand and one foot, and swung around underneath it, springing into the air and then landing on the rope, unmoving, steady on its slimness as she would have been on the solid ground. She leaped over the head of the far Eresthai brother, and then landed on the ground with the barest give to her knees.

The applause was gratifyingly loud.

The rest of the company made their entrances—Evrem the snake-handler twirling a cobra in each hand, Sala of the rings dancing the steel around her body.

Last, of course, was Gray Khuzud, and his entrance was the grandest of all. Superficially, it was like Enki Duzun's, save that Gray Khuzud's moves were perhaps a hair sharper, a fraction cleaner: he tumbled, sprang into the air, and then Large Egda tossed him, too, above the rope.

And then he landed, off balance, teetering on the edge of disaster.

The crowd shouted, but not as loudly as they had for Enki Duzun; they had seen this before.

And, just when it seemed as though all he could do was fall, he fell, onto the field of spikes.

But his body twisted into a blur of motion, and his fall became a handspring, and a cartwheel, spinning him through the field of spikes, some of the razor points missing his outstretched hands only by fractions of a fren. Then he was clear of the spikes, and his cartwheel became a series of handsprings, and his handsprings a leap, and his leap a midair flip.

Gray Khuzud, his full kazuh upon him, broke out of his tuck, landed feet-first in the sand, and accepted the thundering roar of the crowd.

"The Troupe of Gray Khuzud is among you," he said, a particularly deep bow aimed toward the dark window high above.

I clapped as loud as any, not caring how it looked.

The crowd was mostly gone from the courtyard; Lord Toshtai was going to hold an audience, and those who had business with him needed to bathe and change into their finery.

Under flickering lamplight, castle servitors were already busy tidying up, some sweeping dirt and sand and a few stray leaves from the flat stones, others raking the pebbled paths from the old donjon to the larger, new one, yet others watering potted bushes and reaching up to pull dead leaves from the trees.

Enki Duzun tugged at my wrist. Slim as a boy, she was much stronger than she looked.

"Be gone, Kami Khuzud," she said, her lips twisted into a thin smile. "This one might not wait for you." Her bare shoulders and her torso were slick with sweat and caked in places with dirt and sand.

"This one, little sister, is special."

"That's what you say about all of them."

I was going to say something to the effect of *I mean it with her*, but I was afraid that Enki Duzun wouldn't have believed me. Even though, by the Powers, it was true. So I settled for, "You're falling out again."

Self-conscious, she adjusted her halter.

She hadn't been falling out; I was being unfair.

Enki Duzun's breasts had begun to grow over the past few months, and she was paying too much attention to not falling out, at least among outsiders. Dressed in a halter and acrobat's blousy demi-trousers, she drew appreciative looks from the men of the court and intermittent glares from the overwrapped women. It must have been the eyes. My little sister was just fourteen years old, and her chin and cheeks were still too round, barely hinting of the beauty that would surely appear later, and force me to spend much time fending off admirers, but her eyes were those of my mother: old, wise, kind, and very tolerant.

I loved those eyes.

"I'm sorry," I said.

"About what? The usual?" She smiled, again. "Go, Kami Khuzud."

Timing is everything, as Gray Khuzud says. Just as I was about to steal away, Large Egda's massive right hand closed around my arm. I would have tried to get away, but when Large Egda grabs something, it stays grabbed—even though my biceps was well developed, his fingers almost met.

"Gray Khuzud says not to sneak off, not yet," he said, his voice a dull rumble. "Everyone is summoned to audience with Lord Toshtai. Time enough to bathe and change only."

"Well, now." Enki Duzun grinned. "At least we eat well tonight."

"You, little sister, think with your stomach."

"True enough." She patted her naked belly. "You, Kami Khuzud, think with your phallus."

It wasn't true, not with NaRee. But, a true D'Shaian hypocrite, I couldn't say that; I couldn't even agree sarcastically, letting her know that NaRee and I had something special, that it was different here, with her.

Large Egda pulled again.

"Let go, let go, I'm coming."

He thought about it for a long moment, and then released me.

Obedient to command as always, I accompanied Large Egda, rubbing at my arm.

2
Dinner Party

ENKI DUZUN SMILED at me around a bite of lambroll. "I'm sorry, Kami Khuzud. I know you'd rather be somewhere else." She had changed into a blue silk halter and fuller trousers, and put an ochre orchid she had gotten the-Powers-knew-where behind her left ear.

"I'd rather be almost anywhere else," I said. Particularly with NaRee.

"Depends." She took another quick bite, and swallowed it. I never understood how Enki Duzun could tuck away as much food as Large Egda did. "Not in Lord Toshtai's dungeon, waiting to sit on a spear."

"True."

Of all the great halls where we played, the one at Den Oroshtai had long been one of my favorites, although I don't know why. The floor was of rulawood strips inlaid with triangles of green Aragimlyth marble—unsure footing, even bare-foot—and the ceiling was too low, barely two manheights tall, not nearly high enough for the more vigorous of Large Egda's tosses. Even where the walls, delicately carved of teak and porcelain, didn't hold tapestries, they were off limits for the fastening of guys and staples, as was the ceiling, where easily thousands of walnut-carved bats and drelens hung, waiting.

"Why do I like this great hall so much?" I asked, idly.

"Style, Kami Khuzud," she said. "Taste. You actually have some.

"Eat, quickly—he will be out from behind the screen soon."

I picked up something crispy, although I wasn't hungry. Until I took a bite, that is: it was hot, brittle duck skin, still warm, wrapped around a filling of deliciously cold ham and roe. The ways of a kazuh cook are always mysterious.

The salty roe crunched between my teeth.

I looked around the room, and couldn't find Refle. Maybe he was in a sitting room off the main ballroom, but maybe not. It didn't bode well; I could hardly spend time with NaRee while the castle armorer was paying court to her.

NaRee wasn't here, of course; her family was bourgeois, not part of our beloved ruling class. Attending court was probably a once-in-a-lifetime thing for her. At least, I hoped so; with very few exceptions, bourgeoisie are called into court only to swear fealty, or to be tried for crimes.

We D'Shai are a subtle people, but not in all

28

ways; unless the lord turns his face from it, any crime is what the Foulsmelling Ones of Bhorlani call *oi-tadeski*—a life-crime.

Everybody knew that Lord Toshtai was at the far end of the hall, only officially hidden behind the parchment screen. But he wasn't officially in the room until the screen was removed, which meant that we could stand, walk around, eat or pass wind without committing a solecism. A typical bit of D'Shaian hypocrisy, perhaps.

In a distant way, I guess it was sort of interesting to watch the classes mingle in the pre-audience fiction that all are so far beneath the ruling lord that all are, temporarily, equal. Vaguely.

Some brought more of themselves to the role than others. Off in the corner of the room near both a potted pine and a tray of rolled rouxed eels, Fhilt talked intently with a pinch-faced woman, the traditional cut and bear-and-snake needle-point on her robe proclaiming her either old enough or stubborn enough—or both—to defy modern fashion.

Typical for Fhilt to be cornered by some old dowager. I flattered myself that I cut a better figure in my formal tunic and leggings. Fhilt always looked a bit off; his hair was that awkward color between brown and blond that always looks unwashed, and his arms were ever-so-slightly too long in proportion to the rest of his body.

Across the hall, Lord Felkoi, the brother to

Refle, intently grilled Large Egda on what it was like to catch somebody coming out of a triple.

"—he unrolls, and I catch him," Large Egda said, his flat face betraying no pleasure, no pain, not much of anything. "Then when the trap swings back, I throw him back, just right. Not hard. If I throw him too hard, he doesn't catch the trap, and he falls."

"Yes, yes, man, but how does it *feel?*" Felkoi took a step closer, gesturing to urge Large Egda on. I didn't know why he was so interested, and didn't much care.

Neither did Large Egda. "It feels good, I guess."

Felkoi was a compact dark man, his short black beard shot with premature streaks of gray, his precise way of gesturing softened by an easy smile. He was also persistent.

Large Egda could never quite manage doing two things at once, and while he was talking, he wasn't eating. I've always felt protective toward Large Egda, something I don't understand—a man as large and strong as Large Egda should be able to take care of himself. But what is, is: I walked over to where he and Felkoi were standing next to a waist-high table holding a platter of crispy partridge breasts stuffed with saffron and wild rice.

"A good evening, Lord Felkoi," I said. I gestured at Large Egda to take something from the platter, but he missed the motion. Typical.

I picked one up and placed it in his hands. He bit into it gratefully.

"And a good evening to you, Kami Khuzud," Felkoi said. "I was just asking Egda about trapeze work, about the feel of it, the sense of catching a triple tumble." He took a cloth from his tunic and daubed at the corner of his mouth.

"I wouldn't know," I said. "I've never caught one."

"Yes, but you've done one."

"I stick with doubles. You'll have to ask Gray Khuzud about triples." I smiled. "A triple is . . . interesting."

I could have told him about how it's more than that, about how you have to pump the trapeze so hard that your grip on the bar threatens to tear your shoulder off; about the release, hoping that you've done it right because if you haven't— safety harness or no, net or no—you're going to hurt yourself because you've spun your center away into the dark; about the catch that hurts even more than the release, but is a reassuring, comforting kind of hurt, because you know that once Large Egda's hands have closed on your upper arms, that's the end of it.

But I didn't: I didn't really have any grievance against Felkoi—it was his brother, Refle, who was courting NaRee—but I don't do favors for members of our beloved ruling class. I've never liked being around our beloved ruling class, and it's not just that you have to watch how you behave around them. A part of it, of course, is they're allowed to kill commoners without reason.

A large part.

But that's largely overstated. While in theory any member of our beloved ruling class, no matter how minor, can kill any member of any lower class with absolute impunity, other members of our beloved ruling class are known to get irritated when that happens at the wrong time.

Everybody—including members of our beloved ruling class—remembers that one of the things that triggered the Long War was Lord Dilpa, a minor noble of Lasge, killing a nameless peasant in the Ven. As it turned out, Lord Dun Logehaira decided to take that as an insult, and sent his warships across the North Channel of the Inner Sea, and sacked Firth.

Even that probably wouldn't dissuade a member of our beloved ruling class—they like wars, or D'Shai wouldn't have been at war with itself for almost all of the past two hundred years, and at war with the Foulsmelling Ones the rest of the time. What keeps them in line is the memory of ancient Lord Erist, Dilpa's fealty-lord, who later found Lord Dilpa's table manners irritating, and then made Dilpa's children eat sausages cased in their father's intestines.

Lord Erist, so it's said, liked war, but perhaps he wasn't ready to fight it then. A fealty-lord is allowed to kill any of his subjects for any reason, and in this case the reason wasn't that Dilpa was clumsy with spoon and trencher, or because ancient Erist was a secret kazuh cook, eager to try a new experiment.

At least, that's what Gray Khuzud said, and I tended to go along with my father on things like that.

I also tended to go along with him to things like the audience with Lord Toshtai, although I didn't like it. Gray Khuzud did; he was behind the screen, in private conversation with Lord Toshtai. Toshtai was awfully fond of acrobats, which did much for my practical status in Den Oroshtai, if not for my official one. One would almost think the fat one wished he were an acrobat, although I didn't believe it. The Tale of the Lord and the Peasant does end with the lord going back to his castle, and the peasant back to his plow, after all.

Idiot peasant.

"You think deep thoughts, Kami Khuzud," Felkoi said, with a smile that could have been friendly or condescending, although I knew which way I was betting.

"Always," I said. "It's part of the Way of the Acrobat."

Felkoi looked from Large Egda to me and back again, then walked off after a perhaps overpunctilious quarter-demi-bow.

"Thank you, Kami Khuzud," Large Egda said, from around another bite. "He kept asking me about catching and throwing, and you know I don't know how to talk about it. I just do it."

I patted his arm. "Don't worry, Egda. Just eat, while you've got the chance."

The ballroom was filled with people who I knew only casually, and people who I didn't know at all. There were a few who I wouldn't have minded knowing.

Over by a knee-table, one of the ladies of the court knelt on a red silken cushion. Her robes, sewn of that ripple-woven scarlet silk that only the nobility can afford, were quite unfashionably pulled tight together, promising rather than showing a slim waist and full bosom, but I was drawn to the high cheekbones and the wide, dark eyes that examined me frankly for a long moment, then moved away.

Which was just as well. The heavy man near her, his scabbard lying flat on his lap, had started to follow her gaze.

The bit of byplay hadn't gone completely unnoticed: a pinch-faced old woman standing next to Lord Arefai hid a smile behind her fan, then considered me carefully with her cold blue eyes.

I turned and picked up another duckroll.

It's not comfortable to be stared at by women of our beloved ruling class, at least not in public, not when their husbands and brothers and fathers and sometimes—Powers spare us!—their mothers can see them do that.

I admit I am handsome, except for my hands,

of course, but that is a function of being an acrobat. A well-proportioned physique is something
that you have to develop, and you do it without
working in the hot sun, developing a peasant's
tan.

Not that that would stop a lot of the noble
women, or the bourgeois ones. While liaisons between them and peasants are absolutely forbidden, some husbands, brothers and fathers will
turn their faces from that. The danger of not
knowing can add some spice to it. I speak from
experience.

Each of the two Eresthai brothers had picked
out his quarry: Josei had chosen a lovely, delicate
redheaded kazuh courtesan with whom he had
no chance; Eno was working on Hebrid, the wife
of a bourgeois meatpacker, under the muffled
glare of her husband.

By a dyed-grass tapestry of two gazelles in a
glen, old Dun Lidjun was holding forth on some
fine point of swordsmanship, holding out an
eating-stick as though it were a sword. While the
lecture was clearly aimed at the younger swordsmen who watched his every move with careful
eyes, nodding in unison when he paused for
breath, Evrem the snake-handler pretended to be
paying rapt attention, although he absently kept
spinning his own pair of eating sticks through his
fingers.

I didn't like Evrem, and sort of hoped that Dun
Lidjun would take notice and frighten him a lit-

tle, the way Evrem used to scare me with his snakes.

"I hope Dun Lidjun doesn't take notice," Enki Duzun said.

"Just what I was thinking." Well, it was what I *should* have been thinking, as a loyal member of the troupe. Sometimes you have to substitute.

Enki Duzun knelt by the serving board and picked up a lambroll, wrapping it in a chumpa leaf, then ladling bitter brown horseradish sauce over it all, so thickly I didn't know how she expected to eat it without splattering herself. Rising, she twirled it faster than the sauce could drift off before she took it in three bites, like a wolf downing a gopher.

"The arts can have minor applications, as well as major ones," she said, brushing at her hair.

"Just what I was thinking."

Narantir the magician was glaring at me from across the room. I gave him a false-friendly wave, as though noticing an old friend.

"Taunting magicians is stupid and irresponsible," she said.

"No," I said. "Only irresponsible." I half-filled a crystal goblet with rich purple winterwine and headed toward him.

"Good evening, Narantir Ta-Mahrir," I said, respectfully, if informally.

He was an overweight man who had been destined to be immensely fat, but had partly thwarted his obvious destiny, at least for the time being. While he was probably half again my own weight, his face was lined and wrinkled, as though he were underinflated. He was probably carrying an extra half stone as sweat and dirt in his clothes, and as crumbs of food in his beard.

I wonder if it's true that mahrir, wizard's-magic, comes in part from filth. All I can say is that in my travels I've met both wizards and witches, and never want to be downwind of either on a hot day.

"May your evening be one of rain and sleep, Eldest Son Acrobat," he said, too formally for the occasion. Dirty fingers played in his rat's-nest of a beard.

I didn't have a good response. Technically, acrobats are of the peasant class, but we're not all that fond of rain. I didn't even like to practice when it was wet; I tended to slip and fall a lot. Besides, I didn't know how to make small talk with magicians; I hadn't had much practice. So I just smiled in answer, and let the silence hang over him.

"You performed quite well, this evening, Eldest Son Acrobat," he said, finally. "Yes, you did, didn't you?"

I liked the pause between "well" and "this," and the slight emphasis on the latter word. It was clear that Narantir and I were still not going to be friends. Some people just don't get along.

I can be just as excessively formal as anybody

else. "You, Nailed Weasel User of Magic, are far too kind."

Magicians learn levels of self-control, but not the same kind as the rest of us; for a moment, I thought he was going to rear back and shout at me, but then his features softened.

"No, no, don't be that way, young acrobat. I meant no offense by formality, Kami Khuzud."

"I certainly didn't intend to give any where none is deserved, Narantir."

He didn't know quite how to take that, so I turned to leave.

"One moment."

"Yes?"

"I would like your winterwine," he said. "Really, I would."

"I'll fetch you a goblet, Narantir."

"I wish I could express myself better." The wizard shook his head. "You don't understand." He muttered a phrase and passed his hand over my goblet. "I want *your* winterwine."

The golden surface of the winterwine slowly sank, as though it was being drawn out by an invisible straw.

"Do you take my point?" he asked.

"Perhaps." Well, no, actually.

"Perhaps it's too simple. Try this: when you annoy a wizard, you end up with less than that with which you started." He smiled at me with teeth that were neither even nor white.

I thought of responding with a pleasantry like

"Please stick the goblet up your back passage," but decided that that would be neither politic nor safe, so I just watched my goblet drain into nothingness.

I sort of expected a sucking sound when the level dropped to the bottom of the goblet, but I didn't get one.

Typical.

I never do get what I expect.

"Lord Toshtai is here; our Lord receives subjects and guests," two guards, a baritone and a tenor, sang out; a bass and another tenor picked up the song and turned it into a round as two maids slid the screen aside.

Like a field of wheat bending in the wind, everyone in the courtyard knelt, warriors dropping only to one knee, all the rest of us to both.

Toshtai sat on his throne, a robed attendant to either side, two of his sons, Edelfaule and Arefai, kneeling warrior-fashion beyond them.

Now, while Narantir was an overweight man who had avoided being fat, Toshtai was massively corpulent, but there was something majestic in his bulk. His hair was oiled and combed back over a head large enough for a man of his size; his flipper-like hands were comfortably folded over his belly.

The kazuh of the rulers is, according to legend, history and law, an offshoot of that of the warrior, and a warrior is never without his sword. It would have been hard for Toshtai to sit comfortably in his leather chair and deal with a sword and scabbard, so Toshtai's dress sword was a miniature, barely larger than an eating knife, stuck into his sash as though in afterthought.

His eyes always bothered me. Sunken and porcine, they held no trace of humanity, of kindness or cruelty, just of intelligence. Momentarily, they rested on mine, but then they passed me by.

It felt like an executioner had read out another name.

"I am pleased to wish a good evening to all," Toshtai said. "I am further pleased to see all of you on this evening, in particular the Troupe of Gray Khuzud. I would be pleased if you were each to rise." He inclined his head fractionally, and the guards took up the refrain again.

Old Dun Lidjun's joints groaned as he rose to his feet, his left hand on the hilt of his sword, as though that steadied him. His hair was white and thin, and his skin thin and ashen with age, his tunic loose on his bony frame; but he threw back his shoulders and stood straight. Perhaps he could not control his joints, but they would not master him, either.

"I seem to recall telling you not to kneel before me, old friend," Toshtai whispered. I'm not sure if he thought he was talking privately, or not. "Your bones are too old for that."

"If you please." The old general bowed. "I have greeted the Lord of Den Oroshtai properly for more than five decades, Lord; if it please you, Lord, perhaps I'm too old to learn new habits."

"Ah." Toshtai's face was blank. "Perhaps you are not too old to bring me the ears of your favorite granddaughter. Do so. Now."

Dun Lidjun's face went a shade whiter; his shoulders slumped. "Yes, Lord." He drew himself up as straight as he could. "Immediately." He spun on the balls of his feet and stalked toward the door.

"You will have to get past the guards. Ver Hortun, Bek De Bran—kill him if you can," Toshtai called out.

Two guards lowered their pikes, taking up ready stances. Dun Lidjun drew his sword in one smooth motion, his face calm, growing supremely impassive.

The hair on the back of my neck stood on end as his kazuh flared. Enki Duzun had felt it, too.

"I've never seen that done faster," she whispered.

Me, neither. I had seen the look on Dun Lidjun's face before—I had see it that evening, on my father's face—but never brought on so casually. Dun Lidjun had raised kazuh in a heartbeat, like drawing on a glove. Or drawing a sword.

The three of them stood motionless, frozen in time for a moment, until the larger of the guards lunged for Dun Lidjun, his pike stabbing out.

"Don't cut either of them," Toshtai commanded.

41

The guards moved forward.

Dun Lidjun blurred into motion, seemingly brushed past one attacking guard, toward the other. But the first guard staggered and stumbled in the old warrior's wake, and the other brought up the butt of his pike—

"All of you, stop."

The second of the pikemen stumbled, but Dun Lidjun froze in place, like one of the friezes on the wall, his sword reversed, his hand in midsweep; he had almost clubbed the second pikeman with his sword butt.

"Bek De Bran, lower your pike. Do not kill him."

The other, the one who had first attacked Dun Lidjun, had dropped to his knees; there was blood at the corner of his mouth. His eyes were vague and dreamy. They rolled up; he fell on his face, his pike clattering on marble.

"Dun Lidjun," Toshtai said, "I revoke the orders to hurt your granddaughter."

"Yes, Lord." The old warrior let his arm drop, and suddenly he was just an old man again, wearing a tunic that he had grown too small for. Ancient fingers trembled as he tried to slip his sword back in its scabbard, failing twice before he succeeded.

Toshtai gestured twice to his maids; the unconscious guard was hauled away, another from the hall outside taking his place as the screen was pulled back in front of Lord Toshtai. Whispers might not have made it around the curtain, but Toshtai didn't lower his voice.

"It seems, old friend, that you do remember how to obey orders; my orders stand."

"Yes, Lord."

Gray Khuzud patted me on the shoulder. "So? What has this taught you, Kami Khuzud?"

"That if Lord Toshtai tells me to stand up, I'll stand up."

He frowned. "And is that all?"

I shrugged. "Lord Toshtai is either very blunt, or very subtle." Alienating the marshal of his forces—if that's what he had done; I wouldn't have bet a shard on how Dun Lidjun had really taken their little drama—was probably stupid. Reminding everyone in the room that he had the power of life and death over them was a bit obvious, and painfully real to all.

"Or both, Kami Khuzud. I've been wondering that for years."

The three elder members of the troupe and the two Eresthais had gone to sleep; Fhilt, Enki Duzun, Large Egda and I were the last to bed, as usual. The while before bedtime was our time, a quiet time as we sat on Madame Rupon's porch, looking out at the town, and at the flickering lights in the castle above the town and at the watching stars.

Our time, although we often spent much of it

squabbling. I'm persuaded that much of Fhilt's and my arguments were for the sake of arguing.

The single lamp hanging over the steps occasionally sent a burning vastamoth slowly flapping away into the night, the insect too stupid to know it was dying.

Night in D'Shaian towns and cities is quiet, although tonight the quiet was broken by a distant troupe of musicians. It was easy to pick out the deep rasp and thrum of the bassskin, the distant ringing of the chimes, but it was hard to tell if there were one or two drummers and zivvers, two silverhorns or three.

"Any idea which troupe that is?" Fhilt asked.

Except for a few court bands, musicians, like acrobats—and storysavers, lisburns, farriers, and deilists, for that matter—travel the length and breadth of D'Shai, each on their own route.

"No," I said. "I've sometimes thought that it would be pleasant if we could travel with one of the better musician's troupes, and perhaps have them learn set pieces of music to play, to better set off our performance."

"I like the variety," Enki Duzun said.

Fhilt snorted. "Perhaps you can find an earnest young musician who would like you to learn to juggle your balls in time to one of his jigs."

"Shh, Fhilt," Enki Duzun said. "Listen. I like that." She leaned farther back in the wooden porch chair, and relaxed. There's nothing so comfortable as an acrobat at ease.

"Very pretty," Large Egda said, hunched on the porch steps. Ever since a wicker chair in Tiree's Lair had shattered underneath him during an intermission, Large Egda had been nervous about wooden furniture.

"Mmmm . . . maybe," Fhilt said. "But I think the zivver player's leaning too heavily on the scratchbox. Don't you?"

"Leave him alone, Fhilt," I said. It's not right to expect Large Egda to pick up on something subtle, like a zivver player's thumb. "The zivver's just fine."

It was part of the ritual, more of a dance than a reality: Fhilt and I would argue, and sometimes almost come to blows, and then Enki Duzun would stop us before it became serious.

Suddenly the music stopped.

I chuckled. "I guess they don't like your criticism, Fhilt," I said, as though they could have heard us.

"Or your ignorant defense, Kami Khuzud," he said, rising to his feet.

I squared off opposite him. "Ignorant, did you say? From a man who can't tell a zivver from a cow?"

He snorted. "I'm sorry. Make that 'woefully ignorant.' "

A silverhorn purred out a complex phrase quickly, then, note by note, slowly.

"It sounds to me," Enki Duzun said, "like the second silverhorn missed a phrase, like the first silverhorn player is reviewing it for him, and like neither of you two music appreciators knows as much as he claims to." She looked up at the two of us and smiled. "If you're going to beat somebody for speaking the truth, try me."

I looked at my fists, and dropped my hands. Fhilt shrugged and did the same.

"Some day, the two of you will really fight," Enki Duzun said.

"Entirely possible," Fhilt said.

"Very likely." I nodded.

Large Egda shook his head. "Even *I* know better than that."

3
NaRee

THERE'S NOTHING QUITE like breakfast with the Troupe of Gray Khuzud. There *are* things more restful, but there's nothing quite like it.

I sighed. There was no use in putting it off any longer. "Could you pass the fundleberry preserves, please?" I asked.

"In a moment, Kami Khuzud." My father's lips pursed in familiar annoyance. "Egda hasn't had any yet." He looked over at the big man.

"Could you do it for me, Gray Khuzud?" Large Egda asked. His broad face was smooth, childlike, and gentle as always. I guess if you're as strong as Large Egda, you have to be gentle.

"Of course," Gray Khuzud said patiently, as he had a thousand times before. He smiled as he balanced the fist-sized stone crock of preserves on his wrist for a scant second before flipping it over, catching it neatly in his other palm. "Sala: the bread, if you please."

Sala of the Rings quickly dropped her own

spoon, picked up the breadknife, and took to slicing frantically at the remaining quarter-loaf, while, with a tired smile, Evrem picked up a spreading-knife and the theme. Morning seemed to agree with Evrem—his constant frown was a few degrees less intense, and his freshly shaved face seemed somehow less lined.

Evrem twirled the knife through his fingers, spun it on his fingertips, then flipped it, caught it, and presented it to Enki Duzun, who snatched it, dug the end into the crock, and flipped a dollop across the table at Sala's face.

"*Aha!*" Sala slapped two thick slices of bread around the blob, rubbed them quickly together to spread the preserves, and slapped the bread down on Large Egda's plate.

She raised a finger. "Not this time, Enki Duzun, not this time." Even at breakfast, her body mostly wrapped in a bulky gray robe that concealed her curves, her almond eyes lazy with sleep, Sala was oppressively beautiful. Her hair was bound up in her sleeping knot, stray golden tendrils playing with her cheekbones and the corners of her smile.

"What's hurt can be fixed," Sala said, "but sometimes it's a lot of trouble." That didn't have anything to do with anything, but it was typical Sala. It's not that she wasn't clever, or smart, but somehow irrelevant aphorisms always dropped from her mouth like apples from an orange tree.

"Good," Large Egda said from around a huge

bite of bread and preserves. "Very good." Large Egda's table manners, on the other hand, were never particularly good, not even by the somewhat eccentric standards of our troupe.

Fhilt and the two Eresthai brothers were showering soft-boiled eggs across the table, looping them high into the air, each of the three eating with one hand while he juggled with the other. Bite and throw and catch, bite and throw and catch.

Fhilt, by far the best juggler of the three, added a flourish by using his juggling hand for other things—scratching at an unlikely itch on his cheek, moving his glass nearer his eating hand, taking a pinch from the saltwell—letting it arrive at just the right time and place for a catch-and-throw, as though by accident.

"Would you like an egg, Kami Khuzud?" the nearest of the Eresthais asked.

"No," I started to say, automatically, then stopped myself. I *was* hungry for eggs this morning. "Come to think of it, I would."

"I think I've got this one down." Fhilt bounced one of the intact eggs off his biceps, then caught it and set it down on an old, yellowed porcelain eggholder, putting a touch of robbed time into his juggling just long enough to pick up a spoon and tap the egg. He cracked the shell neatly, then added his spoon to the three-sided, one-handed shower.

"I've got it, I've got it." The nearest Eresthai

picked the spoon out of the air, and took another tap at the egg, not missing a beat as he threw the spoon to his brother.

"My turn." The other Eresthai thumb-flicked the top off, then snaked out his juggling hand quickly enough to snare a pinch of salt from the saltwell, drop the salt on top of the egg (actually, he spilled just a little), and return quickly enough to catch the next egg.

A huge wooden serving bowl of boiled oats stood congealing in the middle of the table, largely ignored. Gray Khuzud has never been fond of boiled oats, although they are a staple in Den Oroshtai, and Madame Rupon could be counted on to produce a bowl at every breakfast and supper.

Actually, with a bit of butter and a sprinkling of salt, or perhaps some honey and savorfruit, I *like* boiled oats—but I wasn't good enough to do anything interesting with something so . . . gloppy.

"Preserves coming, Kami Khuzud," Gray Khuzud said.

"I have an egg now; I don't—"

Gray Khuzud rolled the preserves crock down his arm, perhaps trusting to his balance and to the thickness of the preserves to keep it from spilling out.

And then he dropped it.

"Got it! Not this time, old man, not this time do you make a fool of your daughter." Enki Duzun's bare foot had already risen; she caught it neatly on the side of her foot, then foot-tossed it in a high arc that even I couldn't miss.

"Have some respect for your father," Gray Khuzud said, smiling.

"I do. Which is why I don't trust you at all." Enki Duzun giggled. "Go ahead, Kami Khuzud," she said, turning to me. "Your turn."

They all looked at me expectantly, waiting to see what I would do with the crock.

"Please, Kami Khuzud," she said. "You have to do it right."

Sala tilted her head to one side. "Please, Kami Khuzud. Just this once."

I just sat there. I hate mornings, and I hate juggling at breakfast.

Gray Khuzud arched an eyebrow. "Kami Khuzud?"

I sighed. I picked up the knife, spread some of the preserves on my bread, then carefully set the crock and knife down on the table.

A cold silence settled over the table.

Fhilt and the Eresthais interrupted their juggle, Evrem set down his spoon, and even Sala and Enki Duzun stopped eating.

I took a bite. I like fundleberry preserves, and these were nice and sweet, with a hint of tartness that I couldn't quite place.

Gray Khuzud glowered at me. "You call that eating?"

I swallowed. "Yes, I call this eating." I glowered back at him. "I really don't like—"

"Surely you can do better than this." It was a command, not an observation.

"Very well." With both hands, I tossed the bread a handsbreadth into the air, and let it fall back into my hands. I took another bite. "Happy?"

"Delighted." Enki Duzun splattered my tunic with a dollop of butter.

"Thank you, little sister."

"You were *supposed* to catch it. With the egg."

Daubing at his mouth, Gray Khuzud stood. "Finish quickly. Morning practice starts at the hour of the hare, as usual."

"All depends on how you look at it," I muttered.

"What did you say, Kami Khuzud?

"I said, 'And a fine day for practice it is, Father.' I'd best go get ready."

We were quartered in town, of course, although this time not in Ironway—I saw the hand of NaRee's father in that—but down toward the river, in the part of town called the Bankstreets; Crosta Natthan, Lord Toshtai's chief servitor, had managed to get the whole troupe quartered on a quiet corner.

It was a neighborhood of whitewashed wooden houses, none built more than ten years before, since the last time that the waves of war had washed through Den Oroshtai, leaving a river of burned buildings and shattered lives in their wake. Sometimes stone survives; what is wood always burned.

The residents of the Bankstreets were all middle class, rather than the true hereditary bourgeois. Pewtersmiths, stablemen, quarrymasters, daubers, and ranchers; not silversmiths, hostlers, masons, carpenters and orchardmen. Half a lifetime of good work and decent matchmaking, and they would visit their daughters in Ironway, or with hard work, superb matchmaking—and luck—perhaps even Up the Hill.

Quartering can be either a lot of fun for both the locals and the troupe or very unpleasant, and it's impossible to tell which it's going to be ahead of time. I've been treated as a treasured new friend about as often as an imposing relative; I've had the gristle end of the joint more often than the tenderloin, but not much more.

Part of the problem comes from the very nature of the arrangement: while the local lord usually pays well for the quartering of traveling troupes, what he's paying for is room and board, not breakage of crockery or the disorder that flows from having guests. The master of the house can either swallow those kinds of complaints and pretend that they don't give him gas, or complain to the lord.

Which is to say that the master of the house

can swallow those kinds of losses and pretend that they don't give him gas.

While all of us sat table at Madame Rupon's, we slept separately. Father and Sala were across the street at Clink the pewtersmith's; Enki Duzun had a room there, too. The Eresthais were on a second corner, at the house of Vernel the stableman. Fhilt and I split a fairly large room at Madame Rupon's with Large Egda, unfortunately for Fhilt and me. Egda snores.

Fat, friendly Madame Rupon had two daughters, and was keen to show them both as marriageable. Not many of the middle class were eager to arrange a marriage with itinerants, but I could see her predicament: FamNa had a large temper problem and a small mustache; Eliss had a small temper problem and a large mustache.

"It is time for practice, Kami Khuzud," Gray Khuzud said.

We practiced in Vernel's corral, as we had the last time we were in Den Oroshtai: a corral is the ideal kind of place to do almost everything except trapeze and long-rope work.

The first job, of course, was to rake out the horse turds; the life of an acrobat is one thrill after another.

Then we set ourselves up on the dirt, the Eresthais improvising a couple of platforms and then running a tightwire between posts set on two adjacent sides, dividing the corral diagonally.

While Enki Duzun and Gray Khuzud worked out on the low wire, Fhilt and I limbered up with a bit of juggling. A half dozen of the local children, all dirt and smiles, stopped across the street to watch, although they'd soon get bored and drift away.

Sala, stripped to canvas shorts and halter, bound her hair behind her head and began her stretches.

"Keep yourself limber, young ones," she said. "It gets harder every year."

I was skeptical, myself. As she said it, she was carefully fitting her left ankle behind the back of her neck, and I couldn't see flesh split or hear bones break—Sala wasn't even breathing hard as she looked at nothing in particular and said, "No matter which way you turn, most everything is behind you."

Fhilt glared at her. Sala's irrelevant idle musings were a perpetual annoyance to him, although I never understood why.

"Here," I said, tossing him a juggling stick.

He tossed it back, as though he didn't want it, and within moments we were in our usual warm-up juggle. I tended to spend as much time juggling as possible. If you're good at something, getting even better at it is a way toward kazuh, no matter what that something is.

So wands twisted and turned through the air, while the children across the street giggled and pointed. Juggling looks like magic to children. Truth to tell, it often looks like magic to me.

Large Egda threw himself into an interminable series of squatting exercises, while Enki Duzun and Gray Khuzud took the first turn on the wire, practicing quick and slow crossings.

Evrem just played with his snakes. I never liked his snakes. Or him.

"Spend less time with those juggling wands, Kami Khuzud, and more time on balancing," Gray Khuzud said. "The Way of the Acrobat—"

"Yes, Father, yes," I said, reluctantly catching the last of the juggling wands and setting them down.

Practice was always about the same, except when we were working out a new routine, which we didn't do in Den Oroshtai. Den Oroshtai was not the most important stop for all troupes— some of the larger ones played at the Seat, the very fanciest in front of the Scion—but it was the most important for ours. For one thing, as long as we pleased Lord Toshtai, lords of smaller holdings would be unlikely to treat us too ill—Lord Toshtai was known to be fond of acrobats, and fondest of all of the best troupe.

Not the fanciest, not the largest, but the Troupe of Gray Khuzud was always the best.

The only way one gets to be the best, or to stay the best, is by practice, practice, and practice. The world isn't a just one; kazuh, the doing of something naturally with added grace and power, only comes to those who don't really need the added grace and power.

My father was a fine acrobat even without raising kazuh; kazuh made him the greatest that there ever was.

". . . and I became what I am by practice, Kami Khuzud. Practice."

I set myself up with the board, ball and roller. Three simple pieces of apparatus: a board, two shoulderswidths wide; the roller, a wooden cylinder, as long as the board is wide; and a wooden ball, about the size of my head.

First: lay the board on the roller, and stand on the board, your feet widely spaced. Then roll the cylinder toward the middle, and keep it there.

It just takes a bit of balance; you don't even need to be an acrobat to do it, although the better you are, the less the roller has to be moved.

Under me, it yawed and rolled like a ship at sea.

"Far too much shaking, Kami Khuzud," Fhilt said. Picking up the ball, he took my place on the board and gave the wooden ball a quick one-handed twist, spinning it on his finger, then moving it to his nose. His form was perfect: his head tilted back, his back arched, force flowing straight up and down. The board and roller underneath his feet couldn't have been more steady if they had been nailed into place. That didn't impress our audience across the street.

Enki Duzun, over on the wire, clapped her

hands twice. Large Egda interrupted his exercises to move between her and Fhilt.

She stopped herself in the middle of the wire, and then pushed off to a handstand on Large Egda's shoulders.

Fhilt, his head still tilted back to balance the ball spinning on his nose, was beginning to wobble.

"Better hurry, Egda," he said, as Egda walked over gingerly, careful not to disturb Enki Duzun's balance.

She handwalked from Large Egda's shoulders up to Fhilt's palms—a tricky move, harder than she made it look—and then she balanced there for a moment, her hands on his outstretched palms, Fhilt solidly atop the board and roller, the wooden ball spinning on Fhilt's nose.

Then came the hard move: she and Fhilt flowed from her balancing with both her palms on both of his until she was balanced on one of his outstretched hands, leaving Fhilt's other hand free to give the wooden ball another spin. He gingerly reached down—

I couldn't see what gave first, but then it all fell apart: Enki Duzun and the ball fell off in different directions, while Fhilt staggered from the board and fell to the sand, too.

Our childish audience laughed at that, more than a little derisively.

"A bit more attention to what we are doing, if you please," Gray Khuzud said, as the two of them got to their feet, brushing themselves off. "We already know how to fall. Less attention to the informal audience, if you please." He beckoned to me. "Take a turn on the wire, Kami Khuzud."

I've never liked wirewalking, I decided yet again as I pulled myself up to the low platform.

It can get boring fast. Still, there is something special, something wonderful about the most ordinary practice, about wirewalking just at the limits of your abilities, pushing the edge outwards, knowing that if you fall—when you fall—it's only a span to the ground.

"Very nice, Kami Khuzud. Again. Faster."

I left the platform slowly—the hardest part is when you transfer your weight to the wire—and slipped off. Again.

"No, no, no. Don't just *stand* there, Kami Khuzud. You have to really balance yourself, not just plant your feet on the ground and trust to their flatness. Balance, after all—not trickery, not showmanship, not flair—is the Way of the Acrobat.

"Again."

An acrobat has some free time in the afternoon, unless you're doing a matinee. There were no matinee performances at Den Oroshtai: Lord Toshtai napped after his noon meal, generally waking late in the hour of the horse. That was only one of his whole complex of eccentricities—although it's not particularly safe to notice a lord's eccentricities, and particularly not safe to comment upon them as such.

Still, I appreciated Toshtai's tendency to do things his own way. Den Oroshtai isn't one of the larger domains in D'Shai, but Toshtai's line has never been fealty-bound to any of the other lords; he was responsible in strict theory only to the Scion, in loose theory sort of responsible to the Steward, and in practice responsible only to himself.

Doing things your own way was something I understood; while the rest of the troupe was resting up for the evening performance, I bathed myself quickly in the icy water of Madame Rupon's pumphouse, then sneaked off into the heart of town, and Ironway.

Ezren Smith's house wasn't quite the largest in Ironway, but it was among the best kept: the roof had a new course of whitewashed slate laid on; the grasses were scythed to a fine green ripple; the marble slabs of the walk were freshly washed and highly polished.

As I walked up toward the front door, I broke into a staggered jig—skip a walk stone with the left foot, then quickly hit the next three before skipping one with the right.

A peasant gardner was weeding the high hedge on the side of the house. I raised my hand in polite greeting, but he ignored me. The trouble with being of the peasant class without actually being a peasant, without actually working fields and paddies, is that everybody hates you, even before they get to know you. The upper classes—particularly the middle class, for some reason—look down on you for really being a peasant, although they can't always treat you like it; the peasants scorn you for not working the fields.

You can't win. I'd long ago given up trying.

I thought I saw a viewport in the front door open and shut as I ran up the short flight of steps, and then pulled the bell rope.

Far away, a gong sounded, its brassy twang hanging in the air for a long time.

Nothing.

I pulled again, twice, peremptorily. I wasn't going to believe that NaRee wasn't home, not on my second day in Den Oroshtai. Nor was I going to believe that nobody was home.

The front door creaked open, and NaRee's mother Haenno stood there, a patently false smile creasing her fishbelly-white face. If I were the superstitious sort, I might have believed she had been left with child by Spennymore ... but I'm not superstitious. Thankfully, the Powers leave us alone, and we them.

The smile looked uncomfortable on her; it wasn't the sort of garment she usually had to put on for the likes of me.

"Oh, Kami Khuzud," she said, false pleasure dripping from her mouth, threatening to run down her taupe housecoat and drip onto the floor. "How nice to see you once again." Her smile broadened, but she didn't waddle her bulk out of the doorway. "I am so very disappointed that NaRee will have to miss your visit." The door started to close, slightly. "I must beg of you to—"

"The sun," I said, loudly, raising my hand as though to shield my eyes. "The sun now rises in front of me," I said. "And I am dazzled, Lady."

I bowed. Well, she had asked for it. I'm not so constituted as to always return honesty for honesty, but I will return lie for lie without hestitation or guilt.

"I pray of you, lovely Haenno: leave your husband this day, and walk with me to Lord Toshtai, so that I might ask that he divorce you from your husband, and splice our lives together."

It's an old D'Shaian principle: when you don't know what to do, get over-formal, and let the other party worry about it.

Alternately, it's an old juggler's trick: when you know you're about to drop a club, let your whole body and soul decide that, by the Powers, you are Going to Drop A Club.

Proposing marriage to NaRee's mother wasn't part of any plan, but it wasn't a bad improvisation. I hoped.

I smiled broadly and bowed again. "May I wait in your garden for your answer?"—and I was off and around the house before she could answer.

The fence around the garden was of the usual

sort: a weathered wooden palisade, perhaps two decades old—it must have been missed in the last burning—treated with chimney-water and protected at the top by a row of rusty iron spikes. The gate was closed, although the damaged grasses growing up around it suggested it was often used, which was unusual; the usual access to a bourgeois garden was through the house itself.

The gate, though, was locked, and the garden would be secure from most.

On the other hand, few trying to enter the garden would be trained acrobats, part of the Troupe of Gray Khuzud.

It's important to do these things right: I bowed to a nonexistent audience, I took three running steps, leaped, and caught the edge of the wood with my fingertips, pulling myself up to the top of the fence in one smooth motion, just avoiding the spikes. I hesitated at the top for a moment, balanced precariously on fingers and a single toe, then vaulted the rest of the way.

I landed at the edge of the grass, one foot on the grass, the other sinking into the dirt of the flower beds, missing a bramblebush by a fingersbreadth.

I should have had faith in myself; straining to push against unhelpful air and miss the bush pushed me off-balance. Instead of landing square on my feet, I fell, breaking my fall with a sloppy forward roll that strained my shoulder slightly and would have earned me a disappointed sigh from Gray Khuzud, had he seen it.

But I recovered, and rose, and he hadn't seen it, because he wasn't there.

NaRee was.

"Bravo, Kami Khuzud, bravo. Do it again." I couldn't tell whether or not she was making fun of me.

"Which part?"

She tilted her head ever so slightly to one side, wisps of black hair playing with her strong cheekbones and blood-red lips. I wished I was a wisp of hair.

She had whitened her already pale face a few shades, particularly around the eyes, which made them look larger, although I couldn't see the need. I could already have drowned in her eyes. NaRee was, as always, lovely, even though her robes were barely open at the neck, only a glimpse of a starkly white shift and soft white bosom peeking out beneath the thin, rough muslin robe.

The tips of her sandals peeked out beneath the bottom of the robe, her toes tiny and even, the nails silvered and polished.

"The part," she said, her sweet voice echoing of distant bells, "where you almost popped your arm out of the socket. I liked that so very much."

"It takes great artistry to make it look that clumsy," I said. "You should see my father's drunk act."

"Tonight," she said, taking my hand, looking

up into my eyes. She pressed herself gently against me. "Tonight. I will meet you after the performance. For now?"

"For now, we only have a few moments. I think I have your mother confused, but that will wear off."

"Then let us not waste time." She came into my arms, her lips warm on mine.

Too soon, there was a call from the house. "NaRee, Refle is here to speak with you."

She pushed away from me and made a moue. "You'd better leave, and quickly. Over the fence, please."

I could have scrambled for safety most of the time, but not in front of NaRee. "I think that I'm good enough to walk through your front door. In or out, NaRee."

"Yes, yes, my Kami Khuzud, you're always so brave and strong, but now is not the time to prove it, not in front of Refle. He has been . . . pressing me, and this will not—"

She shook her head infinitesimally, and took a step back, away from me.

"NaRee—"

I took a step forward.

"Take your shitty hands off her, peasant."

The hairs at the base of my neck stiffened at the click of clumsy boots on the gravel path.

Refle.

When you're under stress, it's important to move slowly, deliberately; I turned quickly.

I had underestimated Haenno, which surprised me. Normally, people are just complicated puzzles, and I've always been fairly good at puzzles. It was clear what had happened: she hadn't known how to deal with me herself, but she had known enough to send for help, although judging from the amount of time it had taken, Refle had already been somewhere in Ironway.

That wasn't surprising. Toshtai's armorer would, of necessity, spend much time among the ironmongers and ironworkers; he would, by choice, spend even more time there if it allowed him to pay court to NaRee.

He stalked across the stones, his brother Felkoi trailing behind him. Refle's face was flat and emotionless as he approached, his riding crop in one hand, the other resting on the hilt of his sword.

The two of them looked like brothers, but only barely, only around the mouth and eyes. Felkoi was half a head taller, and stood much straighter than Refle, who almost hunched over, one thumb hooked inside the front of his swordbelt, the other hand still tapping the riding crop against his thigh as he glared at me. Where Felkoi was compact, Refle was puffed up, and out; where Felkoi's gestures were precise and understated, Refle sawed at the air with his crop.

I was in trouble.

"Good day, Lord Refle." I bowed correctly, no more.

"Kami Khuzud," he said, pronouncing my name like a curse. "It seems you disturb my intended. Go back to your tossing of little sticks in the air, acrobat." He slapped his riding crop against his leg.

I would have offered to help him hit himself, but I was afraid that he might have taken the suggestion in the spirit in which it was intended, so I didn't.

NaRee stepped between the two of us. "Kami Khuzud was just leaving, Lord Refle."

"He is." His expression softened fractionally. "At your request?"

She hesitated for a moment. "Yes." Well, that was true enough.

"Perhaps a beating will then hurry him on his way." He slapped his riding crop against his thigh, again, harder.

Felkoi grabbed his arm. "No, Refle, leave him be."

It wasn't a contest of strengths, but of status, and of wills. Refle was the older brother, but he was only a hereditary armorer—a noble trade, but still "reeking of trade," as the saying goes, while Felkoi was a blooded warrior, and outranked his older brother. I had the feeling that Felkoi would have gestured an apology to me, but his self-discipline was restraining him better than he was restraining his brother.

My mouth sometimes lives a life all its own. "Please, Lord Felkoi," I said. "Leave your brother be. Let him beat me so badly that I can't perform tonight for Lord Toshtai. It would seem a fair trade."

Refle glared at me with a look of unalloyed hatred as he shrugged off his brother's hand and took a step forward.

It's said that the Foulsmelling Ones of Bhorlani have a whole range of punishments for miscreants, sometimes locking them in small rooms for years—I presume they feed them—but D'Shaian justice, such as it is, tends to be somewhat simpler.

"Lord Toshtai likes to see acrobats, as I recall," I said, standing my ground. "He enjoys them rather a lot. I doubt our act would be as good with a featured player hobbling about in pain."

Refle's jaw clenched so tightly I thought his teeth were going to pop out.

From behind him, Felkoi smiled momentarily. "Let him go, Refle."

Tension hung in the air between Refle and me for a long moment, and I thought that I'd pushed him too far, until his shoulders sagged, and he shrugged.

"Then be gone," Refle said, his feet planted firmly in the middle of the path.

I walked around him—slowly, careful of the audience—and left.

4
Highwire

OF ALL THINGS acrobatic, I hate highwire the most. I'd much rather juggle knives, and somebody as clumsy as me has no business juggling knives.

It's not just that it's not forgiving. Flying is every bit as merciless—even more so—and I've never disliked flying as much as highwire. If you come out of a flying double roll wrongly and miss, you have to grab control of your center in order to be able to hit the net right. When you fall from the wire, you're usually not rolling. It's hard to hurt yourself, but it's dreadfully easy to embarrass yourself.

Part of it, of course, is that when you're on the wire, you're always at the bottom of the pyramid. It doesn't matter what you're doing, if you do it wrong, you fall—and if you're doing it with somebody else, they fall, too.

I hate that. In this world of Nythrea, in this country of D'Shai, it's always been more than hard enough for me to keep my own balance; I don't want to be responsible for somebody else's.

We were going to be doing our standard first-night show. It's important that each of the nights of our appearance builds on the previous evening, but it's also important that those who only attend the first night, or even the preview we do upon arrival, understand that they have been honored by the presence of the Troupe of Gray Khuzud. So we hold back, but only a little, and whittle away at that holding back until our final show.

The troupe had been given access to two rooms: one below, a small room that opened on the courtyard, and a suite above, on the top floor of the donjon. Large Egda, Sala and Evrem were preparing themselves in the dressing room downstairs; the rest of us were readying our entrances on the wire, anchored in the far wall, that stretched out to the trap-platform outside.

The Eresthais had set up the anchor, and Gray Khuzud had checked it, but checking the anchor was *my* job, and while I wasn't a particularly good acrobat, I wanted to be reliable.

It was typical Eresthai work: they had selected a huge mounting staple that was just a little too large, then worked it thoroughly over the edge of the doorframe, and pulled open the legs far enough to slip some ingawood slabs down inside. Then they had clamped the whole thing down tightly, so that it was supported by seven of the massive stones of the wall, before they had tightened up the turnbuckles tightly enough to make the taut wire sing at the tap of a fingernail.

Good, solid work. It's not my favorite anchor—I much prefer the security you get from proper redundant staking—but it was typical of the Eresthais: reliable, competent, unimaginative. My only complaint is that they'd set everything, including the platform out in the courtyard, fractionally too high; I'd be forced to duck as I walked out through the open window.

"Good enough for you?" The older Eresthai smiled as he gave his muscles a practice flex. Naked from the waist up, his torso oiled, his rippling muscles made his skin look almost transparent. Women like all that, so I'm told.

"It's acceptable," I said.

Enki Duzun giggled. "Don't mind him, Eno. He's just being himself." Arms extended gracefully to the sides, she balanced for a moment on the ball of one foot, then dove forward to a handstand.

"My brother," she said, walking back and forth on her hands, "thinks that the trick to being as good as Father is being every bit as unstinting in praise as Father is."

"Really," Gray Khuzud said, from behind.

I started; I hadn't seen Gray Khuzud come in, either.

Folding his arms across his bare chest, he

71

leaned against the doorframe. "Am I really so uncharitable, Enki Duzun?"

She tucked into a forward roll and then came to her feet a fingersbreadth from the wall. It's not a flashy move, but it's a tricky one.

"Well, yes, you are," she said.

Gray Khuzud thought it over for a moment, and then laughed. "I suppose I am. And I suppose you would prefer it if I were to feed you a sweetmeat every time you remembered to hold on to the trapeze with both hands?"

My sister was fearless. "It would be a change, at least," she said.

"It would be a change, at that."

I looked out through the door. Under the flickering torchlight, the rigging stood waiting, taking up half of the courtyard. The rest of the yard was filled, and not just with the nobles of Lord Toshtai's household: minor nobility from holdings all around Den Oroshtai had come into town.

I didn't flatter myself it was just for our performance. Any noble who rejected Lord Toshtai's invitation would likely find that the next invitation would be brought by Dun Lidjun and his army. An invitation by Lord Toshtai didn't have the force of law and tradition that one by the Scion did, but lords less subtle than Toshtai had long noted the effect that the Scion's Invitation had in preventing trouble—for the Scion, at least—and had long taken up the invitation habit.

Still, all mingled with apparent pleasure as they

sat on the chairs that had been hauled outside for the occasion, servants passing among them with trays of meats and candies, and the mugs of hot mulled wine.

I could smell the cinnamon and firemint from here.

Down below, the musicians played something light and inoffensive. Hmm, maybe Fhilt was right: the zivver player did have a heavy thumb on the scratchbox.

I'm not sure that that's *wrong*, mind, but maybe it fits into the category of things that are wrong but that I like anyway; he was skritching out a deceptively complex counter-rhythm.

Gray Khuzud stood beside me. "Very nice, eh?"

"Yes, father."

Absently, affectionately, Father rubbed his blunt, callused fingers against the point of my jaw. "First night, Kami Khuzud."

"I know."

"You'd best be getting downstairs." What he meant was *Don't embarrass us, Kami Khuzud.*

"Yes, father," I said, to both the voiced and the unvoiced command.

Entering to the sound of two silverhorns, Sala opened the first night's show with half a dozen rings spinning on each arm, two each on her neck and waist.

Given that her outfit was silk, sequins, and movement, and given the action that all that entailed, she not only caught the attention of the men in the audience, but—with typical D'Shaian hypocrisy—seemingly bored the women, until the Eresthais lowered Large Egda the rope and loops.

The musicians were good: the drummer took up a slow, hypnotic beat, while the bassskin player dug in his greased thumb for deep, rough notes that sometimes overpowered the silverhorns. The chimer lay back, and the zivver kept time with the music while Sala went into her rope act.

It's an old act, but Sala's delivery was one of the better ones. The basic principle is that the acrobat dangles from a loop tied to the rope, say, two or three manheights above the ground, while somebody below spins the rope, spinning the acrobat.

Beginners hang by the wrist; more advanced work involves hanging by the ankle. Sala, clad only in a jeweled halter and silks, danced up and down the length of the spinning rope.

She hung on by first the wrist, and then the wrist and ankle, and then walked herself up and down the spinning rope, hanging by one foot while she slipped another into the next loop.

Her finale was always the same: facing the rope, she slipped her head into one of the larger of the loops, supporting herself by the back of the neck as Large Egda spun the rope faster and faster, until she was almost horizontal, the sequins on her halter flashing in the torchlight.

It's graceful, but a lot more dangerous than it looks: it's easy to snap the neck.

But then the rope stopped, and she released herself from the loop and slid quickly down the rope, braking only moments before her bare feet gently touched the dirt.

She bowed deeply toward Lord Toshtai, who acknowledged her with a fractional movement of his head that wouldn't have dislodged a fly—for him, a vigorous nod of approval.

My turn.

I bridged the acts with juggling, simple stuff. First night was the easy one; basically, it was just a reprise of my entry routine, without fire. I had been playing with a routine with a single steel ball, but it wasn't ready—I wasn't ready—to play that in front of an audience.

So I tossed three juggling sticks through the air, occasionally holding on to two of them and batting the third around between them, keeping time with the musicians. Which was easy: the zivver player and I did an impromptu rhythm duel, him with his thumb on the scratchbox, me with the sticks, until with a smile and a wave I had to concede him the match and mastery.

His broad, black-bearded face split in a broad smile, and he graciously nodded back, strumming a complex arpeggio as the music slowed, becoming sinuous for Evrem.

I didn't watch. I know that snakes aren't really slimy, but they look that way to me, and they've always scared me. His first-night show wasn't all that spectacular—he only handled two, or three, or at most four at a time, and none of them were the really fierce-looking ones like cobras.

But I still don't have to like snake-handling; I didn't watch until Evrem trotted offstage, his snakebag now bulging with the wriggling creatures.

The music picked up again, and again it was my turn.

Now, while I'm no great acrobat, I have always liked being in front of a crowd. There's something special about standing out in the torchlight, the cold sand beneath your bare feet, with every eye in the house on you.

I trotted out on the sand again, this time with juggling wands, and with Fhilt. Two-man juggling is fun, particularly after you've practiced enough to make it look easy.

I dropped three wands to the dirt and kept three. Fhilt did the same with his. We started off with a simple shower, each juggling his own, then exchanging every fourth wand, rewarded with an *Ah* from the crowd.

Fhilt added a fourth to his stack, and so did I. And again, until each was showering five.

That sort of thing could have gone for another two or three wands, but I had come up with a variation that I thought was kind of special: instead of picking up the sixth wand, I mimed it, added the mimed wand to the shower. It's a tricky move—you have to simulate the natural way that your hand speeds up when you release a wand, slows down when you catch it, all the while treating a phantom as though it were real.

It was a new variation, and it didn't always work, but there was a moment of delicious silence as the crowd held its breath, deciding whether or not to take the move seriously.

You have to help them; it's part of the job. I tried to *see* the wand, hear its gentle *swish* through the air as Fhilt tossed it back toward me, sense the *thwock* as its handle slapped into my palm, feel the weight as I brought it around and up and into my own shower.

And it worked! By the Powers, the audience cheered, the zivver player thumping out his approval on the scratchbox. He nodded to the balding bassskin player, and they picked up the tempo.

It happens, sometimes, when you don't expect it: somebody catches fire, raises kazuh, and it spreads to others, each igniting off the others, like a torch taking fire from another one. This time, it started with Fhilt, and the spark was caught by the lead silverhorn player, as a triple-tongued fanfare both supported and cut through the applause.

I've always been sensitive to kazuh; I could feel its fire burn in my mind.

For a moment, I thought it was going to stop at that, but the zivver player picked up the theme, drawing a sweet stream of inverted, twisted runs out of his strings, his thumb hammering sharply on the scratchbox in counterpoint, while the bass-skin player supported the whole structure of notes with a light thumb, and the drummer shattered the rhythm into a thousand raindrop spatters of accent.

The second silverhorn player and the chimer were the last to catch it, the horn breaking and reassembling his leader's fanfare, the chimer tapping all six metal fingernails against his crystals so hard I thought they'd shatter, his thumbs and little fingers barely able to dampen the notes of old chords as he followed the frantic progression into new ones.

I didn't have to look at them to see that all six of them had raised kazuh, and I didn't have to look up to my father or across to Fhilt for approval to keep the juggling going on longer than we had intended.

I could feel more than see Fhilt smile, and then, with a coldness washing across me, his face went all ethereal and vague as his kazuh flared even brighter.

"Try this, Kami Khuzud," he called out, tossing one of the wands aside, substituting a phantom wand for it, including it in the shower, passing it to me.

No.

But it was too late. We had tried two in practice, but never in front of a crowd. I kept up with him, trying to become motion, trying to be the

78

juggling, not merely do it, but it was all I could do to keep up.

No; I would have to let skill go where kazuh couldn't take me—I tossed one of my own wands aside, and then we were showering six wands, three of them solid, three of them imaginary, and every one of them real to us and to the wide-eyed faces in the audience.

The silverhorn screamed, notes rising and falling in a sweet staccato above the steady thrum of the bassskin and the complex chords of the zivver, rising to a crescendo, then falling back into an introductory arpeggio.

The sound was still sweet and full, but it was practiced, not quite the rich patchwork of kazuh music.

The moment had passed, and I didn't know whether to laugh or to cry.

The crowd knew what to do: they cheered.

I nodded to Fhilt; he gathered up all of the wands, imaginary and real, and showered them as the rope dropped down from above.

I grabbed it in time for Large Egda to pull me and the audience's focus high into the air, dropping both me and their attention on the outer platform of the highwire. Below, Fhilt finished with a flurry of tosses to Evrem, who was waiting in the wings, and left the sand to a loud spatter of applause.

My turn, again.

Actually, this was a simple job—I had to try to

walk from the platform through the window, and as long as I didn't lose control, it would be fine if I fell into the net; my job was to make wirewalking look as difficult as it is, not as easy as Gray Khuzud and Enki Duzun would make it.

I hate highwire, but I took a tentative step out, and called for the deep sense of balance that an acrobat must have, will have, as, arms spread widely, I walked over the audience toward the window, stooping as I fell into the Eresthais' waiting arms.

"Very nice, Kami Khuzud," the elder Eresthai said, as they lowered me to the floor.

Enki Duzun and Gray Khuzud were ready for their entrance: they exited through the window, one after the other, ducking through with more grace than I could have displayed.

Fhilt had followed me up to the platform and was already crossing toward the window in the first part of the highwire act.

Normally, I would have watched them; normally, I could watch my father perform as long as he cared to perform. But the act had left me weak at the knees. I leaned back against the wall, the rough stone cold against my sweaty back, and closed my eyes.

"Very nice, Kami Khuzud," the younger of the Eresthais said, pressing a mug of cold tea into my hands. I drained half of it in one gulp, a trickle of the sweet nectar running down my neck while the rest ran down my throat.

The Fhilt/Enki Duzun/Gray Khuzud first-night highwire act is a flurry of fast motion, not of balance and danger. It's a comedy of dramatic entrances and exits: right on cue, my sister did a forward roll that brought her through the window, dropping lightly from the wire to the deep pile of the carpet, her hand sweeping for the mug that I was already holding out.

She swigged a mouthful of the cold tea, slammed down the stone mug and then dashed away through the door, heading downstairs, giving me only a quick smile and a get-going wave.

Well, it was true enough. I was done for this show, and there was no particular reason to be waiting around for her teeterboard remount of the wire, or for the finale.

"They have porcelain tubs filled down at the baths," the older Eresthai said. "With very hot water. No waiting. And clean clothes."

While the house is supposed to see to the bathing needs of the troupe, too often the locals think of us as Bhorlani—tepid baths in cold bronze tubs.

But hot water, clean clothes and NaRee were waiting for me—I got going.

Still damp from the bath, I waited for NaRee under the old jimsum tree where we had first kissed, over by the south wall of Toshtai's keep.

It stood there starkly alone, just at the edge of an overhang kept in place by a partly crumbling retaining wall, lit only by the crescent moon and the lamps on the castle wall, their light flickering through the long, breeze-stirred leaves.

A warm place, even in autumn: it seemed to generate its own heat, although the real explanation probably had something more to do with the smithy in the basement near the south wall of the keep, and the chimney that rose within the walls of the keep itself.

Below, the harsh blue moonlight shining on the still water made the rice paddies seem austere and alien, a too-loose liquid cloth, perhaps woven for the giants of the land and sea that used to walk Nythrea before the coming of man.

That was a nice image, but perhaps not quite romantic enough.

There's nothing terribly romantic about rice paddies, I'm afraid.

I spread the blanket on the edge of it all, then sat down, and let my feet dangle over. It was pretty, but the Long War was still going on, and some things were not being taken care of. Someday the retaining wall would give way, and the rocks and the tree would fall down the slope on the houses far below.

Well, they weren't my houses.

"We are not children anymore, Kami Khuzud," NaRee said.

I had been too busy working out clever things to say to listen for her. She sat down next to me. Gone were the formal robe and makeup of the day: she was dressed in a pair of leather breeches and a short informal robe, her feet barely protected by sandals. The straps were tight against her skin.

"True enough." I smiled. "Remember when you used to throw rocks at me?"

"You were an evil little boy, always strutting about, boastful of your traveling."

Traveling is either one of the great drawbacks or great advantages of belonging to a troupe; most D'Shai—except for our beloved ruling class, of course, who make their semi-lustral pilgrimage to pledge their undying loyalty to the Scion—grow up, live and die within a day's walk of the place where they're born.

"I still am," I said, slipping an arm around her waist. "Boastful of my traveling, that is."

She leaned close to me, and rested her head against my shoulder, her breath sweet and warm on my neck. "Tell me," she said. Her breath smelled of firemint.

"What do you want to hear about?"

"Anything. What do you see on the road, the roads?"

She'd asked before; she always did. And although I collected stories and images to spread before her, when the moment came to trot them out, I couldn't remember one that I'd saved. Well, I could always start with the Ven, as I had all the times before.

"We were in the Ven two months ago. There are paved and unpaved roads there, but the godboneroads are still the same, and still the same strange things."

"Strange?" she asked, as she had many times before.

"They run along the ridges and hillcrests, some of them from town to town, some of them from nowhere to nowhere. They push up from the ground, smooth, like weathered bone, but yellowed in the sunlight. Grass and trees grow up near to the godboneroads, but never on them."

They are smooth beneath bare feet in the daytime, but slippery in the rain, like they are covered with . . . something.

I remembered, one rainy day, trying to negotiate my way along a godboneroad that led down the side of a hill, and how my feet slid out beneath me, and how I slid helplessly down the smooth whiteness, accelerating, slipping and sliding until the road bent and tossed me into the air and down into a rice paddy.

"Who made them? Who keeps them up, and why?" She ran a sharp fingernail gently down the side of my neck, then planted a light series of kisses where the fingernail had been.

"Nobody knows who made them; and nothing needs to keep them up."

"Godboneroads," she said. "Things must be very strange in the Ven."

"There are strange enough roads in the True Shai and Otland." I closed my eyes for a moment to get my bearings, and then pointed. "A few points north of sunwise . . . there," I said. "If you were to follow the road all the way there, you could walk down to where it leads down the cliffs to the shore of the Inner Sea, and further."

"Further?" she asked, as though I hadn't told her about it before.

"Yes, even further, if you had the desire to follow it. It doesn't stop at the water; the road goes on, down into the sea. I don't know how far."

"Tell me."

"I can remember pushing down into the dark, cold water, fishskin goggles tight against my face, past the long tendrils of seaweed that reached up their clammy fingers for me, trusting to the oaths of Cicela that the distant vague shapes that feed near the Oled outflow would leave you alone as long as you stay within reach of the road."

"Cicela?"

"A friend of mine."

It was hard to tell whether her smile was warm or cold. "You seem to have friends all over D'Shai."

"It comes with the route, NaRee. But there is nobody who means as much to me as you do."

I couldn't tell if she believed me or not, but I tried to persuade myself that I didn't care. I'm a fairly good liar at times; I managed to convince myself, just for a moment, that I didn't care.

Life is sometimes so predictable: that was the moment, of course, when she came into my arms, her mouth warm and wet on mine.

After a long time, she pulled away, although not far. "You were talking about the road into the sea?" she asked.

"I was, at that." I tried to recreate the moment in my mind so I could lay it out before her. "Dozens of divers disappear each year; more come back rasped by the brush of harsh sharkskin, but nobody who stays near the road ever disappears, as far as we know."

"Why?"

"Nobody knows why." I toyed with the drawstrings of her robe, gently tugging at the knot. "It's said that those on the road are under the protection of the Scion himself, but about that I don't pretend to know either much or little."

"Were you very scared?" She toyed with my fingers for a moment, then tugged the knot open herself.

"Never," I said, pressing her back to the grass. "I knew I would come back to you."

"Kami Khuzud, do you always know just what to say?" Her arms slid around my neck.

"Always." I pulled her robe open. Beneath, her belly was smooth and white. I drew my finger across her skin upwards. Each small breast fit neatly in the palm of my hand, as always. "Always."

"Well," I asked, perhaps a bit more exasperated than I should have been, "how *did* you sneak out?" I regretted the sound of that instantly, and shook my head in apology, sealing it with a quick kiss on her forehead.

I pulled at the gate. It rattled, but it was still very definitely locked.

"I just walked through the gate," she said. "Truly, Kami Khuzud, I was careful to leave the bar latched up. Somebody must have dropped it."

That didn't look good. I had hoped that Na-Ree's parents would continue to turn their faces away from us. That was the best I could hope for. I would need their approval to court her openly, approval that would not be given to a peasant boy—but when you're a peasant, even if only in theory, you learn that what matters is what happens, not whether or not others accept that it happens.

But I gave NaRee an encouraging smile. "Walls wouldn't keep me from you; they won't keep me from walking you all the way home."

You don't always need to see what you're doing; I fixed the location of the bramblebush in my mind as I backed off, then ran at the wall.

In midstep, I decided to show off; instead of just vaulting to the top, I'd do a handspring from the edge of the wall, and spring over. Besides, it would give me more room away from the bramblebush, and I didn't fancy another close fall to it.

I ran, and I leaped and sprang, catching the edge of the fence with my fingertips, but pulling my knees in toward my chest in a tuck as I straightened my arms, and sprang off the top of the fence, pulling myself over in a pike position as I looked for the landing spot I'd used before.

I landed with a clatter and fell over, hard.

Two rakes lay on the ground, each with a dozen finger-length iron tines pointing up, toward the sky.

A chill washed up my back, and then back down. If I'd just vaulted over as I'd done that afternoon, I could easily have landed on the tines, crippling myself quite handily, instead of just tripping over the handles.

Not everything that happens is a lesson of which Gray Khuzud would approve. Sometimes it pays to be a show-off, I guess.

"That's a silly way to leave tools," I said, mainly to myself. "Somebody might get hurt."

Or perhaps that was the idea. No, that didn't make any sense. I was reading too much into Refle's look of naked hatred, that was all.

Even assuming it was him, how would he know where to leave the rakes? That was easy: I had marked the spot with my earlier landing, and that was just where the rakes were.

I would have to be more careful. I would have to be very careful.

"Kami Khuzud? Are you hurt?" NaRee's whisper was far too loud. My darling wasn't all that good at sneaking around. Not enough practice, I supposed, at first irritated, then thankful. I didn't *want* her getting a lot of practice sneaking around.

I unhooked the gate, and let her in.

"Your gardener is clumsy," I said, collecting a quick kiss. "Good night, NaRee. Tomorrow evening?"

"As long as we have, Kami Khuzud."

5
Sore Points

HE JUMPED ME two blocks short of the Widow Rupon's house.

I hadn't been paying attention—or rather, I had been paying attention, but not to the right things.

What I had been doing was walking home alone, after. Something I was not unfamiliar with; it comes with the lack of territory, so to speak. I've walked home alone, after, many times.

Above me, the night was full of winking stars, a silver crescent of moon high in the sky; below, the street seemed a bit softer, easier beneath my feet than it had been before.

It was late, well past the hour of the bear and into the hour of the lion, and the streets were quiet and empty, save for the whistling of the wind through the jimsum trees, the clicking of fidgetbugs in the eaves and gutters, and the far-off *taroo* of a hairy owl. I had passed a cloaked nightwatcher in Ironway, and had returned his raised hand of greeting, but I hadn't seen any of the other watchers, which wasn't surprising. I doubt that there were more than a dozen in the whole town, and they would tend to patrol on the eastern side of the town, downwind, where smells of smoke would be blown toward their nostrils, rather than away.

It was time for all D'Shai, good and bad, to be tucked safely in their beds asleep, and while troupers sleep late—very late, by peasant standards; peasants are up before the hour of the cock—I'd long ago learned that the hour of the hare does not wait for Kami Khuzud to finish with his dreams.

Something whistled through the air behind me.

I turned just in time to catch a glimpse of a stick or maybe a truncheon moving toward me, and ducked aside. He missed with the stick, but the back of his fist caught me high on the cheekbone, shattering the night into light and pain, and then the ground came up and slammed me in the back. The streets in Den Oroshtai are of cobbled stones—one of the larger ones caught me just over the kidney.

He kicked me hard in the ribs a few times, and then in the pit of the stomach. My hands flailing uselessly, vainly, I folded over like a damp towel, so much in pain that I couldn't even try to move out of the way of the foot that snapped my head back, exposing my neck for a final, fatal blow.

It didn't fall. I guess he couldn't just do it; he had to work himself up to it.

I knew that it was Refle who stood over me in the dark, a bulk I could more sense than see. It was him, I knew it was him, but he was dressed in the black hood and cape of an assassin; I couldn't have even sworn that it was a man, much less Refle.

I tried to gasp out something, but it was all I could do to groan.

He kicked me here and there—I don't remember the exact order; I was too busy to take extended notes.

I do remember his finale, though: his eyes hidden in the folds of his hood and cape, he didn't say anything; cleanly, neatly, balanced on one foot with an equilibrium I would have admired in other circumstances, he toed me in the testicles.

I gagged, hunched over on my side, my stomach purging itself, although of what only the Powers knew.

He lifted his foot again, then stopped, his head cocked to one side. I couldn't hear anything over the sound of my own quiet groans and the red rush of pain in my head and ears, but I guess he heard something, because he raised a long gloved finger, as though in warning; then, balanced like an acrobat, he neatly spun and stalked off into the night, turning a corner and disappearing.

Footsteps pounded on the stones behind me as I lay there, the taste of sour vomit filling my mouth, cupping myself, trying not to inhale as I retched again.

"Who are you?"

I groaned out an answer, but I guess I wasn't quite coherent.

"The acrobat boy, no?" he asked. Surprisingly gentle fingers pried at my shoulder, and at my side. "Kami Khuzud, is it not? I am Helden, the watcher. Lie still, Kami Khuzud—you likely have broken bones."

The watcher had a keen eye for the obvious.

He cleared his throat as he knelt beside me, and raised his voice, a firm tenor piercing through the night, singing,

"Chief of Nightwatch, you are now called,

"A boy lies broken on Bankstreet,

"Watcher Helden bids you come now,

"Let your steps be sure and fleet."

He cocked his head, listening, then nodding as the song was picked up far away, then was echoed, then quickly answered in a gritty baritone. "Good. He comes." He shrugged out of his cloak, then slipped it under my head.

"Rest a moment, Kami Khuzud, and prepare yourself. When you are ready to rise, I will help you."

There wasn't much I could tell them.

I knew who it was, of course, but I was hardly in a position to swear to anything except what I had seen, and what I had seen was enough to persuade me that I had been attacked by Refle. Still, making accusations against a noble isn't a way for a peasant—even only a theoretical peasant—to guarantee himself a long life.

So I was as circumspect as possible. Which wasn't much; circumspection is one of the many things I've not picked up from my father.

"—I know it was Lord Refle, *you* know it was Lord Refle, let us not turn our faces away from it."

"I look away from little, Eldest Son Acrobat," the chief watcher said. "I do not waive warrants, as you will see if you swear one: if you produce it, I will present it."

A spasm of pain washed over me in a red wave. Enki Duzun, kneeling beside me, gripped me hard around the wrist until it passed.

When I could speak again, my voice was ragged, frayed at the edges. "But I can not do that, Amused By Perching Redbird. I am sure of it, but I can not swear to it; the ordeal would probably kill me."

Chief Watcher Verniem Dar Hartren didn't look like somebody who had been ever amused by anything, much less a redbird; I assumed it was his baby name, and not a changed one.

He was a big man, almost as large and heavily muscled as Large Egda, but was both flabbier and somehow seemed tougher, meaner, which is not unusual for a firewatcher. I wouldn't know for sure, but some say that more towns have been lost to accidental fires than wars have put to the torch. While the notion of armed peasants scandalizes lords of other domains, in Den Oroshtai the firewatch is both armed and allowed to do almost anything to almost anybody—bourgeois, middle class, (of course) peasant, and even a member of our beloved ruling class—to keep that from happening.

Still, firewatchers are kept in their place. A watcher going for the challenge sword was always met by a true kazuh warrior, his kazuh fully upon him.

"It might, at that." He considered the matter for a moment, blunt fingers drumming against thick thigh. "Still, I've sent for the sorcerer; we shall see what he says."

The rest of the troupe gathered in the parlor, hair and clothing disarranged, eyes puffy from sleep.

Sala, kneeling on a cushion near me, a flask of Scarlet Teardrops in her hands, had thrown her robe on too quickly: she had neglected a strategic tie, and the part of me that wasn't preoccupied with aching and hurting and suffering was vaguely amused at the way both watchers tried to keep their gaze and minds on me and my injuries and off her and the way her right nipple tended to peek out when she sipped.

Fhilt fluffed a pillow and adjusted it behind my head. "Such a careless idiot," he said. "Wake us all up in the middle of the night."

I would have liked to hit him with a juggling stick. That was so typical of Fhilt, more irritated at being woken up than upset that a member of the troupe had been beaten.

Sala sipped at her flask, then tucked it away in her robes. "Sometimes there's nothing you can do about a fall," she said. A typical Sala comment: true, but not at all relevant to what was going on.

"He didn't *fall*," Fhilt said, not playing along. "I know you can't pay attention to what's happening in front of you, but he didn't fall. Some misbegotten son of a pig mauled him." His knuckles were white.

Enki Duzun laid her hand on his arm. "Be still, Fhilt; don't snap at Sala. Kami Khuzud will be well."

Large Egda sat apart from the rest, perched gingerly on the edge of a settee. He shook his head, his steak-sized hands gesturing aimlessly as though he wanted to reach out and help, but couldn't. I couldn't tell what he was thinking from the dull expression on his doughy face. Poor Egda; he didn't know what to do.

I forced a smile. "I'll be fine, Egda," I said.

He just didn't understand any of it. When you're that large, you have to be either gentle or a warrior, and while Large Egda sometimes forgot his own strength, he was a mild man who didn't understand violence.

My father brought me another mug of hot urmon tea, the rough stone mug cradled in his thick hands. He brought it to my lips, accidentally splashing some of the hot tea on my chest. That surprised me, in two ways: first, because I'd never seen Gray Khuzud clumsy; second, because it hurt. I didn't think I could hurt any more.

I drank. It tasted like fur.

"Have some more," he said.

"I'd rather have something stronger."

Sala, her every move as always a step in a dance, rose; she then knelt gently beside me, tucking the hem of her shiny silk robes around her knees and clucking sympathetically. She reached into the front of her robes and produced her slim, filigreed flask, which she put into my hand.

"Easy it is, easy it is." She gently bent my fingers around the flask. "It's not a good idea, Kami Khuzud—so take only a small sip."

I thumbed back the silver crown and tilted the flask back. It was hot, and from more than her body. The heat washed the taste of blood and vomit from my throat, and set up a pleasant warm feeling in my middle.

I could get accustomed to drinking a lot of Scarlet Teardrops. Quickly.

There was a firm, peremptory rap on the front door. Fat Madame Rupon, still in her bulky nightdress, scurried away to open it. She returned, momentarily, with Lord Arefai—Lord Toshtai's seventh son, a young scowler too far down in the

line of succession ever to be the heir apparent—
and Narantir, followed by two servitors, each
gently carrying a man-sized burlap bag.

Being woken in the middle of the night hadn't
had any visible effect on Lord Arefai, except perhaps to annoy him. His boots and tunic were of
the same dark brown leather which contrasted
properly with his blousy canvas pantaloons of just
the correct creamy tan; his sword belt was pulled
fashionably tight about his waist. His hair, black
as his father's, was pulled back in a finger-set
queue, freshly oiled and tied; beneath his short-
trimmed beard, his jaw clenched in irritation.

"Well," Arefai said, "what is all this?" His hand
flicked the air, as though to brush it all away.

"Lord," Verniem Dar Hartren said, "it appears
that young Kami Khuzud had been beaten by a
brigand, mauled by a masked man."

"But that is forbidden!"

"That doesn't undo it, Lord Arefai."

Arefai could have taken that as insolence, but
he was used to the chief watcher dealing in sober
realism, I guess. He didn't rear back and chop off
the chief's head, which is always a good sign.

"I'm not used to Lord Toshtai's laws being broken," Arefai said.

They chewed on that for a while, while Narantir stuck the end of his beard in his mouth and
chewed on *that*—wizards have few social graces.
I kept as patient as I could, waiting for them all
to spit it out. It's amazing how patient I can be

when I've got a vial of Scarlet Teardrops pushing the pain away.

I sipped at it again, and again, the warmth penetrating not only my middle, but my tired bones and mind.

Narantir gave up first. "Interesting as this all is, would it offend Your Lordship to take this discussion to the other room while I examine the patient and mend his broken bones?"

Arefai raised an eyebrow. "Why don't you simply move the peasant?"

"Because, Lord," Verniem Dar Hartren said, "the boy has broken bones."

The wizard looked at me as though he was unhappy that he hadn't thought of moving me. I really didn't like that much. Then again, I really didn't like him much.

"Of course, of course. We shall wait in the kitchen," Arefai said, dismissing my fractures with exceptionally good grace. "All of you, out of the room. Let the wizard work," he said, gesturing abstractly at the rest of the troupe. Everybody left except for Narantir, his two silent servitors, and Enki Duzun. I guess the young lord didn't notice, or hadn't meant her.

Still in conversation with Verniem Dar Hartren, Arefai followed the rest out of the room.

The wizard shook his head from side to side as, with grunts, groans and creaking of limbs, he knelt down next to me, taking my right wrist in his surprisingly gentle hands.

He noted how I relaxed at his touch, then looked me in the eye.

"We may not like each other, Eldest—Kami Khuzud, that is, but this is a matter of mahrir. True magic, not this zuhrir of yours. I know mahrir, if I may flatter myself."

Flatter yourself all you want, fat one. Just heal me. I didn't say it; I'm not that stupid.

"The Ten Pulses first." He felt at both wrists, at three spots on my neck, both elbows and armpits, and finally—with a clinical detachment that prevented any embarrassment—at my groin.

"Your pulses are adequate, although you really should see to your balance of forces, when you are up and about. Too much beef and butter in your diet, I suppose; I recommend carrots and whey. Clearly you have some broken bones. Let us see which ones."

I had the impression that he was becoming so involved in showing off that he was forgetting that he didn't like me.

That's generally true about wizards, by the way: once you let them get going, it's hard to turn them off.

He gestured at the two servitors. The first opened his bag to reveal what appeared to be a complete skeleton, wired together like a graveyard marker. The second pulled out a similar skeleton, except that—

"He's in worse shape than I am." It was a weak joke, but the best I could do at the moment.

"That can be changed," the wizard said. "For one thing, he's dead. For another, each and every one of his two hundred and six bones is broken, each once; for yet another, I did the breaking—this won't work for somebody else."

"How did you get it?" Enki Duzun asked.

"It was difficult, persuading Lord Toshtai to have two poachers executed by drowning instead of, well, instead of the usual, but it did keep both skeletons intact, as well as the sinew. There are many uses for sinew." He clucked. "You wouldn't believe how much trouble it is to bone a poacher, though," Narantir went on, unfolding a strange device from his leather bag—it looked like a spike on a tripod, two coils of green-tinged copper wire projecting from the base of the tripod.

He set the tripod down between me and the skeletons, then strung a long wire to the spike. "We shall see. This may not work well; it's possible that you don't have the standard complement of bones."

"Eh?"

"Well, the slant-eyed Bhorlani tend to have an extra pair of ribs, and some people's wrists don't fuse quite properly."

Enki Duzun was getting interested. "Fuse? You mean, like what smiths do with metal?"

"Oh, yes. Babies are born with more than three hundred bones—they fuse as the baby gets older. There are just too many combinations—I don't have a good set of baby bones, not yet. Still collecting, young death by young death—boning a baby is fairly easy." He brightened. "Ever regret not being a magician?"

Enki Duzun shook her head. "Not really."

"Pity. I can usually dispel that regret, but only where it exists."

His wizard's bag yielded two wooden boxes, a glass-stoppered bottle and a wad of cotton.

"Now," he said, warming to the subject—wizards always like to talk too much, in both senses—"we'll have to calibrate the equipment. For that, we pick an unbroken bone. Is there one you're sure isn't broken?"

"Several." I tapped at my arm.

"Very good. We run wires from each of these two ulnas to their coils, and then from both to your ulna." He opened one of the wooden boxes to reveal a row of shiny needles.

"My favorite part," he said, fitting the needle to the end of one of the wires. He spat on a cotton ball and daubed both the needle and my arm, near the wrist.

Then he stuck the needle in my arm, and again, I learned something I'd have been able to work out by myself: that no matter how much you're aching from broken bones and a bruised body, if somebody sticks you with a needle, it hurts.

"*Ow.*"

"You like that, do you?" Enki Duzun glared at him.

"Oh, yes." The wizard smiled.

"That's really disgusting, you know—"

"Shh," I said. "He cares as much about me as Fhilt does."

"Eh?" Enki Duzun raised a slim eyebrow.

"You heard Fhilt, complaining about the way he was being woken up at night."

She snorted. "Sometimes, Kami Khuzud, I despair of you, I really do," Enki Duzun said, with an angry toss of her head that flicked her short black hair out of her eyes. "Some days I think you'll never be able to listen past what anybody says to what they mean."

The wizard had left the needle stuck in my arm while he opened the second wooden box. Sitting inside, cushioned gently on purple velvet, was something that looked like a compass needle; he lifted it and gently set it on the tripod's spike.

"Law of Similarity," he said. "Once I start the device, phlogiston will flow from similar to similar, and back. Now, since the bone is unbroken, more phlogiston will flow through the wire coil between your bone and the unbroken skeleton than between your bone and the broken one. Understand?"

He didn't wait for an answer. Wizards *never* wait for an answer; I don't know why they bother to ask questions, given that—at least, if you listen to them—they always know everything. He just pulled out yet another box, opened it, extracted a piece of ordinary-looking chalk and scribbled a few quick runes on the leg of the tripod.

"Now . . ." he lowered his voice and whispered a few quiet syllables, and snapped his fingers.

The runes flashed into flame, and I felt a strange tingling in my arm—along with the pain. My arm jerked, flinging the needle away.

"I didn't do that—" I started.

"Hush, hush. It was my fault; I will handle it, Kami Khuzud, I will handle it." The needle—the other one, the one that looked like a compass needle—had popped off the spike and now hung in the air between the two skeletons, what looked like little bolts of lightning flowing between it and the two skeletons.

Narantir swallowed a curse; he muttered a quick phrase and snapped his fingers, and the compass needle dropped to the carpet. "That's what you get for rushing me—"

"My brother did *not* rush you," Enki Duzun snapped. "It's your own fault; you were too busy talking to do it right."

"And how would you know what's right and what isn't?" The wizard ran nail-bitten fingers through his beard, then wiped his forehead with his sleeve. "Never mind, never mind; I forgot to make the skeletons dissimilar to each other, and that's just a matter of a moment's work," he said, his chalk at work on each of the white ulnas, scrawling a different set of runes on each before he traced over the ash on the tripod's arm, then rewiped my arm and the needle, and reinserted it, again muttering.

Again, the chalk flashed into flame, but this time, the needle stayed on the spike; it pointed unerringly toward the unbroken skeleton.

"That seems adequate, doesn't it? Now, let's try your fourth rib." He untied the wires, and re-tied them to corresponding ribs, then opened my tunic, felt down the side of my chest, wiped and speared me.

The needle swung, this time pointing toward the broken skeleton.

"Better than zuhrir and kazuh, eh, Kami Khu-zud?" he said, shifting the wires again.

"Not really."

"Better than zuhrir for finding broken bones," he said. "Or do you think you can find your bro-ken bones by balancing a ball on your buttocks?"

By the end of the hour, Narantir had completed his inventory, I had a couple of hundred pinholes to accompany my bruises and broken bones, and Arefai was back for the wizard's report. "Lord, we have six fractures, as well as the bruising."

"And you say that some masked man did this to you, lad?" Lord Arefai asked me. "Answer promptly when I speak to you."

"Yes, Lord. I can't swear who it is, although I wouldn't mind if you questioned Lord Refle. He'll deny it."

The young lord looked over at Narantir. "That could be fixed, if need be."

"Now, don't be looking at me, young lord, don't be looking at me. Truth spells are very unreliable, and, if the truth be known, which it usually is, one way or another, I don't like doing them—they're too . . . subtle, they are. Take far too much energy, too. Law of Similarity, yes, but it's not a precise application of it. I'd have to kill something for extra power, a rabbit, at the very least, and if I've said it before, I'll say it again now: necromancy is a bad habit to get into."

"I wasn't thinking of similarity, Narantir. I was thinking of the Law of Contagion, or of Relevance."

The wizard snorted. "Ah. Of *course*, how very foolish of me, Your Lordship. Yes, yes, just find me the stick that cracked young Kami Khuzud on the head, and the glove that held the stick, and the hand that filled that glove—"

"So, it would work?"

"No," the wizard said sharply, then apparently realized that that wouldn't do. "Begging your pardon, Lord, but it won't work. You can possibly fit the glove to the hand, if the glove still exists, which I doubt. The odds are, though—and I'll cast some bones on it if you'd like—that the stick didn't interact enough with the glove for Contagion to apply. For a certainty, the crack on his head is barely relevant to the stick that made it; to amplify the relevance and make it measurable—if we can—we're back to necromancy again, and again you have me squatting naked over a pentagram with a knife in one hand and a cute little bunny in the other."

Enki Duzun cocked her head to one side. "It doesn't bother you to bone a person, but you do mind killing *rabbits*?"

"Idiot child—those who I have boned were already dead; they didn't mind. The rabbit doesn't like it; I've asked several."

"Father won't like this," Arefai said, lolling back in the chair, toying with a cup of urmon tea on a translucent, almost transparent bone saucer, which was probably the finest thing Madame Rupon owned. "He won't have woken by now, but I will be prepared to speak to him when he rises. Yes, that is what I'll do."

Suddenly, decisively, he leaped to his feet, setting the cup and saucer very gently on the table at his elbow. "In the meantime, heal the peasant boy, good Narantir." He turned and stalked from the room, calling out a loud thank-you to fat Madame Rupon for her hospitality. Not all members of our b ed ruling class constantly make an effort to m..streat the lower classes.

Narantir shook his head and pulled more apparatus from his wizard's bag. "Waste of time and effort, and easier commanded than completed." He clucked for a moment, considering. "Another Similarity spell, and now I have to fix this, too."

He produced a small steel knife and pried the lid off a clay pot. "Glue."

"Glue?" My voice squeaked around the edges. "You fix broken bones with glue?"

"Not for you, idiot," he said. "For it. Him." He gestured at the broken skeleton. "Law of Similarity, like to like—I fix his bones, it fixes yours. I will have to get a new broken skeleton, mind, and poachers are hard to find."

Enki Duzun raised an eyebrow. "Why not just break the bones apart and clean off the glue?"

"Ah. Everyone's a magician." Narantir chuckled. "Because you don't want to have your brother's bones break apart, little one. It won't do your soft tissues any good at all, Kami Khuzud, but I'll have you up on your feet and hobbling around by nightfall."

I was.

But it was the strangest feeling: my bones felt like they were glued in place. Honest.

INTERLUDE:

Way of the Warrior

DUN LIDJUN LET the morning sun wash over his tired bones as he made his way out to the courtyard, Lord Arefai, seventh son of Lord Toshtai, at his side, the four warriors of his immediate guard at his heels, a physician and apothecary—both warriors in theory—tagging along behind them.

The morning sun hit the sides of the granaries just right, the stone shattering the light into rainbow flickers. The stones of the path clicked beneath Dun Lidjun's sandals, while a crow, its feathers glossy as fine oiled leather, mocked them from the branch of a mute, gnarled oak.

"You should let me do the testing, Dun Lidjun," Arefai said, giving an absent swing with one of the pair of wooden practice swords that he carried. "Father left it in your hands."

"Precisely, Lord," Dun Lidjun said, choosing each word as carefully as an artist would choose each brushstroke. "So: when *you* are lord of Den

Oroshtai, you may decide into whose hands to put the testing. For now, the decision remains in these old ones."

"Yes, yes, the decision is yours. And—"

"And so I shall do the testing," Dun Lidjun said. He *had* planned to allow Arefai to take charge this morning, but some distasteful undercurrent in the younger man's manner had made Dun Lidjun change his mind.

Perhaps he was irritated with the easy way that Arefai held the practice sword wrongly: tightly with his thumb and forefinger, loose with the outer fingers.

Pulling at it, not balancing it. Treating it as a toy, not a simulacrum.

That was not the Way.

That was one of the things Dun Lidjun never liked, how men born into the noble class had to be treated as though they were warriors, even when you could see that they didn't have the kazuh, would never have the kazuh.

Unfair, old man, unfair, he chided himself.

Arefai was a true kazuh warrior; Dun Lidjun had felt his kazuh flare a dozen times. The young lord was simply being thoughtless and lazy, a perquisite of youth, one rarely underexercised.

Dun Lidjun worked his shoulders under his brightly burnished bone armor, the reticulated segments of his lacquered pauldron and gorget clicking like dice.

Four young men waited for him around the

challenge sword. They gathered about the stone altar where the sword lay protected from the elements by a silk fly, protected from theft by the certainty of Lord Toshtai's retribution. An occasional killing was perhaps something to be shrugged off, but theft was not permitted in Den Oroshtai, or anywhere else within Lord Toshtai's dominion.

Lord Toshtai did things differently than most lords, and while much of that irritated Dun Lidjun—then again, the old man had to admit to himself, much of much irritated Dun Lidjun; it was part of getting old—some of it pleased him.

The challenge sword was one example. Both the Scion's law and even more ancient tradition required that a sword be kept available to the men of the lower classes who might claim the kazuh and status of a warrior; but in many baronies, the challenge sword was old and rusty or, if a sound weapon, kept within the walls of the lord's keep.

Lord Toshtai's challenge sword was not only of fine gleaming nebbigin steel, it was a Sunder sword, one of the handful of the master's blades remaining, and it lay in the open courtyard at the foot of the hill leading up through Old Town to the castle.

The blade was available to anyone who wanted to challenge a warrior: to be tested, perhaps to the death.

Everything was to be a lesson: the sword was there as a reminder to the lower classes that they were the lower classes, and not noble, not warriors; taking the testing was a reminder to the lower classes that they belonged in the lower classes; and doing the testing was a lesson to warriors on how to handle peasants, bourgeois, and middles who would dare to take up the sword.

Arefai had irritated Dun Lidjun, but he couldn't let his irritation affect the testing. That was not the Way of the Warrior—anger had no part it in.

"Your name, boy," Dun Lidjun asked of the first of the four boys, a well-made lad with brooding eyes and nervous hands.

"I am Ben Der Donesey, Lord," the boy said.

"And you think yourself a warrior?"

Ben Der Donesey cocked his head to one side. "I would hope so, Lord," he said, too eagerly, too confidently.

Far too confidently.

Ignoring the wooden practice weapons, Dun Lidjun drew his own sword, once again reveling in the purity, the density of the dark striations of the fold-forged Eisenlith blade. It was a lovely sword, perhaps only two or three grades the inferior of a bright Sunder like the gleaming challenge sword, or a fine blue Greater Frosuffold like Lord Toshtai's.

It was, as was often true for a warrior, his single most prized possession, easily worth a third as much as all the rest of his belongings put together: his horses, his house, his tributary villages, the collection of ugly ancient Eremai watercolors that Lord Toshtai had given him, the lot of it. Not that he would trade as much again for the sword. His Eisenlith blade had saved his life dozens of times; could that be said for a dozen villages full of peasants?

The boy's eyes widened. "Not the practice sword, Lord?"

"Not for you, Ben Der Donesey. Take up the challenge sword and come at me. Or leave."

Dun Lidjun waited, with lowered kazuh. One thing Dun Lidjun could do better than anybody he had ever met was to raise kazuh instantly.

Not swiftly, quickly, or hurriedly—instantly.

He stood with his head erect, releasing the tension in his mind and body until his forehead smoothed. His eyes narrowed and his nostrils flared as he gripped the sword properly in his right hand: a light, floating grip with thumb and forefinger, last two fingers tight, welded to the hilt, the middle finger neither tight nor loose.

He held his neck straight, his belly tight, his shoulders down. Control flowed from his feet to his scalp, washing over him in a cool stream. He had raised kazuh, although at what moment, he couldn't have said.

His kazuh was a river in which Dun Lidjun was a stone; the water rushed and flowed, and it was the water that was of consequence, not an unimportant slice of it. As a distant stream of kazuh flowed and spurted for just an instant, time washed Ben Der Donesey toward Dun Lidjun, the challenge sword held high. The boy cut downward, a stroke that would have done credit to a trained warrior.

Dun Lidjun's kazuh raged; riding the stream of kazuh and time, Dun Lidjun sliced down and in.

Time split, a river dividing itself into many streams—

In one, Dun Lidjun's sword could have spun the challenge sword into the air and then carved the boy across the waist with a simple backslash—

In another, his sword would have beaten the challenge sword up, and in a continuation of the same motion taken the boy's head from his shoulders—

In yet another, his sword should have parried as Dun Lidjun's own lunge took him past, another stroke opening Ben Der Donesey's back to white spine—

—but in the real stream, in the one, true and only stream, Dun Lidjun gently batted the challenge sword aside and then stopped, the edge of his Eisenlith blade but a blade's width from the frantic pulse at the youngster's throat. Although neither of them moved, the stream of time slowed further, like honey in a honeypot: immobile, but potentially only a sluggish ooze. Time slowed even more, becoming like the years-slow flow of apparently motionless glass in a window, or the gentle seaward march of a mountain range.

Dun Lidjun waited, warm and secure in that

frozen moment, until Ben Der Donesey lowered the challenge sword.

"You are accepted, Ben Der Donesey," Dun Lidjun said, gesturing at one of the guards to lead the boy to one side. The arrogance would be a problem, but a curable one. You could beat the arrogance out of a boy, as Dun Lidjun knew from experience—on both ends of the stick.

Dun Lidjun had felt the boy's kazuh flow. Only a trickle of a spring, barely oozing kazuh out, yes, but kazuh nonetheless. It was rare for such an untutored one to raise kazuh at all. It happened, though: sometimes, under the proper sort of pressure, the hidden spring could be made to flow.

That was a bonus; it was not what Dun Lidjun was looking for in a warrior candidate. He was looking for something more fundamental: for the promise of kazuh, the base of kazuh.

"Your name, boy?" he asked of the second of the four, a skinny dark-haired boy, peasant-bronzed by the sun beneath the band of paleness at the forehead.

"I am called Loud Noise, Lord," the boy said, formally.

"Ah. Well, Evaki Belang, it seems you wish to be a warrior?"

"Oh, yes, Lord."

"Very well. Simply, you have two ways to do so: either defeat me, or impress me," Dun Lidjun said, exchanging his Eisenlith sword for one of the two wooden practice swords that Arefai carried.

"Yes, Lord."

"Take up the sword. Attack me. Now, boy."

All mattered, and nothing mattered, as the boy approached him, the sword held high over his head, intending to slash down at Dun Lidjun.

A simple response was all it would take, really: a smacking parry as Evaki Belang staggered by, followed by a quick slap to the back, across the kidneys. A sword would cut, but the stick could kill.

No. Dun Lidjun had not raised kazuh simply to slap the boy's kidney out through his belly or to snap his spine.

The purpose was to test, to see if he could get even a dim feeling of kazuh from the boy. Like resonates to like, and even the greater resonates to the lesser.

Still, the smacking parry seemed reasonable; the wooden sword, guided by his floating thumb and forefinger, slapped the mirror-bright Sunder blade to one side as Dun Lidjun stepped easily to the other.

The boy surprised him; he turned as he ran by, and tried to slash back at Dun Lidjun. But it didn't matter; Dun Lidjun used a falling leaves cut, slashing down at the challenge sword and riding it down, like a golden autumn leaf descending to the ground on the back of a falling hand.

The challenge sword fell to the grass, and Evaki Belang stumbled on the gravel.

Dun Lidjun dropped kazuh.

"No," he said.

With one word, with a wave of his hand, with no trace of regret or equivocation he dismissed Evaki Belang, sending the now stoop-shouldered boy back to his fields, to a life with his toes full of dung.

A pleasant lad, yes, but not a warrior. Never to be a warrior.

"Next," Dun Lidjun said, gesturing to the third of the four boys.

"I am Erife Ver Hosten, Lord Dun Lidjun." He was a well-made, although gangling boy, moving with too much self-confidence by half as he took up the sword, then tossed his head to clear his too-long hair from his eyes.

This one Dun Lidjun knew: he was the youngest son of a dauber, tired of spending days sweating over his black iron pots. The middle class had higher status than peasants, and often lived better, but sometimes all that meant was that they had more opportunities to be sneered at by both bourgeois and nobility, to be looked at as though no bath could ever remove their stink.

Dun Lidjun remembered that feeling all too well, even after all these years.

Erife Ver Hosten moved in smoothly, confidently—or at least with assumed confidence—the point of his sword rising high.

Trying to take his measure, Dun Lidjun tentatively slashed out at him, and the boy cut down at Dun Lidjun's wooden sword. The Sunder sword sliced neatly through the wood, taking with it more than half the length.

Erife Ver Hosten tried to follow through, but Dun Lidjun raised kazuh and blurred into him, the remnant of his wooden sword catching the flat of the blade as Dun Lidjun came belly to belly with the boy.

Erife Ver Hosten broke away, and tried to slash down, but Dun Lidjun closed, blocked up against the descending hands. The old warrior expanded his body and spirit and cut down, hard, against Erife Ver Hosten's head. The wooden sword split to the hilt.

For a moment, Dun Lidjun thought that his kazuh had deserted him, and in that moment, of course his kazuh *did* desert him; he staggered back, off balance.

But then the boy's eyes rolled up, and his knees buckled, and he fell, stunned as though poleaxed. He would have fallen across the challenge sword if the fourth boy hadn't quickly moved in and snatched it up.

The fourth boy turned toward Dun Lidjun, his head erect, his neck and body straight but not strained, his gaze perceptive.

"And why do you not strike?" the old warrior asked.

"I doubt that you could learn enough from me

right now, Lord Dun Lidjun," the last boy said. "Please take up another sword, so that the examination might continue."

He stood calmly, balanced, waiting.

Dun Lidjun looked down at the broken hilt in his hands. "Don't you think that you could kill an unarmed old man?"

The boy stood, calmly waiting. "No, I don't think I could hurt you, Lord Dun Lidjun. And no, Lord Dun Lidjun, I don't think you are unarmed."

Dun Lidjun tossed the broken hilt away. "Set the challenge sword down, boy—what is your name?"

"I'm called Twan Rebet, lord," the boy said, not lowering the sword, still balanced easily on his feet. "I would like to be tested, if it please you."

"Ah. And if it doesn't please me?"

"Then I will still be tested, Lord Dun Lidjun." He said it not as a challenge, but in a measured way, as though commenting that thunder was loud, iron cool, or salt salty.

"As you will." Dun Lidjun took up the other practice sword, and saluted Twan Rebet. "Lesson the second, boy: remember the first lesson."

"Eh?"

Dun Lidjun raised kazuh, closed and disarmed the boy with one violent sweep, sending the challenge sword tumbling end-over-end into the air, leaving Twan Rebet empty-handed.

Twan Rebet bowed deeply, his eyes on Dun

Lidjun, his feet solid on the ground as though planted. "I thank you for your consideration, Lord Dun Lidjun," he said, starting to turn away.

"*Stop*," Dun Lidjun snapped out.

The boy halted in midturn, almost losing his balance. "Lord?"

Dun Lidjun raised kazuh and kicked him in the buttocks, sending the boy sprawling forward. "Let that be the last time you do that, boy. Stop, stand, sprint, scurry, squat, sprawl, sit—but keep your balance, always."

Dun Lidjun looked around, but he already knew that there was no harm in speaking bluntly. Erife Ver Hosten was still unconscious, and the rest of those in the garden were warriors, and all knew the secret of the warrior kazuh. Except for Ben Der Donesey, and he would have to be not only told the secret, but taught it.

"Now, up, up," Dun Lidjun said, helping Twan Rebet to his feet.

Lord Arefai unbuckled his own everyday sword, a fine Least Frosuffold, and belted it about the boy's waist. "Use this sword well, and in Lord Toshtai's service, Twan Rebet."

Ben Der Donesey's brow seemed to have taken up a permanent wrinkle. A flicker of kazuh, that boy certainly had. But not understanding, the understanding that Arefai demonstrated as he stood next to Twan Rebet, beaming like a proud father.

Dun Lidjun wasn't surprised, although he was disappointed in himself.

I grow old and foolish.

"A good day, eh, Lord Dun Lidjun?" Lord Arefai asked, as they walked back up the twisting path toward the gleaming keep above. "Two in one day?"

"That it is, Lord Arefai," Dun Lidjun said, as though he had expected nothing more and nothing less. Which, in a sense, was true: he had expected that those who deserved to become warriors would, and those who did not so deserve would not.

"Father will be pleased."

"As he should." Dun Lidjun stopped. "Lord Arefai," he said. "The next time, if you're available, I would be pleased to assist you in the testing."

"Ah." Arefai broke into a broad smile. "I am honored," he said. He leaned close to Dun Lidjun. "I hope I'm as successful as you were, today."

"Fortunate, Lord Arefai."

"Well, that's true. But still—two at one challenge? Marvelous, Lord Dun Lidjun."

"That it is."

While Dun Lidjun's kazuh wouldn't desert him as long as life breathed motion into his tired bones, he decided that his judgment was starting to slip away. He should have given Arefai the chance to evaluate these candidates; of course Arefai would have seen how the boy balanced himself, and would have understood.

Even an old fool like Dun Lidjun could see that.

Any trained kazuh warrior could have seen it, simply by looking at the way the boy stood:

Balanced.

It was the secret of the warrior, it was the basic truth of the warrior:

Balance—not the earnestness of an Evaki Belang or the cleverness of an Erife Ver Hosten, not even the fluke kazuh of a Ben Der Donesey—not speed nor power nor strength, but balance—is the Way of the Warrior.

6
Descent

I WASN'T USED to being a substitute Eresthai, and it didn't sit well with me, not even in practice.

I busied myself in the small room on the third floor of the donjon, the one we were using as an entrance and exit for the highwire act, checking the gear inside, and perhaps making an occasional mild comment about how I wasn't completely happy with the situation.

Father, on the other hand, was supervising, and being every bit as flexible as usual.

"—you *will* be of help, and since you can *not* go on, you *will* be of help setting up, and work backstage along with the Eresthais. We will *not* announce that you are not playing tonight; we shall treat it as though that were part of the act."

It's shameful not to pull your own cart, and I was having none of it.

"I can go on," I said, giving another tightening twist to the turnbuckle that kept the highwire straight, then rapped on it with the rubber hammer. "I can play."

Not enough treble. You can keep them singing-taut at all times, but it's a bad idea; the song tires the cable strands.

It's not a good idea to loosen them all the way, either, not between shows—that wears out the joints. The best way to preserve the life of the equipment is to treat it gently, tentatively: keep it reasonably taut after you set it up, tune it up for practice, then back down after, and then tighten it back up before the performance.

It's a compromise, and compromise is closely related to balance.

"No, you can't, for two reasons. For one, you are badly bruised—"

"Not that badly."

"—and for another, you cannot go on because I say you cannot go on."

I was hurting, but I could perform. He was having none of it, though, and that was that.

"Gray Khuzud?" Fhilt was outside; he had been going over the trap rigging. "I don't like this hawser—I think we'd best replace it."

"I'll be along in a moment," Gray Khuzud called out. "There is no need for discussion," he said to me, already heading for the door. "I will see you at showtime. Finish here."

I did.

The room was cooling as the evening came on;

I walked over to the trunk and pulled back the straps so I could open it and get at an overshirt.

I looked down at my chest, wishing for once that it had a mat of hair covering its blank slickness—purple isn't my color.

But the bones weren't broken, not anymore. I ached, but I could function.

Across the quadrangle, just barely within the walls of the inner bailey, the old donjon stood in the dusk, its walls a weakening gold in the fading light.

Long ago, it had been the main building, perhaps the only building within the walls, possibly built under the direction of Oroshtai himself when he originally founded the town as his winter retreat from his duties to the Scion.

But some time after the fall of the Oroshtai Tenancy, or perhaps during the fall of the Tenancy, Den Oroshtai had become the lord's seat, and the old donjon had become too cramped for his full array of staff. These days, it was the residence of retainers—everyone who Lord Toshtai didn't particularly want near him—and had a third-floor guesting residence for visiting nobility.

Narantir had the basement all to himself. Nobody likes to bother a wizard while he's at work, and few like to be near one when he's at play. In the big cities—Patrice, Der Field, Thurrock—it's different: the wizards' schools can't be solo affairs, for obvious reasons.

The second floor held both the secondary barracks and the main armory of Den Oroshtai—including Refle's workshop. It was easy to tell where the forge was; anybody could have seen where the ashpile stood against the wall below, beneath what had once been a garderobe. The armorer's forge was clearly a later addition: its chimney, built against the outside of the wall, was of a lighter stone than the rest of the old donjon.

And if *that* hadn't been enough of a clue, I could see the top of a rack of swords through a partly open window.

It would be difficult to get in, but not impossible. Anybody who could get to the third floor or the roof could tie a rope and climb, letting themselves in through the window.

If they could get past the guards and to the roof, which they couldn't.

An old oak tree stood near the building, and a long branch reached out toward it, missing by a man-length. It wouldn't have been allowed to stand there, not in the old days—it wouldn't have made a *good* road for an assassin, but it might have made a credible one, back before the kazuh of assassins was declared profane and anathema, and extinguished.

The branch ran along the morningwise wall of the old donjon, the wall facing the curtain wall of the inner bailey—not quite concealed, but not out in the open. Only an assassin could have kept his balance as he ran along the branch, building up enough speed to make the leap to the window-sill, catching himself carefully with toes and fingers, then releasing the hooks and swinging the windows open.

Only an assassin, or an acrobat. And a good acrobat, at that. There would be no way to practice it. I would have to be a good acrobat.

I've been a good one, for a few moments, now and then.

"I doubt he has stored it in there," Enki Duzun said, touching me on the elbow. I hadn't heard her walk up. Not listening to what was going on was getting to be a habit with me, and not a good one.

"So do I, but do you have any better ideas?"

"Yes," she said. "Give up the girl; forget about the beating. On with the show, and then when the show is finished here, onwards to Minnae, where there's another girl, and then on to Bergeenen, Wei, and Patrice. Before you know it we'll be high in Helgramyth, headed for Otland, and I know how you like Helish and Ots."

I didn't answer.

Enki Duzun sighed. She knew what my silence meant.

Fhilt leaned in through the window; I'd forgotten he was just outside, on the platform.

"You're being more stupid than Large Egda, you know." He raised a hand. "Not that I've always thought that possible, mind, but it's clear that it is. Egda wouldn't be able to come up with a reason for doing anything this dim."

I glared at him. "You leave Large Egda alone. You're always picking on him."

"Hey, hey," Fhilt said. "That's all in fun. He knows that, and you ought to."

"You're trying to change the subject," I said. "And—"

"And not doing a very good job," Enki Duzun muttered.

"—and I won't have it." I tried to explain. "I can't help it—I've always been stubborn." It's how I've mastered, or at least learned, what skills I *have* learned: it's always been sheer, pure, unadulterated stubbornness.

"There is that." Enki Duzun frowned, as though she didn't like the taste of her words.

"There is also growing out of it," Fhilt said.

Enki Duzun was silent for a long moment. "It isn't impossible," she went on. "You'll be exposed as you go in."

"Not terribly exposed," I said. "If I were to be challenged, I'm merely working on a new entrance for the act tonight."

Fhilt nodded judiciously. "Once you get in, then you should be safe. As safe as you could be, in the armory. Which is not very, Kami Khuzud."

"We have the run of the castle, save—"

"Save where guards or locks block our way," Enki Duzun said. "Technically, you couldn't be faulted for going in that way. But, technically, brother mine, Lord Toshtai can take your head for any reason, or no reason at all, even if you do find what you're looking for."

Fhilt stepped in through the window. "This is a silly idea. Haven't you ever heard the old saying, 'Don't carry your footprints with you'? Leave it all be, Kami Khuzud."

"He won't be expecting it." Refle was an arrogant man; he might not even have gotten rid of the cloak and gloves, and perhaps kept the truncheon. Armorers, like the warriors they are in legal theory if not in frequent fact, have a reverence for the tools that they create.

It was worth a try.

"I should ask if she's worth it, but it doesn't matter at this point, does it?" Enki Duzun asked.

"Eh?"

"Even if NaRee were to dust you off now, you'd still want to expose Refle, for beating you. I know you, Kami Khuzud; you've never learned to leave your footprints behind you." She sighed.

Fhilt stripped off his jerkin and worked his shoulders. "Very well, then. I'll do it." His mouth tightened, making him look vaguely toadfaced.

"Eh?"

"This is not a job for clumsy Kami Khuzud." Fhilt spread his hands. "It's going to take a better acrobat than you are to get in through the window. I'm a better acrobat than you are. So I do it."

Sometimes, I just don't understand Fhilt. When I'd been hurt he was more concerned about his loss of sleep than my broken bones and spilled blood, and here he was offering to risk his life on the small chance that he could find some evidence against Refle.

I was about to agree, when he looked over across the courtyard. "Now, which room do you think is the armory?"

No. I couldn't let him. Fhilt was a better acrobat than I was, but if he couldn't see something as obvious as which room was the armory, he didn't have the right kind of mind to figure out what was evidence.

"No," I said. "I'm good enough, and I'd better do it."

There was a long silence, and then Enki Duzun nodded. "I'll go and get Large Egda. You're going to need him."

"Now?" Fhilt asked.

"Now," she said. "We don't have much more than an hour until the show, and Large Egda has to be back for it."

I had finished checking the gear. It was fine. "Let's go."

Less than an hour left to showtime, and the show must go on.

"Again, Egda, again."

I guess I must have let a trace of my frustration

show in my voice, because he dropped the rope and sighed.

"I am not *that* clumsy," he said, "except with things that I haven't practiced. I haven't practiced this, Kami Khuzud." Slowly—deliberately slowly—he tried again, throwing the end of the rope in a long arc.

Nobody was watching us; the security within Lord Toshtai's walls lies in the walls themselves, and in the watchers on the walls, and in the warriors surrounding Lord Toshtai.

This time, the rope snaked over a branch better than the best-trained of Evrem's pets.

But it wasn't the branch I was going to walk over on; it was the branch just above it.

"Egda, you put it on the wrong—oh."

Oh. Of course; that was precisely the right branch to be looping it over.

He smiled, tolerantly. Large Egda is usually patient with the rest of us, even when we're not patient with him. He let me get a good grip on the rope and then hauled away, just like it was part of the act. I sailed up and into the air, and dropped down onto the limb.

For a moment, I teetered, and almost lunged for the trunk.

But an acrobat keeps his balance, and I had to be an acrobat, so I reached down into me, and found balance, if not kazuh. Balance alone would have to do.

Waving Large Egda away, I pulled the rope up, and coiled it.

Time to reconnoiter, if I could do it. I was a bit low; I couldn't quite see into the armory, so I climbed to the limb Large Egda had used as a fulcrum, skinning my shins in the process.

It looked good—there was a clear space on the marble floor inside the armory, lit by the lamps overhead. The only trouble was that I couldn't tell whether or not there was anybody inside the armory; the fact that the lamps were lit was a suggestion that, whether or not there was anybody inside, the armory wasn't shut for the night.

Then again, armorers are renowned for working late, and for having to keep long hours, for the same reason that smiths have to.

What could I say if he caught me?

"Well, good evening to you, Lord Refle, and how is Your Lordship this evening? Theft? No, no, Lord Refle, my entry here is just a new routine in the ever-expanding attempts of the Troupe of Gray Khuzud to give new entertainments to our beloved ruling class."

No. I could probably come up with better last words than that.

It was time either to commit myself or to give up.

I took the coiled rope and pitched it into the armory, through the open window. Now I would have to go get it. It would be good to raise kazuh, but I wasn't a kazuh acrobat.

But perhaps, even if I couldn't raise kazuh, I could make everything real.

It's important to visualize, I remembered Gray Khuzud saying, to make a routine concrete in your mind before you do it.

You have to—

—see the world spinning around you as you tumble through the air,

—hear the roar in the rush of blood to your head as you pull yourself into a tuck, spinning the world around you twice,

—taste the dryness of your mouth as the catcher pulls you out of the sky,

—feel the unyielding smoothness of the trapeze beneath your hands and the resilience and vigor of the wire beneath your feet,

—take the stuff of dreams and fantasy and spin it around your mind, twisting it into reality, making it happen.

I lowered myself to the branch and visualized the routine, just as though I was planning a tumbling run.

Two little steps, and then one big bound, and then a push and dive—if it all worked right, I'd catch myself on the windowsill, and complete the tumble, rolling gracefully to my feet, sorry that there was no appreciative crowd to give me my well-earned applause.

I visualized it, tried to spin reality out of my

wanting: the first step, my shod foot slipping on the rough bark—

No, that wouldn't do.

I slipped my shoes off and set them in a branch crotch, trusting to my bare feet to grip the bark tightly.

So: I would—

—take the first step, rough bark hard beneath my bare foot, my body's inertia resisting the motion as I pushed hard with calf and thigh, to

—move myself into the second step, arms out to my side for balance, my speed increasing, the second step fading into a

—bound, giving momentarily at the knees, while I took in a last breath of air, and then

—spring, putting neck, back, buttocks, thighs, calves, ankles and toes into a leap that would

—push me outwards in a flat arc, somersault me over the windowsill into a roll in the room, coming up to my feet solidly, my only regret that there was no audience.

I would bow, though. Just for the practice.

I smiled. No use waiting any longer.

I took the first step, the rough bark painful beneath my feet, thighs straining, and pushed hard with calf and thigh, moving myself into the second step. My arms fluttered for balance and found it as my speed increased, the second step becoming a two-footed bound as I bent at the knees, then put my whole body, from neck to toes, into a push that sent me into a flat arc toward the window, the world rushing by.

I caught the edge of the windowsill and pulled myself over into a tuck, but I over-rotated and my hands slipped from the sill.

I slammed down on the marble floor.

Hard.

7
Fall

IT WOULD HAVE been convenient if the world had gone away for a while, while I lay there, breathless, in pain.

But it didn't, and eventually I found that I could breathe again, if not particularly well, nor with anything resembling comfort. Slowly, gingerly, I tried to move, then thought better of it. I think I had cracked my head on something—probably the floor—but it had been after I hit; I had reflexively curled properly. If Refle had walked in on me, he certainly would have been within his rights to draw his sword and pin me like a beetle against the floor, and he probably would have done it.

But the door was closed, and it remained closed, and after no more than a few centuries of shock and pain I was able to roll over on my side and then to my belly, and then to get my hands and knees under me.

My back and shoulders were a mass of bruise and pain. I'd definitely cracked my heel and head against the floor, and my left shoulder hurt too badly even to try to move it.

But, amazingly, I didn't think I'd broken anything. While I resented the amount of my life that practice took, one of the nice things about the upkeep of an acrobat's body is that well-developed muscles can protect the body against certain kinds of damage, and it seemed that being slammed against a stone floor was among those kinds of damage.

I vaguely remembered doing some of the right things: tucking my chin down toward my chest to protect my head, slapping back with my arms to suck up some of the motion into my chest muscles, slamming my feet down so that my feet and legs would drink up some of the rest, arching my back just a trifle so that my spine would bend instead of snap.

Even when the mind is clumsy, the body remembers, and an acrobat has to learn how to fall.

As Gray Khuzud always said, an acrobat also has to learn how to get up after a fall.

With a grip on a nearby workbench and a superhuman effort I stood, wobbly as a baby, hurting as much as an old man.

Pain or no, I had to finish up here. My coil of rope lay in the corner; I almost blacked out as I picked it up and slung it around my shoulder, but I held on.

If Refle was going to dispose of the evidence, the obvious place was his forge. The forge, a hulking monster of steel and stone, stood waiting in a corner, the coals banked, the ankle-straps of the bellows neatly coiled.

Large as it was, it still didn't look big enough to be the source of swords and armor plate, but I really didn't know enough about the process, and was neither likely to learn nor there to learn.

I took a piece of metal and poked at the ashes.

Nothing; just banked coals, waiting for air and fuel to bring them to fiery life.

Over against the opposite wall, two racks of spears and one of swords stood waiting. I couldn't tell whether they were waiting to be repaired or waiting to be run through some peasant's belly, but I expected that they'd do for either.

I scratched at my own belly, although the motion hurt.

I hefted one of the swords, the wooden grip warm against my fingers. I hadn't ever held a sword; it's not something that peasants, acrobat or no, do a lot of.

It seemed strangely light for its size, perhaps compared to the knives we used in the act. I always thought of them as remarkably heavy things, but this weighed about as much as a juggling wand, perhaps less.

The balance was wrong for my hand, or maybe not—the sword seemed to want to slash through the air, but my aching body definitely didn't want to slash anything through the air, or move quickly at all.

I wasn't here to play with swords; I put it back.

A rack of miscellaneous weapons hung on the wall—a pair of battigs, a daw, three small maces, and a dozen truncheons: leather-wrapped rods, suitable for smashing bones when you didn't want to kill, or wanted to kill slowly, by crushing bone after bone. Any of them could have been the one he had beaten me with, but all of them looked new, the leather polished to a high shine, the wrist-thongs unworn.

Refle was a diligent worker, either as a would-be assassin or as an armorer. Or both.

Battered worktables, covered with all sorts of devices, lined the adjacent wall. I took a quick inventory.

There were weapons in recognizable states of assembly or repair—Refle seemed to be in working on the lock of a coward's bow—some of the items were clearly tools, and there was one table with half a dozen stone pots about the size of preserves pots, each containing an oily liquid.

I didn't think they contained preserves, and I didn't stick in my finger to check what it was. There are some things you don't need to know.

Nothing there, but what had I expected? A box, neatly labeled "EVIDENCE NECESSARY TO PROVE I AM GUILTY OF A COVERTRY. (signed) REFLE"?

I went to the wardrobe next.

It was larken-built; the sides and doors were made of thousands of separate apparently randomly shaped pieces of wood, some as large as a thumbnail, some as small as a splinter, each one carefully glued into place. Like all of the best larken-built work, there was no evidence of the glue used to hold it all together—the pieces were individually beveled in from the surface.

They do larken woodwork in many of the domains, but this wood had the burnished redness of Agami mahogany. A friend of mine in Agami was the daughter of a woodworker, and this seemed much like what I had seen in her father's shop, except that this was huge—there would have been enough room inside for Large Egda and me not only to stand, but to play a game of lopses while we stood.

I slid my finger down the front of the door, looking for a catch.

Agami woodwork, be it larken-built wardrobes or apparently simple pine boxes or wall panels, tends to have hidden catches, and often several abditories. The Agami woodcrafters are tricky: one or another of the pieces of wood actually conceals the catch, and the hidden, spring-loaded metalwork is so finely made that it can be worked simply by pressing on the proper place, or places in those with more complex lockwork.

I guess I must have pressed on the proper place, because the wardrobe door swung open, sliding smoothly and silently on lacquered bone hinges.

My heart beat painfully hard as I stepped inside, over a pile of blankets and tarpaulins, pushing past hanging cloaks and robes, looking for a specific hooded cape.

Coats, tunics and capes hung inside; some of the capes were hooded, but most were filigreed or embroidered, except for one that was decorated with silver-thread edging.

Not one of them was the plain black cape that Refle had worn when he had beaten me.

No luck there; I'd try for the gloves. The first drawer I opened was empty; the second was filled to overflowing with gloves. I guess the hands of the members of our beloved ruling class are always cold.

I had been looking for a cape and gloves. There were enough gloves here to satisfy Evva Ugly Hands of the children's tales, but none of them was the plain pair that I remembered. It probably shouldn't have surprised me, but I had been counting on finding the evidence. Properly confronted with the clothing he had worn, Refle might have made a break, or perhaps if he had found the cape and gloves missing from the place where he had concealed them, he might have had to sue for peace.

That would have been fine. I wasn't exactly eager to forgive him for trying to beat me to death, but if it was the choice between that and his finally succeeding, I was willing to be the forgiving type. A peasant, even an acrobat, has no need for the sort of pride that gets a kazuh warrior challenged.

Time to go.

I was halfway out of the wardrobe when a key *snick*ed in the lock, and the hall door started to swing open. My heart thumping loud enough to hear, I was barely able to swing the door back toward me, closing it almost fully, leaving just enough of a crack to see through.

Closing the hall door behind him, Refle stalked across the armory, a canvas bundle under one arm, a leather roll of tools under another. He set the tools down, then turned to lock the door behind him, all the while muttering something to himself, something I tried to catch but couldn't.

I pulled the wardrobe door closer to me, not quite daring to shut it. For one thing, it might have made a telltale click; for another, I wasn't at all sure I could work the lock from inside.

That would be less than wonderful.

There was a rustling, and a clumping, and then some creaking noises.

I pushed the wardrobe door open a fraction, to see him over at the forge. He was pumping it up, his right foot in the bellows strap, whipping the bellows into a hot fury, although there was nothing in it to heat.

And then he carefully, gently, opened his canvas bundle, and laid a black cloak and a set of gloves on top of the fire, and worked the bellows even harder, maniacally.

I watched as he burned the cloak and gloves, then stirred the ashes.

He left; I heard his key *snick* in the lock.

* * *

I poked at the ashes.

Nothing.

Oh, the poker turned over a scrap or two of cloth, and I was able to dig deep and find a small piece of very well-charred leather, but Refle had been thorough; certainly nothing large enough to be recognizable remained.

I knew that he was guilty, but I couldn't prove it. I slammed my fist down on a table, then regretted it immediately, both for the noise and for the pain it caused me.

Thanks to Refle and to my own clumsiness, I had taken two serious beatings in as many days . . .

. . . and there wasn't a thing I could do about it.

It was dark outside, and the show would be starting soon, so I doubled the rope around a beam, and then climbed down to the ground, pulling the rope after me.

I had time for a quick dinner before the evening show, but I wasn't really hungry.

Injuries happened not infrequently among members of the troupe, with the decided exception of Gray Khuzud himself, who always seemed immune to both disease and damage. Not the rest of us: every once in a while, Sala would slip off her rope, or Evrem would get a minor bite, or Enki Duzun would twist an ankle, someone would come down with a fever, or come down with a cold and lose their sense of balance. Fevers were usually minor, although we could never really forget that it was a fever that had taken Davana Escabay, Enki Duzun's mother and mine, shortly after Enki Duzun's birth.

So the company was used to substituting; it didn't even count as an improvisation.

Under the light of hissing lanterns, Fhilt and Enki Duzun split my opening, rolling onto the sand in parallel cartwheels that blended swiftly into a duet tumbling act that Large Egda joined as catcher and thrower.

Even from the third-floor window, it looked good. Their three sizes, from little Enki Duzun to Fhilt to Large Egda, played off each other, making their double shoulderstand appear even taller than it really was, and Enki Duzun's fall, land, tuck-and-roll even cleaner, more impressive. Three oiled bodies twisted and moved in the flickering light, and then left the sand to loud applause.

The musicians just kept up, the lead silverhorn purring out a complex, if uninspired, set of scales.

Sala was next. Instead of watching her, I tapped at the highwire, rewarded by the right twang. Nice and tight, which was good, considering how Enki Duzun planned her transition from the floor act to the sky act.

I thought for a moment of crossing the wire over to the platform so I could go up into the rigging and check the trapeze. The argument I would have given Gray Khuzud would have been that, what with Sala and Evrem doing a duet down in the sand, in the light, nobody would be looking up in the dark at the wire for a simple crossing. But we had already checked out the traps earlier, and Gray Khuzud had told me that I was just going to do support for this show, and to keep out of trouble.

So I stayed there.

One of the Eresthais patted my shoulder, gently enough that it didn't even hurt.

"In just two days, Kami Khuzud, we will be back on the road, and by the time we reach Bergeenen, you'll be back in the show."

"Imagine my joy."

Gray Khuzud joined the others down in the sand, and the juggling started: he, Fhilt, Enki Duzun and Sala passing juggling sticks back and forth between the four of them in a complex-appearing weave that had the crowd oooing and aaaahing.

I was so jealous I could have spit—that was something I could have done, something I should have been in on.

The juggling segued into Evrem's normal second-night act, the shower of cobras. I turned away from the window until I knew it was over. I *don't* like snakes.

Gray Khuzud and Fhilt rejoined us in the third-story room. Both were sweaty, their naked torsos

gleaming in the dim light, except where sand
stuck to their bodies. Gray Khuzud exercised his
seniority by being first at the washbasin, splashing water on with quick, economical cupping
motions, then holding out his arms so that I could
quickly towel him off.

"Very nice juggling," I said, sincerely. "Good
snap on the tosses."

Fhilt bowed dramatically, his arms widespread.
"Thank you, Eldest Son Acrobat. But you only
speak the truth." He slapped his hands together,
then splashed water on his face and chest. "Ah, I
am hot and sharp tonight. As soon as you're
healed up, let's see if we can take the phantom
club routine all the way."

I loved the idea, but I was a bit nervous about
it. The notion of taking the audience all the way
along from juggling only real clubs to only phantom clubs was risky. Gray Khuzud could have
done it, I'm sure, but maybe I couldn't.

As I dried him off, Fhilt leaned next to me.
"What did you find?" he whispered.

"Later," I whispered back.

"That's what you said before. Tell."

"Nothing." I shrugged. "Nothing I could use at
all."

"That's a pity," Fhilt said, as though he meant
that stands to reason.

Gray Khuzud cleared his throat. "Let us play
this town tonight, and leave the road for the road.
Time for highwire."

I moved to the window.

As always, Gray Khuzud's timing was impeccable: as I looked out, Enki Duzun had gripped the tow-rope, and Large Egda was hauling her rapidly into the air, two full manheights above the highwire.

She let go of the rope and lithely dropped to the highwire.

There was a sudden crunch, and a twang, and something whizzed by my ear.

"No!" I'm not sure whether I shouted it or heard it, or both.

Enki Duzun fell the full three stories, off-balance.

For a moment, I thought, I hoped, she was going to make the net, but she only hit the edge of it, then twisted and slammed down hard on the hard ground below, so hard I swear I felt it more than heard it.

I was already running for the stairs. I stumbled and staggered down to the ground floor.

The crowd was on their feet, voices raised in useless cries. I tried to shove my way through, not mindful of rank or status, but the press of bodies pushed me back. I shoved in, and out of the corner of my eye saw a thick hand snatching at a swordhilt, another fist raised to strike, both of them freezing in place when a harsh voice cut through the noise.

"Let him through, all of you. Quickly, Arefai,

Edelfaule, run and get the wizard." Lord Toshtai's voice was level, but powerful.

The crowd parted for me.

Somebody was trying to pull at her arms, but I
pushed him out of the way and knelt over her.

She was bent in the wrong places, like a broken
toy.

"Help her up," some idiot said.

"No." You don't move a fall victim until the
wizard arrives, you don't let a fall victim move
until the wizard arrives—you have to let him
freeze their bones in place first.

I brushed at her face, clearing the sand and
blood away from the corner of her mouth, gently
cupping her cheek in my hand. She tried to say
something, I think—I could feel the muscles in
her neck and jaw try to work—but then she vom-
ited blood onto my arm, and then she died in
front of me.

Just like that.

I held her in my arms, but her body was already
cooling when Narantir got there.

8
Stormy Night

MY FATHER SAT alone in the dungeon. The barred rooms were empty; few remain long in Lord Toshtai's dungeon. A dungeon isn't where our beloved ruling class stores living people, not like the Foulsmelling Ones of Bhorlani do. No; our dungeons are for dead people, for those who know that they're about to die, and for those who don't know that they're dead yet.

Enki Duzun lay under a shroud, only her face visible. She looked more asleep than dead, if you didn't look too closely.

I didn't look too closely.

Gray Khuzud gripped my arm. "How could it happen, Kami Khuzud?" he said, more statement than question.

Equipment fails, but not our equipment. Not if it's properly checked.

"Are you asking me if I checked the rigging?" I asked.

He looked at me for a long, long moment. It

was all clear. He was supposed to say something like:

Of course I am not asking that of you, Kami Khuzud. Of course I trust you, Kami Khuzud.

Of course I know that you checked it, that you would not have been careless with the lives of us all.

Of course I know that you are not your sister's murderer, Kami Khuzud.

But he licked his lips and swallowed hard.

"Yes," he said. "I am not accusing, Kami Khuzud," he said, grasping my shoulder. "Truthfully, I am *not* accusing. I am just asking."

I didn't answer; I just turned and left, leaving the old man alone.

The truth was out in the rain; it only took me a few moments to find it.

The threatening clouds had rolled in, the storm was dumping rain down on the empty courtyard, and Enki Duzun was dead. Rain washes away dirt and blood; sometimes, if it rains hard enough, if it just slams down hard against you, it can wash away feeling.

I stood in the cold rain, a bag of tools at my feet, the end of the highwire in my hand, and the storm raging overhead, skeins of lightning sometimes so bright they left the patterns behind in my eyes. The water mixed with tears as I stood out in the cold rain, the twin columns of the granaries looming darkly above me, just within the walls of the keep.

The walls may have been high enough to repel an invader, but they provided me no cover from the rain; I was chilled to the bone. But perhaps a distant fury warmed me, if only a little, as I stood there, the evidence of my sister's murder in my hands.

The light flickered in the armory window, but it might as well not have. There was nothing I could do—even if I could make my way into the room, something I'd been barely able to do under favorable conditions, what was I to do? Challenge Refle to a duel?

Assume for the moment that he wouldn't summon the guards to have me hauled away before Lord Toshtai, postulate that he didn't simply run me through, pretend he chose to turn his face from the fact that I was a peasant, what good would that do? I wasn't a swordsman; he could simply toss me a sword and then hack me into little, bloody chunks. The members of our beloved ruling class didn't turn their faces from a peasant's impudence, not when they didn't have to. It had been one thing to face Refle down in NaRee's garden, but this was another.

Lord Toshtai would hardly complain about him hacking a burglar to death. Or killing an attempted murderer.

The lamps at the periphery of the courtyard still flickered in the dark and the rain. Even in that light, it was easy to tell that the wire either had been worn down by rubbing against the bracket or cut, and cut smoothly, by hard steel.

I knew for a fact that it had not been worn down against the bracket. That would have taken weeks and months, and I had checked the gear just that afternoon. The Eresthais had checked it the day before; the troupe of Gray Khuzud does not go into a performance without its tack in order.

So, strands had been cut. It was all clear.

Refle had not been satisfied with simply beating me, simply breaking my bones and bruising my flesh; when he had heard that I had been put back together, he had decided to take the next step, beyond hurting me. Most people who don't use mahrir, wizard's magic, assume that it can do anything; Refle didn't know that Narantir had put only my bones together, leaving the muscles broken.

The first use of the highwire in our show was when Large Egda lifted me up to the wire; he had just seen that yesterday. Clumsy Kami Khuzud was always first on the wire, because that made everybody else seem even more graceful.

The wire was supposed to snap, sending clumsy Kami Khuzud dropping to the ground, removing Refle's competition for NaRee's affections with a dull, sodden thud.

I wished it had happened just that way. I

wished, as hard as I could wish, that I was a warrior.

But wishing only makes wishes come true for wizards, and then only sometimes. I was just a clumsy acrobat, standing out in the rain, doing nothing of any value or importance.

I threw the bag of tools over my shoulder as I went to the rigging and climbed up, into the night, into the storm. My bruises protested against the strain, but I didn't care. It didn't matter.

The wind picked up, snatching at me, its cold fingers clawing at my face, but I climbed up to the highwire platform. The other end of the wire was still bolted there, and the bolt properly wired tightly in place, then glued into place.

You don't want the inner end of the highwire to loosen. Somebody might die.

The adjustments are always done from the far side, whether that's attached to a local surface or to our own outer platform, carried with our gear.

I took out a chisel and hammer, and knelt on the platform in the wind and the rain, and hammered the glue into shards that were picked up and taken away in the wind and the rain, until I revealed the nut wired into place beneath.

My fingers clawed at the wire, blindly. Tears in your eyes can blind you, if only for a while.

Or perhaps they can make you see more clearly, if only for a while.

I finally worked the wire loose, coiled it and stuck it in my pack.

"You want to *what*?" The servitor on duty at the entrance to the residence wing of the donjon couldn't have looked more surprised if I had told her I wanted to have her youngest child for dinner.

"I would like to see Lord Toshtai, please," I repeated as I stood there, dripping on the carpet.

Anger plus judgment equals a constant, and there was a black fury inside me. I know that I was supposed to phrase my request for an audience formally, indirectly, euphemistically, making it impossible for somebody who wasn't already determined to take offense to do so. But my sister was dead, cold, stretched out on a stone slab in the dungeon below, waiting for her funeral, and the light still flickered in Refle's window.

Across the tiled floor, the two warriors on duty eyed me expressionlessly, as though I was just a piece of furniture. I didn't suppose that benign neglect would last if I were to barge through, past the slim woman in the rose tunic.

Her fingers reached toward a bell rope, then stopped. I wasn't sure whether I was supposed to be relieved or angered. I couldn't have been much more angered.

"No," she said, as though to herself, then faced me directly. "Return to your quarters, Kami Khuzud; bathe yourself, and dress in your finest. I will have word sent to Lord Arefai and Lord Toshtai's secretary that you, with all proper humility and formality, respectfully request an audience, should that at some point amuse him."

She reached out and touched my arm. "I am so very sorry about your sister, Eldest Son Acrobat." Her eyes were wet.

I turned and walked away.

"You did *what*?" Evrem's head spun to the side so fast that he startled the snake he was holding; it almost bit him. "Have you no consideration at all? For your father, for the rest of us, for me?"

"Stick a cobra up your back passage, Evrem," I said, tightening the drawstring of my trousers, then tying the knot with a quick, angry flourish. I'm good at flourishes.

He looked at me for a long moment, then kissed the snake on top of its flat head with a gentleness that made me shiver, and put it back in its basket.

Large Egda's face was grave. "I could have caught her. If I had been there. Stop her with my body."

Fhilt looked pityingly at Large Egda. "The fall still would have hurt her, probably killed her." He turned to me. "You don't have enough to persuade Toshtai. I'm not even sure you're right."

"I have to try."

Can't you understand, Fhilt? Trying is all I have.

Naked from the waist up, barefoot, I padded across the carpet and went through the mess that was my trunk until I found a clean silk tunic, and pulled it out. I checked it over for loose threads, finding one and trimming it with a candle flame.

I slipped into the tunic and belted it tightly around my hips, ignoring the way the belt cut into my bruises. I picked up my shoes.

No. A peasant is always properly dressed with or without shoes, with or without dung squishing up between his toes; and an acrobat spends most of his time barefoot.

I will go before Lord Toshtai as I am, not as I wish I was. I am just an acrobat, not even a kazuh acrobat, and an acrobat is only a peasant.

"You really think it was Refle." Fhilt tilted his head to one side, as though something had occured to him. He shook his head as though to dismiss the subject.

"Say it," I said.

"What?"

"You're thinking something—say it."

Fhilt raised a palm. "No, it's not fair."

"Say it."

"Very well, then." He pursed his lips for a long moment. "It won't do any harm; you've thought the same thing. If it wasn't an accident, if you're right that Refle boobytrapped our gear, then if you'd only have left NaRee alone, your sister would still be alive."

Large Egda loomed over him. "You take that back. You don't say that to him."

"Egda, you idiot, it doesn't matter whether or not I say it: it's true."

"You take that back."

Large Egda's hands reached out for Fhilt, but the big man was slow, always slow. Fhilt ducked beneath Large Egda's arm and swung his elbow, hard, into Egda's side.

Egda's breath left him in a whoosh. Fhilt brought back his elbow for another strike, but I slipped between them, shoving Fhilt aside, and turning toward Large Egda.

"Stop it, the both of you."

Large Egda, ignoring the pain, was still reaching out for Fhilt.

I put my hand on his chest as he moved forward. It was like trying to stop a falling tree: my feet slid back on the floor.

"*Stop* it, Egda," I said.

The words did what force couldn't. Large Egda didn't stop looking at Fhilt, but he did stop walking forward.

Fhilt stood apart, a thin smile creasing his face. "I don't need your help, Kami Khuzud."

I didn't much care whether or not he did. A bit of innocent roughhousing is part of troupe life; fighting among troupe members is wrong, it's not part of the Way.

Egda rubbed at his side, his dark eyes never leaving Fhilt. His face was flat and gray, clay molded by a careless sculptor. "You don't say things like that about Kami Khuzud," he said.

"Just leave it be, Egda."

Egda's forehead creased. "I know I'm stupid, Kami Khuzud," he said, his voice plaintive. "Can't help it. I will never get any better. You are smart. You tell me where I'm wrong. What could you do to make it fair for Refle to hurt Enki Duzun?"

I shook my head. "It's not a matter of fair."

"Should be." He turned to Fhilt. "You *think* you are smart. You tell me, you tell me how Kami Khuzud being with NaRee makes it right for Refle to hurt Enki Duzun."

"It's not that simple. It's not a matter of right, it's a matter of—oh, I can't explain anything to you." Fhilt threw his hands in the air and stalked out of the room, just as Sala bustled in, her eyes red and puffy.

"Oh, Kami Khuzud, he didn't mean it. Your father is sorry, really he is." Always watching after me, after us, as usual.

"Sala." I swallowed, but couldn't go on.

"It's so hard being accused of something you didn't do, I know, Kami Khuzud, but you have to live with it, sometimes."

"Why, Sala," I said, forcing a smile, "that almost made sense."

"What? Don't try to confuse me." She pressed

me to her ample bosom. "Kami Khuzud, I am so sorry. I didn't have a chance to tell you, to tell her, to . . ."

One of the many things I don't understand is why we all talk only in halting, stilted voices to people in grief, saying only that which has been said a hundred thousand times before, a pliant procession of moving mouths going back through time, to the beginning, when the First God made man out of dung, water, and straw.

I held her tightly. Sala was the closest thing to a mother I'd had for more years than I cared to think about; she was the only thing that Enki Duzun had ever had as a mother.

Those that we love sometimes soften us. My anger, at least for the moment, was gone, and with that, my resolution.

Of course, that was the moment that two of Lord Toshtai's warriors, each wearing light bone armor, a sword, and a grim expression, stopped in front of the door.

"Our Lord Toshtai will see you now," the senior said, each word carefully paced. I had once watched a woodcutter chop down a tur tree with just that even rhythm.

The guard at the door held out his hand for my pack; I handed it over without protest. He dumped it out on the table and examined it, silently handing back the pack itself, then dumping my various tools in it, as well as the cable coil.

He opened a wooden box. "What might these be?"

"Practice knives," I said, reaching for one. "They're for juggling when you don't—"

"No." One of the warriors at my side grabbed my wrist, neither gently nor roughly. Firmly, as though he had strength to spare.

The guard extracted one and tested the edge against the side of my arm. It was cool and smooth. Unsurprisingly, it left only a white mark on my skin that vanished momentarily—it was a practice knife, after all; surprisingly, he tested each of the other five knives against my arm before closing the box and slipping it back in my pack.

The search concluded, the door opened, and two guards led me down a long hall, the white stone smooth and cold beneath my feet, past screened-off rooms, some of them dark and silent, others with flickering shadows playing enigmatically on the surface of the translucent paper screens. Lord Toshtai's compartment was marked only by the twin swordsmen standing outside.

The door slid aside and again I was in Toshtai's presence. He wasn't alone, of course. I wonder if even his wives ever saw him alone. I didn't ask; it never came up.

Two blades slid from their sheaths; the two

guards had drawn their swords and had stepped forward into a ready position, not quite eying me, standing like statues, waiting. To Toshtai's left, Arefai raised a finger as though in warning, echoed by Felkoi.

Between them, his beefy face a mirror of his guilt, was Refle.

A warrior would have shouted a battle cry and leaped for him, but even a warrior wouldn't have gotten within ren, cut in half by the guards, or by Arefai. A peasant wouldn't have gotten that far.

Toshtai sat on a low cushion at a knee-table, bent over a puzzle, trying to fit some square bone tiles into a rectangular stone frame, his flipper-like hands surprisingly graceful as he toyed with one of the tiles, *tick*ing it against another, his attention focused on the puzzle, not on the rest of the room.

He was fresh out of a bath, too, apparently; his hair seemed wet, not merely slicked back.

Toshtai finally deigned to notice me and my guard; we dropped to our knees.

"Puzzles," he said, quietly, possibly to himself; then his eyes caught mine. "Do you like puzzles, Kami Khuzud?" He spotted a move, and set a tile down; it clicked into place, bones rattling on stone.

I've never given it much thought, I thought. That wouldn't do as an answer, but I couldn't lie to Toshtai, not with him looking at me.

"I haven't ever given it any thought, Lord

Toshtai," I heard myself say. My anger had faded to fear, and hopelessness, and desperation; I trembled.

Arefai glared, but Lord Toshtai smiled.

"Ah. Come here, young peasant acrobat, and give it some thought." He spread his hands. "Now, we have two dozen square tiles, from this one," he said, picking up a tile the size of a fingernail, with a single hatch mark on it, "of one fren square, to this one," he said, picking up another much larger one, marked with the symbol for two dozen, "which measures precisely twenty-four fren across. The box measures seventy fren across. The problem, and a pretty one it is, is can the tiles be laid into the box?"

I've never had a mind for figures, but I tried to calculate it out. *One plus two is three. No, it is two tiles across, so it is four tiles . . .*

"Pretend your worthless life depends on it, shitfooted fool," Arefai said, his hand on the hilt of his sword. Arefai may have been friendly for a member of our beloved ruling class, but he was a noble and I was a peasant, after all.

Toshtai silenced him with a quick frown. "No, no, Kami Khuzud, don't calculate it—solve it." Toshtai placed the smallest tile in my hands. "I've always had a fondness for puzzles. My son says that you have a puzzle for me. You will try to solve my puzzle, and I shall look at yours."

The trouble with dealing with members of our beloved ruling class is that they make the rules, and I didn't have any idea as to what the rules were. Except that I had better try hard to figure out the problem Lord Toshtai had set me.

Actually, I've always liked games and such, and a game is a puzzle. My sister did, too—but Enki Duzun had never been able to beat me at inverting draughts.

There didn't seem to be any obvious way to do it, so I picked up the largest tile and set it in— wait. The box was seventy ren on a side, and the largest tile was twenty-four ren on a side. So the others running down the side had to add up to no more than seventy fren.

It was a strange thing; a pattern snapped into my mind, and I laid the tiles in the box quickly.

Lord Toshtai raised an eyebrow. "Amazing. I thought it unlikely," he said, turning to the writing desk at his elbow. The fat lord picked up a brush and inkpot, quickly sketching a diagram of the tiles' arrangements, before unceremoniously dumping the tiles back on the table. "The tiles were a present from Lord Ronoda," he said, "and I thought intended to frustrate me." He popped a sweetmeat into his mouth, and then rubbed his hands together, whether to clean them of crumbs or in pleasure I couldn't tell. His fat face was passionless, as always. I couldn't even tell if he was just idly toying with me or if he really was up to something.

"Now, I understand that you have another puzzle for me, another puzzle of life and death, Kami

Khuzud," he said. "Is it in there?" He quirked his fingers. I didn't understand what he meant by it, but Arefai did—he slapped my hands aside and took my pack, and dumped it on the floor.

"Well, boy, what is the puzzle?"

I didn't understand, but I at least had a way to proceed. "This cable is the puzzle, Lord Toshtai. It was the highwire. It snapped while supporting my sister."

I couldn't go on. My voice caught in my throat.

I tried to say something, but Arefai shook his head and held up a hand, silencing me. *Wait*, he mouthed.

"I *told* you, Lord Toshtai, I told you," Refle said. "The peasant—"

"Acrobat," Toshtai said, correcting him.

"Whatever pleases Lord Toshtai. The acrobat, then, sniffs after my intended, and seeks to blame me for the clumsiness of his sister."

"Interesting," Arefai said. "I didn't note Enki Duzun's clumsiness. I thought the peasant girl quite nimble." His voice was deceptively smooth, like the edge of a knife, but his lips where white. "Tell me how grace is supposed to balance someone in midair. Tell me *now*, armorer."

"Arefai." Toshtai hissed once. "Be still, Lord Arefai. I am displeased, my son," the Lord said, gently. "You bring fire and anger to a pleasant discussion of puzzles. Is there a reason?"

"I am *very* angry, Lord Toshtai," Arefai said.

"Somebody beat this boy—and secretly, hidden in a hood. Now his sister has died in a suspicious accident—this is not permitted in Den Oroshtai. It's an attack on your rule, Lord."

"A great friend of the peasants is Lord Arefai," Toshtai mused. "I hadn't observed this. Nor have half the peasant girls on the outlying farms, I'll wager."

"No, Father. Not the peasants. I am your man, always. If any person or even a bourgeois wants to chastise or slice up a peasant, let him do so. Look." Arefai stalked over to me and slapped me twice on the face, hard. My face stung. It wasn't the first time I'd wanted to kill a member of our beloved ruling class, and if I kept still, it likely wouldn't be the last.

I kept still.

"But there are standards to be kept," he went on, "obligations to be met. If Refle wants this acrobat dead, let him kill him openly, in daylight. Let him do it cleanly, not try to steal a life in the dark."

"You would shame me unfairly, Lord Arefai," Refle said, "if you say that I would skulk and run."

"Please, Lord," Felkoi said. "My brother didn't kill the girl. He wouldn't do such a thing."

"Or beat the boy?" Arefai asked. "I saw Kami Khuzud's bruises—they're still there, under his tunic."

Refle almost started at that, but he kept his composure.

"Narantir," Arefai went on, "will speak of his broken bones. Were these self-inflicted?"

"A footpad, perhaps. It may not be permitted, but it happens, even in Den Oroshtai," Felkoi said.

"And the death of his sister?"

"An accident, manifestly," Refle said. "Or his own clumsiness in not taking care of his tools."

"Ah."

Lord Toshtai smiled, although at what I wasn't sure. "I commend you on your vision." He returned his attention to the coil of cable. "It is a pretty puzzle, indeed. You see, Refle, most of the wire strands appear to have been cut, perhaps, or long rubbed against something else smooth. Did it long rub against something smooth, parting the strands, Kami Khuzud?"

"No, Lord."

"Perhaps then the strands were cut?" He looked to Refle, then back to me. "An interesting puzzle, Kami Khuzud. You seem to be good at puzzles. Solve this one for me, Kami Khuzud." For a moment, a glimmer of anger crossed his face. "It would be a shame if my evening were ruined deliberately, would it not?"

His evening ruined . . .

My sister lay motionless in death on a stone

slab, all that she had been, all that she was to be gone forever, and the fat lord of Den Oroshtai thought that less than his ruined evening.

Sometimes I wonder if our beloved ruling class is really of the same species as the rest of us.

"Yes, Lord," I said, the words cold, salty ashes in my mouth. "It would be a terrible shame for your evening to be deliberately ruined."

I thought I'd kept the sarcasm out of my voice, but Refle started to rise, stopping only at a glare from Arefai.

"Such sulking," Toshtai said, ignoring the by-play. "One would think that an indignity has been visited upon your person just now, Kami Khuzud," he went on, "if I did not turn my face away from it, for it never happened. Go, acrobat—I will think on the puzzle, and you will look into it for me. You will need to bury your sister tomorrow—begin the day after. See if you can find the solution."

"Lord?"

A shadow of irritation crossed his face. "Find out how this wire came to be cut, how your sister came to die. Examine things. Talk to those in the castle; see if they saw someone cutting the wire during the time in which it must have been cut. Then tell me how your sister came to die, show me how your sister came to die." His lips thinned fractionally. "I want to know.

"You may leave now."

As I rose, Toshtai turned to Refle. "You have the honor of pouring, Lord Refle. It would please me to drink some of the Crimson Bud Essence; yes, yes, sprinkle the peppers heavily on the surface."

9
Breakfast and Burial

ENKI DUZEN'S CHAIR was empty at breakfast, and we just ate.

"Could you pass the preserves, Sala?" Fhilt asked.

Morning sunlight flooded through the window of the breakfast room, gaily splashing across the table, across plates and pots piled high with rashers of bacon and mounds of steaming boiled oats. Sala picked up a fundleberry crock for a moment and balanced it on the palm of her hand before shaking her head and simply setting it down gently in front of Evrem.

My father looked at me, and I looked at him, the two of us wordless. I had always thought of gray as a lively color, because it was the color of Gray Khuzud, and there wasn't anybody with more life and kazuh in him than Gray Khuzud. Not this morning. This morning, gray was a dull, dead color.

His eyes were red, his lined face sallow, not

merely with sadness, it seemed, but with an infinite weariness. I doubted that he had slept any more than I had.

One of the Eresthais quietly elbowed his brother and whispered; the other—no, Eno; Enki Duzen had always remembered them by name— Eno pulled the bread over and carved off a slice.

Fhilt took a hard-boiled egg from a serving bowl and made a quick flourish with it, then sighed and set it down on the table, rolling it under the palm of his hand to crack the shell, peeling it with no grace at all.

"You aren't eating, Evrem," Gray Khuzud said. "We have much to do today; and you must eat."

"But—" Evrem started to say, gesturing to the half-eaten slice of bread and jam on the plate in front of him, and to my empty plate. He started to rise.

"No," Gray Khuzud said. "Don't leave."

Large Egda gripped Evrem's arm, and while he is not the most dextrous of men, when Large Egda grips something, it stays gripped.

"No," Gray Khuzud went on, as though he was talking to Evrem, "you must eat. It's important that we all eat, that we go on."

I gestured to Large Egda to let Evrem go. The big man thought about it for a moment, then opened his hand. Evrem shrugged and sat.

"We all must eat," Gray Khuzud said. "The show goes on tomorrow, and we must rehearse today. I've been thinking about how to change the act, now that Enki Duzun is . . . is no longer with us, and we will have to practice, and make it smooth."

Evrem didn't answer; he just rubbed at his arm and glared at Large Egda.

We all must eat.

I cut myself a piece of bread and took a bite. It tasted like an old tunic.

Sala spooned some boiled oats onto her own plate, then dropped a spoonful of butter on them.

Egda picked up the spreading knife and held it in the palm of his hand, staring at it as though . . . as though, I don't know, maybe as though he wanted it to get up and dance around, maybe as though he expected it, needed it, to get up and dance around.

But it didn't. Nothing moves itself. The rings, wands, traps, and all the rest of the equipment are without spirit; we lend them ours.

Or not. Fhilt just quietly ate his egg.

Large Egda bounced the spreading knife on his palm, once, then took it by the blade and flipped it up into the air, holding his palm out, as though he expected the knife to smack right into it.

It didn't; the knife clattered on the table, sending other cutlery flying.

"No," Large Egda said. "Not right." He picked it up, and tried again. Again it clattered on the table.

"No. Not *right*." He slammed his hand down

on his thigh with a meaty thunk, then picked up the knife. "I have to do it right, not just do it."

My father raised his eyes. "Egda," he said, wearily, shaking his head. "Shh. No. Leave it be, for once."

"Oh, yes," Large Egda said. "Oh, very much yes," he said, with a quiet conviction that brooked no argument. "We will not leave it be today," he said, reporting not an opinion, but a law of nature, a fact about the world.

"No, not today, not of all days." Sala's eyes were almost glowing.

Fhilt's jaw was as tight as mine.

Large Egda bounced the knife again. This time, it would have knocked the saltwell over, except that Fhilt's hand was already there, and by the Powers the knife slapped firmly into *his* palm.

He lifted the breadknife up and let us all see it.

There are brothers and sisters of flesh, and of spirit, they say.

While we never much liked each other, at that moment my brother of the spirit Fhilt gripped the knife tightly, his hand shaking, his knuckles white, then his grip loosened, and with a quick "Don't move, Egda," he tossed the knife high into the air, so perfectly high, so beautifully high that it almost touched the beam overhead before, falling and spinning, it slapped into Large Egda's palm.

The big man gripped the spreading knife eagerly, his grin broad. "Sala. Preserves."

"Pass him the preserves, Gray Khuzud," Sala said. "Sometimes unexpected troubles solve other problems."

Gray Khuzud looked at her woodenly.

She tossed her head, then reached over and stood as she picked up the stone pot.

"Very well," she said, her voice high and shrill. "If you won't, then I will." She dropped it, catching it deftly on the side of her naked foot, then foot-tossed it into a high arc that took it forward and over her shoulder, and then—"Quickly, Kami Khuzud, quickly"—caught it on the instep of the same foot.

The foot fell, and rose, and I stood quickly to snatch the pot out of the air, leaning back as I rolled it across my chest to my other hand, flipped it high and caught it on my own heel, and then tossed it to Fhilt.

He couldn't have seen it through his tears, but he caught it anyway, snatched the spreading knife from Large Egda's loose grip, and slowly, tauntingly dipped it into the pot while Evrem and Sala each sawed away at an end of the breadloaf.

I picked up the two slices and slapped them around the gobbet of preserves, catching it but a fingersbreadth in front of my father's face.

Yes. We mourn you, Enki Duzun, but we won't stop celebrating your life, not for a moment.

I set it down on his plate. "Eat, Gray Khuzud."

For a moment, it all hung in the balance, and I knew it could go either way . . .

. . . but then he picked up the bread and preserves, and then he just ate.

Sunwise, the sky was clear and cloudless. Too clear; too cloudless. It would have more in keeping with our mood for there to be a storm holding off just long enough for us to bury my sister at the edge of a cornfield.

There had been a storm yesterday, and it had felt like it would last forever, but it had fled.

If Narantir had been a Great Wizard, I would have wondered if it had been his doing; he had seemed to like Enki Duzun. But he was a simple sorcerer, a minor magician, and the storm had run away of its own doing.

Peasants are always buried in fields. From dirt and straw and dung were we created; to dirt and straw and dung we return.

So-be-it.

Large Egda dug the hole all by himself, and made it so deep that he couldn't even climb out of it; Gray Khuzud, Fhilt, Evrem and I had to haul him out on the end of a rope. I'm not sure why he dug so deeply; even if there were foxes and wolves in the area, they couldn't have dug down very far.

Or maybe I do know, at that. Maybe when you can't do anything that addresses the heart of the matter, you have to do what you can, and if the only thing you can do is to dig a hole in the ground, then you dig that hole with all the will and strength and dedication at your command.

He came out of the hole half-naked and dirty, as were the rest of us: a typical D'Shaian peasant funeral party.

Except for two. Felkoi was up on the road, and while he didn't rush out and lend a hand with either the rope or the body, I had the feeling that he wanted to. I understood, or at least thought I did. Shame is something subtle, and if his brother had done what Felkoi perhaps thought he had done, it was shameful for their whole family, were anybody to find out.

They would find out.

Everybody would know, if I had anything to do with it.

If.

If that were Lord Toshtai's decision, which I doubted. If he decided that Refle was guilty of a covertry, it was much more likely he would order old Dun Lidjun to take offense at something Refle said than shame the whole family by exposing him.

"That which is not seen is not," and all. All he would have to do is turn his face from it, and handle the matter in the manner of D'Shai.

Not good enough, not good enough by half. Our beloved ruling class erects monuments of steel and stone for their fallen; I'd erect one of shame for my sister.

But how?

Fhilt and I lowered Enki Duzun's body into the hole. It seemed lighter than it should have been, as though the old stories about how the soul flees the body the morning after death are true, as they may even be. I don't know; I don't know much.

The other person up on the road was NaRee, sitting on a rented white pony, it whitewashed from ears to hooves, she immaculate in her finest funeral whites, as though this was a bourgeois burial.

That earned her an occasional glare from Sala, who didn't understand—it was NaRee's way. NaRee wasn't flourishing her status; she was trying to honor my sister.

But none of us was on balance that day. When NaRee gestured to me, the hesitant quirk of her fingers almost eloquent in its awkwardness, all I could do was shake my head.

I needed her, but I couldn't be with her. Not today.

We D'Shai lie to ourselves too easily, if incompletely; the troupe began practice in the corral as though it was just another day.

Almost . . . Nobody wanted to walk on the low wire. It waited in the bright sun, the cable burnished to an almost mirror brightness, a balancing pole leaning up against the platform on either side, one of the Eresthai brothers waiting at each platform.

While Gray Khuzud and Fhilt practiced tumbling run after tumbling run, Large Egda went through his usual set of squats, perhaps grunting less than usual. Sala's stretches flowed into dance, and then into juggling, until she had a full eight of her rings flying into the air, flowing around her in a silver stream.

The low wire stood waiting in the sun.

I balanced easily on the board and roller, whipping a wand, a knife and a small wooden ball first through a simple shower and then into a circular juggle.

Perversely, everything worked well: not only didn't I drop anything, but the board held every bit as firm and steady beneath my feet as solid ground could have. I almost wished that I couldn't do as well; I kept looking for Enki Duzun's smile of approval, and of course it wasn't there.

Everybody kept deliberately not looking at the low wire, as though that would make it go away. Every once in a while, one of the Eresthais would check a turnbuckle or clamp, as though that would do any good.

Finally, I couldn't take it anymore. I let my gear drop to the sand, and climbed up onto the fence, leaning on a balancing pole for support. I let the balancing pole fall away, stepped out on the wire, my arms out to my side.

And fell to the sand.

One of the Eresthais helped me back up to the

platform, holding out a balancing pole in silent offer.

"No," I said, with a shake of the head, as I stepped out once again onto the cold wire, my arms out to one side. Balance is everything. The long arms of a balancing pole put your point of balance safely beneath the wire; the pole does the work. But when you're walking the wire by yourself, you have to do it all yourself, to move your arms and more importantly your balance, your center, directly over the wire.

Or fall. I fell again, and tried again.

Gray Khuzud reached out a hand and helped me to my feet. "Enough for one day, Kami Khuzud. Tomorrow."

The three elder members of the troupe and the two Eresthais had gone to bed, to pretend to sleep; Fhilt, Large Egda and I were the last to bed, as usual. Fhilt, Egda and I sat on the steps of Madame Rupon's porch, looking out at the town, and at the flickering lights in the castle above the town, and at the stars above.

Our time, for the three of us, sitting out under a star-splattered sky that refused to be dulled by the sadness that should have had the stars weeping.

Three, instead of four. I knew what it felt like to be a wagon with three wheels.

The musicians practiced off in the night, the silverhorns moaning a slow dirge, broken only occasionally by a listless run on the zivver, dragged down by the thrumming of the bassskin. Fhilt toyed with a stick, drawing in the dirt for a few moments, then scratching it out with his foot.

"They're not good tonight," he said.

I didn't say anything to that; I just stepped off the porch and walked a short way onto the path, out of the light.

I'll always miss you, Enki Duzun.

But missing her wouldn't bring her back. Proving that Refle had killed her while trying to lay a trap for me wouldn't bring her back.

Sometimes I have to wonder about what happens after we die. Do we await another turn on the Wheel, the way the Bhorlani claim?

Or do peasants return to the soil in spirit as well as in body, the way we were taught? Does anybody know? Can anybody know? My father used to say something about how if you live your art properly, you can't die, because the art lives on, but Enki Duzun hadn't had the chance to live it out, not yet.

"Is it better if we don't talk about it?" Large Egda asked.

"Stupid question." The stick snapped in Fhilt's hands. " 'Is it better if we don't talk about it,' " he said, slurring his voice to mimic Large Egda's awkward mouth. "Yes, it's better if we don't talk about it. It's better if we don't think about it, it's better if it never happened."

"Idiot," I said, turning around.

"It's not Large Egda's fault that the Powers gave him three men's strength and a hare's brain."

"Not him. You," I said. "You're the idiot. No, not an idiot. An idiot doesn't know what he's doing. You're worse: you're a traitor to her memory."

"Me?"

"Did you ever see Enki Duzun make fun of Egda? *Once?* In her memory, you'll treat him like dung? In her memory, you'll make things worse?"

He squared off across from me. "Don't say that to me. I loved your sister, Kami Khuzud. She could not have been dearer to me if . . . she couldn't have been."

I laughed in his face.

And he slapped me, hard, then staggered back, as though I had been the one to slap him.

"No, no." Fhilt's eyes were wide and white. "Kami Khuzud, you can't, I mean—" In all of our mock battles and threatened confrontations, neither of us had ever actually hit the other. Enki Duzun had always stopped things before they got that far, a brake on our misbehavior.

Fhilt called out for me as I turned and walked off into the night.

When I came back, they had both gone to bed.

10
Tears on a Pillow

WHEN YOU DON'T know what else to do, go back to the beginning. That's what my father always taught me, and that's what I believe.

The beginning.

I stood alone in the dark, in the street outside Madame Rupon's, the wands and balls and rings scattered at my feet.

The night was cool, and dark, barely lit by the lanterns on the porches of the houses of the Bankstreets, and the stars above.

One ball.

It's the most basic juggle: you throw one ball up in the air, and let it fall into your hand. You really only have to control one thing at a time, but you have to control that fully.

You really do.

I threw one ball up in the air with my right hand, and let it fall into my left hand, not snatching it out of the night, but merely throwing and placing it precisely, thinking about each step as I did it. And then I did it the other way, throwing the ball from my left to my right, precisely, perfectly, the way you can do it only with practice or kazuh. It's important to get the form right. Get the form right, and everything else falls into place.

And then two. First throw the ball in the left hand toward the right, and before it arrives, throw the ball in the right hand toward the left. Then do it the other way: the right hand first. Throw-throw. Pause. Throw-throw. Pause. That pause, that moment of robbed time makes it harder to juggle two than three, but you have to do it in order.

Three. Adding the third ball is simple, and turns a herky-jerky motion into a flow of catch-left throw-left catch-right throw-right.

I reached out my right foot and worked a fourth ball onto my instep, then kicked the fourth ball into the flow. And then a fifth, and a sixth, turning the simple shower into a constant motion of catch and throw.

I held the flow, stayed in the stream of catch and throw until my shoulders began to ache, and my eyes began to hurt with concentration.

So I relaxed my shoulders, and closed my eyes, and kept up the shower as I called for the kazuh of the acrobat, to let it propel my arms for me, to guide my way for me.

Nothing happened, except my arms got more tired, the tendons in my shoulders burning.

I couldn't find it; it wasn't there. They say that any problem can be solved with kazuh, or put into proportion. Keep everything in balance, they say, and the rest falls into place.

Hah.

I let the balls fall about me, into the dust, into the night.

"Very deft, young acrobat," a harsh voice whispered from out of the night.

Refle stood behind me, his brother at his elbow. "But not quite deft enough, eh?"

"Shh, Refle," Felkoi said. "The boy's lost his sister; be still." He didn't apologize to me; a noble doesn't apologize to a peasant. This was as close as he could come.

"I'd venture the young acrobat wonders what we're doing here, eh, brother?"

Felkoi didn't answer him.

"We are returning home from an evening visiting with my intended, Kami Khuzud," Refle said. "A very pleasant evening. You know, Ezren Smith told a story that you might find amusing—"

"Be still, Refle," Felkoi said, with less patience. "Leave him be."

Refle looked at me silently for a long time, not a word passing between the two of us.

I wanted to say, *I know you murdered my sister, and somehow I'll prove it.*

He smiled, and in that smile was a confession. *You'll never prove it,* he mouthed, and, after a quick glance he mimicked raising and lowering a truncheon, his body blocking his brother's view.

Just as you never proved I broke your bones.

I took half a step forward, but Refle's hand dropped to his swordhilt. No. That would make it too easy for him.

"Let us go, Felkoi," he said.

The two of them turned and walked away.

"Very interesting," Fhilt said from behind me. "Everybody seems to be out of balance tonight."

I turned. He stood on the porch, leaning idly against a column, a couple of braces of knives—real juggling knives, not practice knives—in his hands. "Not a good night for juggling, eh?" The apology was in his tone, and it was as much apology as I was likely to get. Somehow, I never seem to get a real apology.

"No," I said. "Everything seems out of balance." Which was all the acknowledgment Fhilt was going to get.

He nodded, briefly. "Ever wonder," he asked, "if you could juggle the knives differently? I mean," he said, taking up a position to my side, about a bodylength away, "instead of being sure that they rotated half a turn, or a turn and a half, or two and a half turns, making them rotate a whole turn? Or two? Or three?"

He tossed a knife to me; it flipped end-over-end through the dark, thunking comfortably, hilt-first, into my rising palm.

"Try it," he said. "Throw it at me, point first."

I looked at him a long time. "Don't tempt me."

"What was it you said, Kami Khuzud? 'In her memory, you'll make things worse?' Will you, Kami Khuzud? Throw the knife to me, or at me."

I threw it, but it *felt* wrong; at the last moment, I tugged wrongly at the knife.

Fhilt snatched it out of the air, anyway.

"Not good, Kami Khuzud." He stooped to the flower beds and took up a clod of dirt, setting it on the top weatherbeaten step. "Try to hit that, or the riser, just above that."

He put the four knives into an impromptu shower, catching some by the hilt, snatching at the blades of others.

Knives flickered in the lamplight, and then one twisted in the air toward me.

I caught it by the hilt, and threw it. The knife thunked into the wood, just above the dirt clod.

"Very good, Kami Khuzud," Fhilt said. He pulled the knife from the wood, and considered the blade for a moment before wiping it on his tunic. "Good night." He turned away, and then stopped himself. "I'll probably forget, again. Things are so out of balance."

"That they are, Fhilt."

Obedient to command as always, I picked up the props, cleaned them, and put them away before I went to bed.

There was a flask of Crimson Tears on my pillow; I drained it and slept without dreams.

11
Trapeze

OBEDIENT TO COMMAND as always, I started the investigation, such as it was, the next morning. I didn't know when Lord Toshtai was going to send for me, and with a bit of luck, perhaps I could find out enough by then to fix the blame on Refle.

I started with the door frame, the place where we ourselves had clamped the cable into place.

The mounting staple was still in place; I didn't have the tools to remove it, and the Eresthais, who did, were still in town. They would be in sometime in the hour of the horse. I could take a look under it later, and maybe find something. What, I wasn't sure—perhaps Refle had been considerate enough to impress his signature ring into the wood.

Sure.

I looked down the hall as though I was seeing it for the first time.

In a sense I was; it just hadn't occurred to me

to wonder what the three other rooms down our side of the hall were for. The other side was a long expanse of bas-relief between two circular stairways, broken in the middle by another hall that led toward the central wing of the donjon.

Refle had a residence somewhere in the castle, for certain. If it was one of these rooms, that might be another loop in the knot of his noose.

Down at the far end of the hall, a pair of maids were down on their hands and knees cleaning the floor, one washing, one drying. Members of our beloved ruling class don't like to slip on marble. Neither do the rest of us, although we all too rarely have a chance to walk on it, to feel the mirror-smooth coolness beneath our feet.

"What are these other rooms used for?" I asked.

"*You there*, what are you doing there?"

I turned to face Lord Crosta Natthan, the castle's chief servitor. Today Crosta Natthan was all in off-white, from the creamy silk ribbon binding back his hair, down through a soft cotton tunic of almost formal cut, tightly belted with bleached leather. His pantaloons were primly blousy, their cuffs tucked into the tops of his soft slippers.

There was no hint in his manicured nails, precisely cut hair, or supercilious sniff that he had been born bourgeois. Lord Toshtai had elevated him probably in small part in recognition of his abilities in managing the house as the previous chief servitor's assistant, probably in large part because it enabled Crosta Natthan to better handle noble residents.

Or perhaps I'm just being skeptical. Perhaps Lord Toshtai had elevated him because he had decided that the Powers had made an error, and that Crosta Natthan had been born from the wrong womb.

Of course.

"I asked what you are doing there," he repeated. "Answer me. Quickly, now, boy."

"I am asking questions, Lord Crosta Natthan," I said. "Of the maids."

"And why are you doing this?" He arched an eyebrow, as though he was examining a full chamberpot that some poor liar had sworn empty.

"Lord Toshtai told me to." I thought that would be enough for him, but it wasn't.

"I will not believe that Lord Toshtai told you to ask them assassin's questions."

"Your pardon? Assassin's questions? I'm sorry, but I don't understand."

"Who sleeps in this room and who sleeps in that room is no concern of somebody who does not live in the castle, young peasant."

I bowed. "As you say, Lord. It's my stupidity; I apologize."

"Very well." He dismissed it with a wave. "You may be gone, then."

I opened my mouth, closed it, and opened it again. "Yes, Lord. When may I see Lord Toshtai?"

"Why would you wish to do that?" There was just the tiniest touch of alarm in his voice, although his expression was still blandly correct.

"To have my stupidity corrected, Lord. In my idiocy, I thought that he said to me, 'Do whatever is necessary to find out how this wire came to be cut, Kami Khuzud. See if anybody knows something that will let you discern who cut the wire during the time in which it must have been cut.' "

That wasn't exactly how Lord Toshtai had put it, but it was close enough.

For a moment, I didn't know how Crosta Natthan would react, but then his shoulders loosened just a trifle, just the way a beginner's do, when he knows he's going to drop the clubs and can't do anything about it.

I seized the moment.

"Here, Lord. Come with me," I said, quickly walking down the hall to the room we had been using. I tapped the mounting staple. "I think somebody cut the wire. Probably by slipping a very sharp, very good knife underneath, here, and cutting at the cable."

"Mmm." He was interested, despite himself. He rubbed his fingers across it. "How could you tell?"

I shrugged. "If so, there ought to be some marking underneath, no?"

He nodded. "Metal is stronger than wood. —What would that tell you?"

I shook my head. "I don't know. I've always liked puzzles, though, and one thing I know about them is that you can't tell what matters ahead of time."

"Ah." He nodded. "So, you look at everything?"

"Yes, Lord."

"Well, then," he snapped his fingers, beckoning to the nearest maid. "You there—run down to the quarters and bring back an artificer—Merk Ven Dun; he's got a strong arm. Quickly, girl, quickly."

The wood was not quite notched—it was more compressed, indented, along where the knife had slid.

I measured the distance from where the line of compression was to where the cable had been. It seemed about the distance from the edge of a sword to a part I didn't have a name for.

"May I, Lord?" I asked Crosta Natthan.

"Eh?"

"Your sword?"

"Oh." He drew it quickly, and reversed it with a too-practiced flip. Those who become warriors late in life never quite seem to get that sword-as-an-appendage way of handling it.

I took the cord-wound hilt in my hand. Just like the one in Refle's workshop, it seemed lighter than it looked—a large juggling wand is much heavier.

I slid the sword along the doorframe. "What is the name of this part? The edge of the part where it's ground?"

"The break, it's called," he said. "This part of the sword is the break. It was the break of a sword that made that indentation in the wood?"

I shrugged. "Perhaps," I said, handing the sword back.

He slid it into its sheath. "And what has this all told you, Kami Khuzud?"

"It's hard to say," I said. That was true enough. It was hard to say that it didn't tell me anything useful, but I didn't see any point in letting anybody else know that. "Now, these rooms, along here—what are they for?"

Crosta Natthan frowned for a moment. "I still do *not* care for assassin's questions, but it probably won't do any harm, not this time. This room," he said, indicating the one next to ours, "is occupied by two of Lord Edelfaule's concubines; the next, by three men of our lord's personal guard."

"Who has access to the rooms?"

"Eh?"

"Who comes and goes here?"

Not that it would make any difference; I'd already known that once you got inside the donjon itself, there were guards only on the residence wing, where Lord Toshtai and his family and their closest retainers lived, not in the servants' wing, not in the main tower, the kitchens, the dungeon, or the stables.

Crosta Natthan shrugged. "Not Lord Edelfaule—his women visit him in his quarters. The scullery girls go in and out all the time, of course—the chamberpots are emptied and cleaned every morning, and the linen is changed every third day. The florist delivers fresh flowers once a day to the concubines, and twice to the soldiers. Meals are sometimes taken in the rooms, so one of the cooks' runners might be up here at any time."

"Might Lord Refle come up here?"

The Chief Servitor nodded. "Of course. There is always work being done on some piece of armor or armament, and Refle is hardly going to trust the delivery of arms to bourgeois or peasants, is he?"

"Would you know if Refle was here the night before last?"

He pumped his sword in its sheath with a loud snap. "*Lord* Refle," he said, his voice cold, "may have been here, or he may not. I would not know. Will there be anything else?"

I shook my head. "No, Lord."

He turned and walked away.

I sighed as I watched Crosta Natthan's retreating back. For a moment, I'd been treating a member of our beloved ruling class—albeit a raised member—as another person, and not just a dangerous object.

I'd forgotten myself; assumed humility is as much a key to one's safety as . . .

. . . as the clamp that held the cable tight, and taut.

"Kami Khuzud?" Large Egda was behind me. I hadn't seen him come up.

"Yes, Egda?"

"Practice. The Eresthais have to put up the new cable and clamp."

I shook my head. "Not until I'm done."

I hate flying, particularly with the safety harness on. There's something insulting about the long rope attached first to the broad waistbelt and then to the pulley overhead, the end of the rope belayed below by the Eresthais.

But, even free, I hate flying. It *hurts*.

From the ground, it looks effortless: you grab on to the trapeze, then let it carry you into the air easily, gracefully, momentarily a bird in flight as you leave one for another, or for the waiting arms of the catcher, sometimes spinning as you go, other times simply flying, back arched in pleasure and tranquillity.

All is illusion.

From the ground, they don't hear the grunts of strain and pain, the creaking of joints that can't be completely cushioned by even the most powerful muscles. And—every man does this at least once; I've done it precisely three times, and remember each incident intimately—the uncontrollable scream you make when you catch the bar properly, grip it tightly, jerking your body to an instant stop . . . and suddenly realize you've forgotten to tighten your crotch-strap.

It is *not* funny.

I spat on my aching hands, then tried to work a knot out of the middle finger on my right hand. It felt like a betel nut under the skin.

It doesn't matter how thick your calluses are, or how strong your hands: letting your whole weight fall, repeatedly, onto a wooden bar only a bit thicker than a sprained thumb *hurts*. Being caught is only a bit better. Maybe it is like being a bird in flight—but maybe birds don't like flying any more than I do.

Large Egda, sitting uncomfortably on the far trapeze, pumped up into a vigorous swing, then sat back, catching his ankles on the padding surrounding the trapeze's wires. It's not comfortable, but the padding is the difference between feeling discomfort and having the wire cut into muscle and tendon.

Time for me to go. Timing is everything, and everybody knew my timing was off.

Holding the bar of the outer trap, I started to count down. "Three. Two. —"

"No." Gray Khuzud gripped my shoulder. "You're rushing. Don't be in such a hurry—you want to land squarely, not abruptly. Count with me," he said, gesturing at Large Egda to maintain his pace, then waiting for the right moment. "Three. Two. One. *Go.*"

Gripping the bar, I pushed off. Wind whispered vague threats and imprecations in my ear.

Swinging is worse than simply hanging from a motionless bar: at the bottom of the arc, the spirits of the trapeze pull down, trying to pull you off the bar and smash you down into the net or ground below.

I swung, and just short of the top of my swing, I brought my legs up and let go, pulling my knees into a gentle tuck. The universe spun once around me, no center to cling to, until Large Egda's hairy hands rolled out of the insanity and gripped my wrists, and then pulled me back through the long arc of his upswing. My back and shoulders were still badly bruised, but I held my groans inside; I couldn't let out a scream in front of Gray Khuzud.

For a moment, at the top of the swing, I can understand why better acrobats, why real acrobats, love flying most of all: for that one moment, at the very peak, you're free of the bonds of gravity, of the spirits of earth and rock that try to pull you down.

Large Egda released me at that moment, and we used that time, that instant, to turn me around. This time I gripped his arms, above the thick fists he formed to make his wrists firmer for my clasp, and pulled him through his swing.

I looked up and spotted the empty trapeze high

above me, and as Large Egda and I rose, I pulled up on his arms and released almost perfectly, flying to it, only having to adjust my hands at the last moment as I gripped the bar, then flew up to the platform, where Gray Khuzud's and Fhilt's eager hands reached out and secured me.

"Adequate," Gray Khuzud said. "Barely adequate. Again."

None of the servants were used to being interrogated by the likes of me, including Varta Kedin, the leading third-floor maid, a slim, older woman whose white hair seemed more drained of color than the vibrant gray of Gray Khuzud's. She never put down her cleaning-rag as we talked, crooked fingers wrapped in the linen, working sinuously as she caressed the shoulder-level woodwork of the upper hall with polish and affection.

The carvings were a series of good Mesthai bas-relief—middle period, single-knife work, from the time before the traditionalists gave way to the modernists' innovations of fitting the tool to the task, and the vigor and strength of Mesthai carving was lost to an unending war of various styles, ignoring the content.

They are always faces; even now, the Mesthai consider any other subject beneath their notice. This series of carvings was part of the Comedy of Pain cycle: hurt expressed in the frown of a young girl and the open-mouthed shriek of a middle-aged man, by the false laugh of a roly-poly graybeard and the grim clenched jaw of a sweaty-browed woman.

Some details of the pained faces had been blurred and softened by the same decades of polishing and rubbing that had brought out the fire and color of the wood—must everything be a trade?

"But exactly when were you in the hall outside the room?" I asked, trying to put it another way.

"It was the hour of the bear, but I am always in and out of the hall in the hour of the bear." She stopped to examine one of the carved faces, then work some polish deep into a high wooden cheekbone. "I always polish the woodwork during the hour of the snake, and prepare the rooms during the hour of the bear."

"Who did you see the night before last?"

Who did you see, the night that Refle murdered my sister?

She considered one of the faces: a flat-nosed woman, her wide eyes and barely open mouth probably originally intended to portray horrid fascination, now rubbed down to mere horror.

"I don't know. The usual. Lord Crosta Natthan came through, as he always does, checking on my work." She spat on her cloth and buffed harder at an invisible blemish. "As though I need it. Ver Hortun, and Bek De Bran, I think. Their—" she stopped herself.

"Yes, yes, that's their room there," I said, waving away the issue of assassin's questions. "They're in and out of it all the time, I suppose. And Lord Refle was around, of course, and—"

She nodded.

I kept my smile inside. "Do you know where Lord Crosta Natthan is at the moment?"

"Lord Crosta Natthan," I said. "I need your help."

"Yes, Kami Khuzud?"

"I would like guards put on the doorframe we were examining—the wizard and I are cooking up a solution to the puzzle, and it's important that it not be disturbed. The Eresthais can put up another clamp, but they're not to move this one." I didn't want the Eresthais disturbing the evidence, such as it was.

Or anybody else.

"Yes, Kami Khuzud." His eyes were cold and gray. "Is there anything else I can do for you?"

I had been going to do it myself, but I couldn't help pressing my derivative authority, just to see how far it would go.

"Yes. In half an hour, you can have a runner sent to Narantir's workshop and ask him to join me. Tell him I'll be in the bath."

The wizard, accompanied by Lord Arefai, caught up with me in the bath.

I was stretched out on the hot stone bench,

letting the steam wash all over me in preparation for my final plunge into the cold spring water that burbled into the oaken tub outside the bathhouse.

The idea is that first you clean yourself thoroughly, with soap, tepid water, and sponges—and then you sweat, and then you wash, and then you sweat again, and wash again. It is supposed to make women's skin softer and men's muscles harder, but I like it because it makes me feel clean, deep-down clean in a way that I never get any other way.

Members of our beloved ruling class use the bath, too, but for them it's traditionally done late in the hour of the octopus, as a preparation for dinner; it was only half past the ox, and I had plenty of time. The classes do not mingle in the bath, but it's no more socially awkward for peasants like me and members of our beloved ruling class to use the same bath than it is for us to eat carrots that are pulled from the same dirt. "That which is not seen is not," and all that.

I had taken the tongs down from their peg to wrestle another few rocks from the fire in the center of the bath, and thrown on a handful of wet chumpa leaves, inhaling the steam and mildly heady smoke before pouring a pail of water on the bench and stretching out. Stone is usually cold, but the constantly stoked fire in the pit under the bath house keeps everything somewhere between achingly hot and literally blistering—the water provides a few moments of respite, before the stones again grow too hot.

I had grown comfortable in the heat—I can adjust to anything, given enough time and patience—when the door swung open and an icy blast of air chilled my back from the ankles to the scalp.

I looked up to glare at Narantir, opening my mouth to say something indiscreet, but I changed my mind and quickly rose and bowed as Arefai walked in behind him, my hand coming up as of its own volition to rub at my cheek.

They made an odd couple. Narantir was, as always, a walking pile of rags and fat, his stained robes belted with a simple piece of rope, barely containing his belly, his smile a mocking leer in his untrimmed hedge of beard. Arefai, also as usual, was arrayed in a carefully matched outfit of forest green tunic and wheat-colored pantaloons. Earthy brown leather sandals, belt, and scabbard completed the field-and-forest effect.

"Your pardon, Lord," I said, grabbing at a cloth and wrapping it around my waist. While most peasants are body-conscious, that isn't a problem that a member of a traveling troupe can maintain; you too often are sharing close quarters. "I'd thought it only the hour of the ox, and—"

"It is, lad, it is," he said, dismissing my concern. "Sit-sit-sit. No, better—we will accom-

pany you as you sluice yourself off and dress.
You may do that now."

And a great honor it is, I didn't say, to have
your lordship watch as I dip my buttocks in icewater.

"Yes, Lord," I said, dropping the cloth and
walking past him. Arefai and Narantir following, I stepped through the dangling leather straps
of the heat-curtains and vaulted into the tub,
splashing through the floating ice chips on the
top—the castle bath was regularly stocked from
the ice cellars.

The shock of hitting the water took my breath
away, as it always did, but I managed to keep
my scream under water, letting it bubble away.

Control, after all, is just another form of balance.

Still, as I got out, wiped myself down, and
quickly dressed in drawstring trousers and a ma-
crame tunic, I couldn't help shivering. I was
chilled to the bone.

"Walk with us and talk with us, Kami Khuzud," Arefai said. He smiled, as though he
wanted it to sound like an invitation, not a command. Not that there's a lot of difference between one and the other, not in D'Shai, not
when issued by a member of our beloved ruling
class.

The three of us walked out into the afternoon,
two of the castle's warriors falling into step three
paces ahead of us, another two behind. I didn't

like the way that the one in front, on the left, kept his short horn bow in his hand, but while there was menace in their manner, none of it seemed directed at me.

I glanced behind—both of the warriors following us had their bows strung. Out of the four-man guard of honor accompanying Arefai, only one was solely a swordsman.

The wind picked up, bowing the branches of the jimsum trees and whipping dirt and dust into the air, and into my wet hair.

"This way, perhaps," Narantir said, indicating the path down through the bracken to the east of the castle.

The swordsman, a gaunt fellow with funereally sunken eyes, shook his head momentarily. "Let us have it cleared, Lord. I'm concerned about your safety."

"The bracken is thick enough," Arefai said.

"Yes, Lord, but the path itself? I think not; we will take the proper precautions, if it please you."

"Wait." Narantir held up a hand. "It will take only a simple spell, Lord," he said as he reached into his plain canvas wizard's bag, pulling out a piece of blue chalk, beckoning at the nearest bowman. "Come here and extend your arm, if you please?"

The bowman looked skeptically at him, but then, at Arefai's nod, came over. Grunting, the wizard bent to rub his fingers on the packed dirt of the trail, and then rose to rub the same fingers against the bowman's arm. He made a few quick chalk marks on the arm, then produced a bluish stone hanging from a thong—I'm sure he took it out of his pouch, but it looked like he snatched it out of the air.

Narantir stroked the stone, then the arm, and lifted the stone to his lips for a moment. The chalk marks on the arm flashed into flame, and the bowman's arm jerked momentarily, although he didn't make a sound. Silence while in pain is a mark of honor among warriors.

I've always wondered why they don't just get themselves muted.

The stone hung from the end of the thong, doing nothing more active or interesting than just hanging there as Narantir studied it.

"It would appear to be safe, Lord," Narantir said. "There is nothing resembling a warrior down the path." He eyed the stone skeptically. "And probably no human at all; I made the runes sloppily on purpose."

Arefai scowled. "All this just to take a walk."

One of the guards smiled, but it wasn't a pleasant smile. "Part of the Way, eh, Lord?" he more said than asked.

I expected Arefai to snap at him, or rebuff the familiarity—warriors are only barely part of our beloved ruling class—but he just nodded casually.

Two warriors preceding us, two following, we

made our way down the path. I tried to follow Arefai, as both courtesy and my safety demanded—members of our beloved ruling class tend to punish discourtesy promptly—but he tugged at my sleeve and indicated that I should walk at his side.

"How, Kami Khuzud," Arefai said, "does your . . . solution to the puzzle go?"

The puzzle. *Have you,* he was asking, *either found or created sufficient evidence to prove that Refle is your sister's murderer?*

Again, a storm was moving in; gray, threatening clouds gathered to sunwise.

"Possibly quite well, Lord Arefai," I said. I had a feeling for it all, that maybe if I just asked around enough, just walked around and looked certain enough, Refle would panic and make a mistake. It would have to be a serious mistake, if it was to be him that ended up dead instead of me.

But it was worth a try.

"I'll need Narantir's help, though. And his cooperation."

The wizard snorted. "I am at your service, Lord Kami," he said.

We walked in silence for a while. Arefai bit his lip for a moment. "If I ordered you to leave this matter be for the next five days, what would you do, Kami Khuzud?"

"I am obedient to orders, as always, Lord. But the troupe is supposed to leave Den Oroshtai in four days, and I expect that Lord Toshtai will want to hear my guess as to the . . . solution to his puzzle before then."

"Ah. *His* puzzle, indeed." He smiled at that, and for a moment he looked almost like a person. But then the mask of dignity that members of our beloved ruling class wear like a suit of armor slipped back down. "Lord Orazhi himself is coming here; he arrives this evening. It would be . . . convenient if no trouble were to mar his visit."

Glen Derenai and Den Oroshtai had always been loosely associated, if not allied, in the wars that wash up and down our narrow island like a brush painting a fenceboard. But that's none of the business or concern of peasants or of troupers; we are subject to all, supportive of none. It's better that way.

But for Orazhi to be on the road here spoke of at least a potential close alliance, or something more complicated; I've often wondered if members of our beloved ruling class would have as much time for intrigue if they had to work for the food they eat. In no case was it any concern of mine, and I didn't understand why Arefai was bringing it up.

"It's both political and personal, Kami Khuzud," Arefai said, looking away. "I understand that you're rather fond of NaRee, the ironmonger's daughter. Lovely girl."

Was he threatening to take NaRee as a concubine?

"Yes, Lord, I am," I said carefully.

"Those sorts of feelings aren't restricted to acrobats, acrobat."

I didn't like the tone in his voice, but I couldn't say anything about it. Not and expect to live.

Narantir snickered. "Lord, you're acting more stupid than usual."

Instead of lopping his head off, Arefai grinned at the wizard. "I didn't think that would be possible."

"Neither did I. You just threatened Kami Khuzud."

"I did *not*." Arefai drew himself up straight. "I did nothing of the sort."

The proper form to disagree with a member of our beloved ruling class—to the extent that there is a proper form—is to use words to the effect of "I am sure that that is so." The words should be pronounced carefully, softly; you must let the lord or lady hear the sarcasm only in the context, not in the tone.

"Wrong again." Narantir snickered. "You just implied that if Kami Khuzud doesn't do as you request, you'd either harm his beloved, or perhaps take her as one of your women."

"Are you certain?" Arefai looked at me, and then back at Narantir. "I did?"

"You did." Narantir nodded. "Subtlety is not your strong point, Lord. Leave it to your father.

Try telling Kami Khuzud what you want to tell him."

Exasperated, Arefai threw up his hands. "What I *thought* I was telling you was that I am as fond of Lady ViKay, Orazhi's daughter, as you are of the ironmonger's daughter, and that any disturbance during his visit might create problems for me." He spread his hands. "Wasn't that obviously what I meant?"

"Of course, Lord," I said.

Absolutely obvious, as soon as it was explained in complete detail.

"I thought so." Arefai smiled, favoring Narantir with a quick frown. "See, Narantir? You don't know as much as you think you do." He stopped, suddenly. "I'll leave you two; I have preparations to make," he said, turning about and jogging away.

All four of his guards, never missing a step, simultaneously broke into a trot to keep up.

Narantir waited until he was gone. "Your blood boils, doesn't it?"

I shrugged.

The wizard reached up and snapped a dead twig off a gesmyn tree, quickly stripping the bark with surprisingly deft fingers, and inserted the naked twig between his lips.

"Well, try to keep it at a simple simmer for the next few days." He chewed on the twig, and then sniffed the air. "Both Orazhi and a storm are coming in, and I'll have enough problems to deal with. You told that sour-faced Crosta Natthan that you wanted to see me?"

I nodded. "Yes. I want you to prepare a spell that will find the hand that held the knife that cut through the cable, notching the doorframe."

He snorted, irritated. "Idiot. What law am I supposed to apply? And how? Do you know what it takes to make a blade relevant to the hand that wields it? Sunder himself could barely make a Relevant blade, and I know of only three of those. And a blade relevant to a notch in the doorframe? I might be able to make a relevant notch with a gap-toothed saw, if it were bent enough. But not a smooth knife."

I shrugged. "Perhaps you could apply the Law of Pathos?"

"Pathos will never do anything for you that Relevance can't." He snorted. "You've fallen for the pathetic fallacy. Personify a doorframe as much as you want, it simply doesn't *care* what notched it so smoothly. But do it as much as *you* want; I don't care to waste my abilities on something that simply won't work."

"This sort of thing is well known?"

"Nobody listens to magicians. Those of you who can't work magic think magic can do any—" His eyes widened. "Oh."

I smiled. "Finish the thought, good Narantir. Finish the thought."

He looked me straight in the eye. "Those of

you who can't work magic think that magic can do anything. Refle can't do magic."

"Precisely." I cocked my head to one side. "This spell should take several days to prepare." We were due to leave in four days; if I turned up the pressure sufficiently, the accusation itself might be enough, enough to break Refle.

Now it was Narantir's turn to smile. "Very nice."

"Yes."

INTERLUDE

Way of the Cook

"No, no, no. You get the skin off the duck this way, not that way, not another way. When you're a master cook, *then* you can do it your way. Not that you'll want to; you will have learned to do it correctly by then.

"If you've survived.

"In the meantime, this is my kitchen, and we will do it correctly.

" '*Which* it?' *Every* it, you fool.

"No, no, it doesn't matter a fig that the dinner is for both our lord and Lord Orazhi. Concentrate on the thing itself, not on who is going to eat it. Pay careful attention to what you are doing, and let it carry you along. Feel it all. If you do, you will know what to do, most of the time. Yes, yes, timing is everything.

"For example, I can tell you that the stockpot has been over the charcoal long enough now, and it's near the boil. Yes, yes, you had better slide it to the side and watch it carefully—if it boils, we'll never be able to make the broth clear again.

"Oh. Idiot. Yes, yes, yes, you know so much, so very much, that I shouldn't waste your time with your Master's instructions. Yes, yes, you can clear a broth with egg whites, but that takes the flavor out of it, too. If you want a perfectly clear broth with no flavor, boy, then why bother adding the vegetables and spices and the chicken? Why bruise the peppercorns and toss them in—it would be so *very* much easier your way.

"No, no, you go ahead, you make a tasteless broth—set a bowl of hot water down in front of Lord Toshtai, sprinkle some thyme leaves on its surface, hand him a spoon and tell him it's soup. I don't think he'll be impressed.

"So, you want to do it my way? Very well.

"Good, good, stir the broth, but don't get your thumb in it. Not so vigorously—let the spirits of the fire do most of the work. Taste it, and try to taste what it will be like when it's done, not just what it is now. Will it need more salt? No? Correct. Pepper? No? It should need more pepper. Hmmm ... let me taste. Yes, yes, bruise another five of the green peppercorns, I think, and two of the black ones. Add another few thyme leaves, and maybe a carrot. Definitely no more onion.

"Now, where were we?

"Ah. Of course: we were getting the skin off

the duck. Just insinuate that tube into the slit, yes, yes, you've seen me do it a hundred times before, and now puff in, and watch it pull away from the flesh. Yes, you have to hold the tube in, and if you keep hacking away at the poor dead bird you're going to have to do more than sew up the rents in order to keep the air in.

"Good. Very nice—the skin is separating, so we sew the hole shut, put the duck in a pan, and pop the pan in a medium oven. Oh, good boy—you think that's a medium oven? You don't think that's a medium-*hot* oven?

"Well, bank the fire a bit, anyways. Good.

"Next, the fish. Simplicity, simplicity is everything, boy. Yes, yes, you've cleaned the trout adequately, but you've handled it far too much—all of the slime is gone from the skin. Let's try it again. Get one from the tank, and set it on the board. Yes, yes, I know it flops around rather a lot, but you gauge it by eye as you pin down the tail and with one whack of the cleaver—there. Without the head, he flops much less, eh?

"Very well. Now, again—notice that I'm just holding it by the tail—with one cut, we open Lord Trout's belly, and pour out all those nasty viscera. You run the pump for a moment, and we'll clean out the insides. Good.

"See? Now, into the pan we put the peppercorns, and the juniper berries, and the salt, and cover it with the boiling water, and then add the

vinegar. Oh, fundleberry wine vinegar, you think?
Perhaps—let's try it.

"In goes the trout—and see? See how the skin
is turning that beautiful blue? Another few moments of this—you can chop some onions while
we wait; much of what happens in my kitchen
starts with a chopped onion—and Lord Trout is
fully poached; we slide him onto a warm plate,
garnish with a few carved radishes, and that
lemon-butter sauce you worked so hard on. And
then, we taste. Mmm . . . nice choice of the vinegar, young one. There may be some hope for you,
appearances to the contrary. I think a bit more
dill and a few mussels as a garnish would make
it better, don't you? Now, the trout doesn't need
to rest—you there: quickly, quickly, bring it out
to Lord Toshtai. And you there: start another one
for Lord Orazhi.

"Now, we are going to work on the beef strips.
Do you think the loin is cold enough? Well,
you're wrong, it is—if we leave it on the ice any
longer, the ice will steal some of the flavor. No,
we don't want any flavor stolen. It's different
with those ham-and-roe balls—they have to be
absolutely icy for their flavors to balance out
right, when we wrap them in the hot duck skin.

"So. I'll have to do the beef myself. Be quiet
now. Yes . . .

"I've been thinking about getting the potter to
glaze a plate with writing on it. You should be
able to read through the beef, it should be so thin.

Ah. So good you are with the knife, you think you can slice the beef so thin, so thin—look at this: as it sits in my hand, you can see the lines of my palm through the redness. Mmm . . . dodn't tasht bed—lemme swillow. There. I was saying that it doesn't taste bad either.

"So. We slice the beef thinly, and carefully deposit it on the plate, fanning out from the center. The first ring will take about twelve slices—yes, I'm leaving a space in the center. While I do this, you will start the sauce.

"Beat the egg and the sunflower oil together. A pretty oil, isn't it? Vigorously, now, put your back into it. Good. Add a squeeze of lemon, and beat some more—you forgot to taste it, see if the balance is right. Let me taste. Mmmm . . . no, that egg had started to turn. Throw it out, and do it again . . .

"Better. A bit more lemon, and then the ground mustard, and the mustard seeds. Very good, and very well. Now you do the last ring of beef slices, and I'll get the basil leaves out.

"Sloppy cutting, but I've seen worse. We'll try a couple of rolls now, and see if it's right. Do it in this fashion: take a basil leaf in one hand, and set a beef slice on top of it. Good. Sprinkle with a bit of pepper, and roll it up. I'll dip it in the mustard sauce, and then, we taste.

"I'd say that everything's in balance, wouldn't you?

"Oh, you would, would you? You think everything is in balance, you young fool? What, tell
me, what is so balanced about that duck that's
about to burn in your so-called medium oven?"

12
Courting Disaster

WE WERE OUT to steal what time we could; I met
NaRee in her father's garden.

The storm was moving in, the setting sun ob-
scured by dark, oily clouds. From our usual place
by the south wall, we probably could have seen
the far-off lightnings, instead of merely being disturbed by the distant roars of their thunder cous-
ins as the cold wind breathed against our faces.

For a long time, we sat on a bench quietly, and
I just held her. That was enough, for a while.

"Tell me," she said, finally, "tell me about the
mountains of Helgramyth."

She was always wanting to talk about distant
counties and distant lands. Sometimes it was irritating, sometimes it was arousing, but now it
was comforting, NaRee's way of consoling me,
distracting me.

So I told her about climbing through the mountains of Helgramyth; about how when you're ne-
gotiating the high passes, you camp on the narrow

roads themselves, because night falls quickly that high, and you're never more than a few steps away from a long fall.

And I told her about the nights high in the mountains, about how it feels to be camped out on the side of the world, on the edge of the world where the stars shine more brightly, more steadily, more bravely than they can on the plains; and I told her about how sweet the wind blowing up the mountain passes is, filled as it is with mint and the remnants of the warm tang of sun-baked grasses, and the far distant foresty smell that never goes away, and about how distances in the mountains stretch and shrink, about how you can sometimes see a light in a window that feels so close that you think you could reach out and touch it, only to find that it's four days away.

And I told her about the mornings in the mountains, about the dim, chilly mornings when the clouds have blown off from the mountain-locked lakes in the night, and how when you wake and can barely see your feet on the road next to you—and you never leave the road, you never leave the road—you're not sure sometimes whether it is fog or cloud that parts every now and then; and I told her about how you can see vague, hulking shapes off in the mist, sometimes, and then how the fog or cloud thins even more with the oncoming day, and how you can see sometimes dark things, you're never quite sure what, moving across the surface of the lake, and how all is mist and shadow until the sun, not caring whether it is fog or cloud, simply burns it away and leaves behind the bluest water, the greenest grass, the clearest air that there ever has been in the world, and you feel you can see from one end of D'Shai to the other, and how sometimes maybe you really can see from Wyness Tongue in the north to Everai in the south, from Bitter Bay in the east of the Ven, to Wisterly, where the Tetnit stands watching the Sleeve.

I didn't tell her everything, of course.

I didn't talk about how the pack's straps cut into your shoulders with a pain that doesn't become one whit less intense with great familiarity, or about how, late in the day, when you finally take too long a rest—only a few moments, it's supposed to be; you must rest, but you mustn't let your muscles cool, or your feet will realize how very much they hurt—you let yourself remember how each step is agony when you resume.

And I didn't talk about the days of eating cold food, the beef and chicken salted too heavily, the onions too pungent, the waybread always stale and sometimes wormy, and how you have little enough of that, or about sleeping on cold ground that will suck the life and heat from your core, or about how, if you've found a soft patch of grass on which to stretch your blankets, more insects than you've ever believed existed will choose to share them with you, or about how you can never quite get the damp and dank out of the blankets, because it will take at least an hour of sun and wind to fully air them, and you can't wait in the morning, and you can't stop until the sun is down. And I didn't tell her about how, sometimes, when the road slows you down too much, and two villages that were three days apart become four days apart, you arrive in the next one too beaten down with hunger to even be able to sleep properly, because you never carry more on the road than you have to, and you already have to carry a lot.

And then she leaned her head against me, and sighed, and said, "Today, my father has given Refle permission to marry me."

I thought about how I felt up near the top of Aragimlyth, the mountains of Helgramyth, where I could see it all, and how clear it all was, and how good that felt, how it made me feel a part of everything.

And I thought of the supposed spell Narantir was preparing, and about how quickly gossip travels, and then I thought about Refle sitting up in his workshop looking across the courtyard at the donjon, and at the room where, for all he knew, the spell that would reveal him for what he was being prepared.

And then I thought about that vague crease of irritation that had crossed Toshtai's face at the thought of the murder of Enki Duzun interrupting his entertainment, and I smiled into her hair, and I said, "We shall see about that."

Because of the storm, we were performing indoors for the two lords and their entourages; for the same reason, Crosta Natthan had arranged for us to be quartered in the donjon, even better rooms than I had expected—we were to use the room we had been using as equipment room, and the three next to it.

The room with the doorframe.

The doorframe that had held the clamp.

The clamp that had held the cable.

The cable that Refle had cut through, plunging my sister, Enki Duzun, to her death.

The top of the doorframe was covered with a plaster, from which several small wires projected, draped down over the clamp. Some of the wires were of gold, some of silver, three of some green metal I couldn't have named. Several runes had been scribbled over the frame, and the wall beyond it, no doubt thrilling Varta Kedin and the rest of the maids.

One swordsman stood guard over it. Actually, he sat guard across from it, lolling in an armchair that had been moved there, drumming his fingers against the arm of the chair, alternately singing and humming a complex minor-key scale. But he wasn't just for show, perhaps; his naked sword was flat on the arms of the chair, and any sound, any movement from either end of the hall got his immediate attention, his whole body tensing into sudden motionlessness until he identified the source of it.

He eyed me levelly as I walked out the door, closing it behind me. I was late; the others were already downstairs, outside the ballroom.

"Dinner performances are always difficult," Gray Khuzud said, as we waited outside the double doors. Inside, the silverhorns had picked up a three-note theme and were tossing it back and forth, occasionally letting the zivver take part of the melody.

"It's a simple matter to overpower the food and talk, but it's higher art to complement it, as we do the music. We do not—" He stopped, swallowed, and started again. "We do not attempt to create the fear in the audience that if they don't watch at any moment they will miss something forever, but rather we want to create the comfort of knowing that should they look in our direction, they will find something interesting to see.

"Or, more accurately, we only insist upon all of their attention occasionally, as with the entrance.

"Similarly, all of the acts are built so that almost all of the interesting moves are repeated, at least once. When Egda tosses Fhilt into the air for a double roll, it comes after a fairly quiet moment, and the attention of many may be on their plates—so, Sala will do the same move next.

"Is all that understood?"

"I'm never sure whether a road is Kami Khuzud's river, or his wall," Sala said, eyeing me.

"Some day, Sala," Fhilt said, "you'll come up with an aphorism that suits the occasion, and we'll all faint in astonishment."

She raised an eyebrow. "We take what victories we can, Fhilt." She reached out and laid a hand on Gray Khuzud's shoulder, and then on his cheek, cupping it. "We understand, Gray Khuzud," she said. "We understand all of it."

He smiled, and just for a moment was the Gray Khuzud that I had always known; and before the dull gray mask slipped back over his face again, he mouthed his thanks to her.

I never really understood the two of them. I knew that there had been no woman for my father since my mother died, and that he wanted it that way, but that Sala loved him, in a way both complicated and requited, but in a curious fashion, one that permitted but didn't require they touch each other as lovers.

Enki Duzun had always said that she understood it, and that the trouble with me was that I thought too much not with my heart and head, but with my phallus, but that that's not where all love is, not even where all passionate love is, even if you'll never understand that, Kami Khuzud, not until you grow up, and never mind that I'm younger than you, I understand these things, I—

Fhilt gripped my arm. "Kami Khuzud, pay attention," he said, not ungently. "We are on in a moment."

"Sorry."

Beyond the doors, the two silverhorns were playfully, lightly dueling at the top of their registers, supported below by easy rhythms on the zivver, smooth, heavy notes from the bassskin, an even flurry of drumming and a delicate tinkling from the chimer.

The doors swung open, and I entered the hall with a simple tumbling run: a quick dash, followed by a pair of handsprings, and then a solid landing. I quickly moved off to the side to pick up my juggling sticks while Fhilt made his entrance, his run the same as mine, except that he finished with a punch-back, to a spattering of applause.

He took up his sticks, and we each began to juggle three, occasionally banging two together in time to the music, but not loudly enough to distract from Evrem's entrance—he was using a single watersnake tonight, keeping it spinning straight—and Sala's.

It was a banquet in the traditional style of our beloved ruling class: a forty-person, staple-shaped table that cupped the far end of the room, with all the diners on the outside of the staple, their backs to the wall; members of our beloved ruling class were always nervous about leaving their backs to the open room. Near the legs of the staple, two serving tables stood, one holding a rosette of golden-roasted capons, another a single roast kid, white-clad servitors slicing to order.

The diners at the table itself were broken into eight or so smaller groups of four and five by interposed islands of serving foods, each similar, but variations on a theme: the soup bowls were all up on legs, heated by candles beneath, but one had bits of bright carrot and dull chard floating on its surface, another was clear; on yet another, three carved turnips, each shaped like a coil of a seadragon, poked out of an oil-slick bowl.

It was a magnificent spread, from the traditional first course, the pyramid of roasted aborted piglets, each the size of a small chicken, to the finale: a spiced potato pie, a wall of cinnamon sticks arranged around its edge like logs in a stockade.

The only foul note in the room was Refle. He and his brother sat with the group at the far end of the table, the farthest from Lord Toshtai, with Dun Lidjun's group in between him and the lord. I wished that it had been a place of dishonor, but it wasn't: all seats with the lord are a place of honor; this was only one of lesser honor.

His face studiously blank as he watched me, he toyed with his food and he kept from looking over toward Narantir.

Felkoi didn't have as much self-control: he

kept glancing over to where the wizard was busy staining his beard with the juices of an aborted piglet.

Lord Toshtai and Lord Orazhi, each with the traditional counselor at his side, were the center foursome. They chatted amiably, occasionally gesturing with their eating sticks, Toshtai politely tasting from Orazhi's plate and vice versa. Arefai, arrayed in black and silver, sat at his father's side, and in a bit of typical D'Shaian hypocrisy, Orazhi had chosen Lord Edelfaule, the older of Toshtai's two resident sons, as his counselor, and even dipped his head toward Edelfaule every now and then, nodding as though receiving a confidence.

Where Toshtai was magnificent in his rotundity, Orazhi was quiet in his compactness: a lean, beardless man, thinning yellow hair slicked back neatly across his head and glossed to a high shine, formal black and gold tunic cut tightly across his shoulders.

His movements were both quick and sudden, even as he reached out an eating prong to spear a marinated mussel from the serving tray in front of them; Dun Lidjun, part of the group to Orazhi's left, eyed the younger lord with unconcealed suspicion.

The food looked marvelous, and smelled wonderful; it filled the air with the scent of roasting meat, and of garlic, and a distant tang of firemint, probably from the hot apple stew. I paid particular attention to a plate of roast turkey legs, each one beautifully crisped on the outside.

While the crowd was watching Sala, Large Egda and the Eresthais quietly entered the hall, picking up their own equipment as Fhilt and I reclaimed the crowd's attention with a flurry of exchanges, the wands first tumbling once around as they flew through the air between us, and then one and a half times.

Kneeling next to Fhilt, Sala opened the large oaken box containing the juggling knives. The appearance is part of the effect: the box was of deep rubbed oak, lined with crimson silk; the knives were polished to a high gloss.

She picked up one, and all eyes fell on her as she walked to the horseshoe-shaped dining table and took an apple from a fruitbowl, smoothly moving the knife through the air, slicing the apple a dozen times as she walked back to Fhilt's side, and then cleaned the knife.

It's a fool-the-mind trick: deep inside, the audience knows that we're flipping the wands over one and a half times, and knows that if we do that with the knives, we'll be cut to ribbons. So all eyes were wide and upon us as, one by one, Sala reached up and took one of Fhilt's juggling wands from his hand, replacing it with a knife.

I wondered about that, too.

Fhilt, effortlessly, as though it didn't affect his timing at all, quickly worked the knives into the stream, careful to give each knife only a half-turn flip as it flew across the air to me.

We picked up the exchange pattern: throw-throw-exchange instead of throw-throw-exchange-throw. The crowd broke into a polite patter of applause. Perhaps Refle paid more attention, wondering if he would be quick enough should I turn one of my throws to Fhilt into a throw at him.

The door again opened: it was Gray Khuzud, carrying three juggling sticks, and he was weaving as he walked.

He was quite obviously drunk.

Gray Khuzud threw one of the sticks in the air with his right hand, and then hesitated, as though unsure when to throw the next, but he barely got it out of his left hand in time to catch. The flipping pattern was almost random; some sticks flipped half over, some all the way, some one and a half times, and every once in a while one wouldn't quite rotate out of the way, and he would snag a horizontal stick, and barely throw it in time.

Gray Khuzud kept walking forward, though, approaching Fhilt and me almost blindly. One stick dropped from his shower, but it bounced on its end off the hard marble, and Gray Khuzud snatched it and worked it back into his rough shower as he walked.

He caught himself barely an armslength from

our exchanges, and bowed to Lord Toshtai as he continued his staggered juggle.

And then it happened: another stick fell and bounced off the marble, but this time it bounced forward, directly beneath where Fhilt's and my knives were whipping back and forth, through the air.

Any sane person, any sober person would have let it fall, but Gray Khuzud leaned forward, through the path of our knives, a pair of knives barely missing his head.

And then he rose, the juggling stick firmly in his hands. The knife I had just thrown to Fhilt passed barely in front of his naked chest, and the one from Fhilt to me barely behind his back, but Gray Khuzud juggled through our exchanges, the knives and sticks coming close together, but never quite touching, the applause of the audience almost deafening as he dove through the space where, only half a heartbeat before, a knife had been flickering through the air.

Those of the audience who hadn't seen my father's drunk act before sat stunned, while those who had grinned.

The knives still flickering through the air behind him, Gray Khuzud took a step forward.

And his right heel came down firmly on a slippery apple slice, and he fell backwards, toward the exchanging knives—

—and *through* the turning, flying knives, as his

fall became a backwards handspring, and then a forward handspring back yet again through the shower of knives, a handspring that brought him almost to the table and into yet another handspring that turned into a leap to the surface of the dining table.

Dun Lidjun was already on his feet, a sword in his hands, but Gray Khuzud had cartwheeled away in the opposite direction down the surface of the table, his flying hands and feet avoiding plates and bowls and cups and fingers as they had planted knives in our entrance act, and then he was again on the floor, but he had somehow seized six turkey legs, and had them in the air in an intricate shower.

Fhilt and I caught our knives, and bowed in his direction, as the applause thundered.

Gray Khuzud smiled as he tossed the turkey legs off in different directions, one toward Fhilt, another toward Sala, and three others to the Eresthais and me. He flipped the last turkey leg through the air, end over end, then caught it and took a bite.

"The Troupe of Gray Khuzud is with you," he said, with a bow to where Toshtai and Orazhi sat, and then another, perhaps deeper bow, toward Dun Lidjun.

The old warrior eyed him blankly for a moment, then sheathed his sword with a smooth motion . . .

And bowed to Gray Khuzud.

* * *

After a performance is a special time, always; nothing can take away from that. I've never known much about mahrir, wizard-magic, and I doubt I ever will, but there is some sort of magical energy that passes between the audience and the troupe, draining one kind of energy, leaving us charged with a different sort.

Usually you just know what to do—usually, when you're both charged and drained, you find the nearest place to sit down, to lie down, not to rest. But sometimes you don't. The banquet was over, but the servitors had gone to bed, leaving the cleaning for the morning and what leftovers we wanted to the seven of us.

A quarter of the leavings wouldn't have fed more than a troop of famished soldiers; the troupe of Gray Khuzud could barely finish half. Outside, past the half-open glass-paneled doors, the rain beat down with a steady patter, punctuated only occasionally by the crash of thunder or a distant flash of its cousin, lightning.

"I'm not sure," Philt finally said, sprawled on a rug runner, "that this is the way things would be done if it was my castle, my banquet." He toyed with a plate on the rug next to him, dipping a piglet haunch in raspberry sauce, then taking a delicate bite before offering some to Sala.

She smiled. "For some reason old Crosta Natthan didn't think to ask you."

235

"Foolish man."

"Every problem its own solution; every solution its own problem," she said.

I looked over at Large Egda. "Good food?"

"Mm." Large Egda had piled his plate high, and was working from the top down, stoking himself without concern for how the flavors mixed. "Very good food," he said, when his mouth cleared.

Evrem, despite the fact that he had been the last to start eating, was already on the potato pie—the snake-handler was like one of his snakes, I guess, tucking away immense quantities of food, figuring that he could digest anything he could squeeze down his throat.

The Eresthais, Josei and Eno, just ate.

I wasn't hungry, although I had a bowl of apple stew in front of me, and had tasted some. The firemint had been laid on with too heavy a hand for my taste, although perhaps it was less intrusive when the dish was hot.

But I tried to talk anyway.

Gray Khuzud sat alone, eating without tasting whatever Sala set in front of him, chewing with an even rhythm, like a machine. We hadn't exchanged any words at all, not privately. Not since Enki Duzun died.

Fhilt pitted a cherry, so purple it was almost black, and with a quick, "Egda, open wide," thumb-flicked it into the air and into Egda's mouth.

The big man smiled as he chewed and swallowed.

"I will see you all in the morning, in the courtyard, at the hour of the hare," Gray Khuzud said, rising. He walked out of the hall.

Sala made as though to get up and go after him, but she looked to me for confirmation, first, as though I had the slightest idea what was right.

I didn't understand Sala. I spread my hands.

Enki Duzun was dead, and nothing said or done right or wrong would ever change that. Everyone was silent for a long time.

Fhilt finally broke the silence with a loud sigh.

"I miss her, too, Gray Khuzud," he said to the air in front of him. "And were there anything that could bring her back, I would do it. Failing that, I'd do anything that would expose her murderer." He looked steadily at me. "But it appears that you and Narantir have that well in hand, doesn't it, Kami Khuzud?"

"I hope so. If you put too much strain on a cable, it breaks," I said, then realized what I'd said.

Sala didn't like that. "The spell, though, will tell who did . . . oh."

I didn't answer.

Evrem stroked the rug, his fingers moving sinuously. "I watched Refle. He worries. He tries not to show it, but he worries."

"I don't understand all this," Large Egda said. "Too complicated for me."

Fhilt started to say something, but I interrupted. "Just leave it to me, Egda. I've got it well in hand, I hope."

Egda grinned, his smile a yellow gash in his porridge face. "Whatever you say, Kami Khuzud."

Fhilt twisted an eating stick between his fingers. "If you put too much strain on anything," he said, "it breaks." He snapped the stick cleanly. "But if not?"

Lightning crashed outside; I picked up my juggling sticks and left.

When you don't know what else to do, you go back to the beginning, the basics. The root of acrobatics is juggling.

I stood in the courtyard and the rain and the thunder, the rain beating down so hard at times that I couldn't even see.

One ball; the most basic juggle. Never mind that the rain beats down hard, never mind that your sister is dead, never mind that crash of thunder or this flash of lightning; you can't control that. What you can do, the only thing you can do, the thing you have to do is throw one ball up into the air and then let it fall into your hand.

You have to get at least one thing right.

Throw and catch, throw and catch. It isn't the most important thing in the world; it has to be the only thing in the world.

Throw, and catch. Not quite. Oh, it was close enough for catching, and easy enough to make part of a juggle, but the ball hadn't fallen onto exactly the spot on my left palm that it was supposed to.

It has to be perfect, the form is everything, because you can't raise kazuh without the proper form, and once you raise kazuh, everything will be correct, in proportion.

Again.

Not quite. But closer. Again.

A flash of lightning and crash of thunder overhead rocked me, but I didn't drop it, by the Powers I didn't let the ball fall.

Feel the ball, Kami Khuzud, you must feel the ball, you must find your balance, find your center, and throw and catch it from the center.

Again.

That felt better. No—it felt right, there was even a distant tingling, a far-off spark of something. I added the second ball, and then the third, and kept them going in an even flow of catch-left throw-left catch-right throw-right, each ball falling perfectly into place, despite the rain battering at me, despite the thunder, despite the lightning, and I held that moment of time for as long as I could.

And, once again, it wasn't enough. There was a distant spark somewhere, perhaps, but it wasn't the kazuh of the acrobat.

I don't know what I am. But whatever that is, it isn't a kazuh acrobat.

INTERLUDE

Way of the Servitor

HE HAD BEEN the last noble in the castle to sleep, but Crosta Natthan was the first to awaken.

That was part of the secret of his success: even before his joints had started to ache with advancing age, he had never needed more than two hours of sleep a night, and always woke toward the end of the hour of the dragon, the hour before dawn, and was well in possession of his faculties and his day before the hour of the cock.

Now, he couldn't sleep through the night. But that was acceptable; sleep had never been as satisfying as his work.

His hair still damp from his ablutions, he stalked the dim halls in the predawn light, a harsh eye alighting on an ill-dusted nook here, a stained spot on a rug there.

Being servitor, even chief servitor, is not one of the fifty-two kazuhin, but Lord Crosta Natthan, great-grandson of peasants, didn't mind.

His grandfathers had been the first of their families ever to rise to the middle class: his maternal grandfather had been a tradesman; his paternal, a pewtersmith. Crosta Natthan was a noble, and while his shrewish wife had long been banished from both his life and Den Oroshtai as an unpleasant distraction from his work, his sons were both nobles, and his daughter was married to Lezear Ahulf, a favored retainer of Lord Nerona of Oled.

It was worth some effort to be worthy of this, he reminded himself, then chuckled, quite silently, at his own D'Shaian hypocrisy.

Being worthy of it had nothing to do with his passion for his work. He enjoyed all of it, even this, the first pass through the castle.

The guards at the door of Lord Toshtai's morning room were alert but appeared tired as Crosta Natthan opened the door and passed through, shutting it silently behind him. Of all those in the castle, there were only three who could pass through any door, at any time, without let or hindrance: Lord Toshtai himself, old Dun Lidjun, and Crosta Natthan.

Not too bad for the grandson of a pewtersmith, the great-grandson of a dungfooted peasant.

The morning room was dark and cramped in the dull light, but it would brighten in but a few moments, as the dawn came on. A pitcher of icewater, the proportions of ice and water correct, waited next to Lord Toshtai's chair, and a yellow silk robe was neatly folded over the back of the chair. Ignoring the pain in his right hip as he moved, Crosta Natthan bent and sniffed—yes, it was freshly washed, and lightly scented with rose and lemon.

Crosta Natthan examined the straight razor, the shaving bowl, and the soaps over by the washbasin. Yes, all were ready, although he would want to strop the razor a few times before running it over Lord Toshtai's countenance. Nobody else, not even Dun Lidjun, was permitted to hold a razor near the lord's throat, and Crosta Natthan took that responsibility, as he did all of his responsibilities, with the utmost seriousness.

There was really one too many apples in the porcelain bowl; it *looked* overstocked. As a matter of policy, Crosta Natthan didn't formally break his fast until after he had finished his morning rounds, but what is not seen is not, after all. He selected one with a slight green tinge, and tucked it into his pocket as he left the room; when he rounded the corner and passed out of the view of the guards, he took the apple out and bit into its tart sharpness as he slowly, painfully made his way up the steps to the second floor, pride preventing him from leaning on the wall. Stairs were the hardest, and it was best to walk them when nobody else could see his weakness.

He liked the apple. It tasted like retribution.

When he was but a boy, careful matchmaking

had matched his elder sister, Ilda Verken, to a true bourgeois, an orchardman. Ilda Verken and Trevan Idn Abeta had looked down on the little middle-class boy, and had shunned him when he had entered Lord Eveshtai's service.

But that was long ago, and now the best of Trevan Idn Abeta's son's apples graced his table, and—every once in a while, when his duties allowed—Trevan Idn Abeta's young niece, one of the bourgeois attendants to Lady Walasey, warmed his bed. Altogether a perfectly pleasant arrangement, he decided, slightly disappointed that there was nothing requiring his attention on the second floor.

He took a last bite of the apple and set the core in the salver on a hallstand. It would be gone within the hour. It had best be gone within the hour.

He made his way to the third floor, and stopped outside one of the rooms assigned to the acrobatic troupe.

The guard was sitting in the chair across from the strange contraption of plaster and wires that the wizard had put up. That was acceptable; there was no need for him to stand when he could do his job sitting.

But the carpet!

Crosta Natthan shook his head. It wasn't that Lord Toshtai would ever see the dirt on the carpet; the lord of Den Oroshtai hadn't been above the first floor of any wing of either donjon in

Crosta Natthan's memory, and Crosta Natthan's memory was perfect.

But it was a wrongness, and would have to be corrected. Even though the acrobat-peasants would dirty the carpet again that night, it would have to be rolled up and taken out back to the laundry to be gently beaten, cautiously washed, carefully shade-dried, and then replaced.

Still, as his father used to say, in every bruise there was a lesson to be learned: Crosta Natthan would wait until midmorning and see if old Varta Kedin noticed by, say, the hour of the hare.

She was getting old; it might be time to retire her, send her back down to the village to live with her children and grandchildren, have her drive her daughters and daughters-in-law mad with her insistence on polishing already well-polished woodwork.

He completed his rounds of the donjon and staggered down the stairs to the foyer, kicking off his sandals and tying up the ends of his pantaloons before he headed out into the quadrangle, toward the old donjon.

The ground between the flagstones was muddy and squishy between his toes. He liked the feel of it; it almost made his old bones feel young again, he decided as he washed his feet in the foyer of the old donjon, dried them with a clean towel, and donned the sandals hanging from a peg on the wall.

His tour through the old donjon always took less time than the rest of his rounds did, but that was just because it was smaller; it was not indifference. The old donjon was where the first rulers of Den Oroshtai had lived, back when the whole domain was only a summer residence of Oroshtai himself, and it deserved the respect due to an aged and trustworthy servant of the family.

Today his rounds were even shorter than usual: the entire top floor was occupied by Lord Orazhi, his guards and personal attendants, and was to be considered part of Glen Derenai, not Den Oroshtai, while Lord Orazhi was in residence.

Downstairs, the guard had changed at the beginning of the hour of the dragon, a doubled shift out of tradition, not necessity. The hour of the dragon was the traditional time for a surprise attack, and while it would be ridiculous for Orazhi to be here in some complicated political maneuver culminating in a surprise attack, others had done ridiculous things in the past.

He passed quietly through the barracks on the first floor. Most of the soldiers slept on their pads undisturbed by his passage, a few waking momentarily to turn a bleary eye on him before rolling over and going back to sleep. Over in the corner, a foursome was quietly working a harmony, their voices low, almost singing in whisper, the tenor emphasizing the high notes with sharp, chopping motions of his hand. Two others, apparently having come off shift insufficiently sleepy, quietly played a game of singlebone draughts, a third watching the board with hawklike intensity, like a referee at a sparring match.

Walking past the guards on duty at the other end of the barracks hall, Crosta Natthan made his way up the stairs to the second floor, and took a quick look down the hall.

Something wasn't right.

His steps picked up as he walked down the carpet toward where a dark stain spread from underneath the closed door to the armory.

He knelt and dipped his fingers into the carpet. His fingers came up red and sticky with blood.

Crosta Natthan rose quickly, ignoring the pain in his joints, and knocked on the door, at first calmly, then in a rapid tattoo.

No answer.

There were two master keys in all of Den Oroshtai, only two that fitted every door within the walls. One, made of fine silver, its bow covered in enameled bone, hung from a slim golden chain around Lord Toshtai's neck; the other, of simple burnished brass, hung from a plain leather thong around Crosta Natthan's.

Crosta Natthan had used his master key twice to test it, after it had been presented to him by his predecessor. He had never used it since; there had been no need.

He didn't hesitate for a moment: he slipped the thong over his head, inserted the key in the lock, and turned it firmly. The bolt snicked aside.

He pushed the door open, but it only gave a little. Something was blocking it. Crosta Natthan could have slid inside, but there was no need. The door was open wide enough for him to see that Lord Refle, Den Oroshtai's armorer, lay dead on the floor, quite thoroughly hacked to pieces.

He wasn't sure how long he stood there, but he hoped it wasn't long.

"Guard," he called out, hoping that his voice wouldn't carry far enough for Orazhi's soldiers to hear him. And then, *"Guard."*

Feet thundered on the stairway: the troika of draughts-players, each with a naked sword in hand.

One started to speak, but Crosta Natthan held up a peremptory finger. "One of you—*you*, go and wake the rest of the castle guard. You, keep guard here; I don't want anything disturbed. And you," he said to the third, "go get Kami Khuzud and throw him into a cell in the dungeon."

The guards were all well-trained. The first guard, after a quick, "Yes, Lord," had run off already. The second, his face grim as death, assumed a watchmanlike position in front of the door, and the third was disappearing down the stairwell.

The boy should have waited. He should have found the evidence to show that Refle was guilty; he shouldn't have simply killed him.

Crosta Natthan spun on the ball of his foot and walked off. It would be necessary to wake the lord of Den Oroshtai and tell him that his armorer had been murdered.

How to do it, though? Crosta Natthan would certainly stand outside the Lord Toshtai's sleeping room, and invade it only with his voice, not with his person. But how would he begin? What would he say?

Lord Toshtai, I hope you will think me right to wake you—No. That wouldn't do at all; it was not Crosta Natthan's job to predict Lord Toshtai's thoughts, but to obey his orders, to anticipate and divine his needs.

Lord Toshtai, it is with sadness that—no, that was just as bad. Not only had Crosta Natthan never cared for the armorer—and lying to Lord Toshtai was absolutely forbidden—but Crosta Natthan's sadness was properly none of Lord Toshtai's concern, and it would be wrong to wake the lord with the suggestion that it was otherwise.

Lord Toshtai, it is necessary that I wake you, perhaps?

Better.

Yes. That would be it: *Lord Toshtai, it is necessary that I wake you.*

Crosta Natthan had never woken Lord Toshtai before; but not having done it before would in no way excuse doing it other than promptly, or properly.

13
Apprehension

IT'S SOMETHING I think about, every now and then:

I've decided that my favorite way of being woken from sleep is for a lovely black-haired woman, fresh but dry from a hot bath and heated towels, her skin scented with soap and lemon and roses, to slip under the blankets with me, and gently, carefully, lay her head on my shoulder. Her breath smells of firemint and tea; her long, glossy hair floats around me in a warm, silken cloud.

At least, I *think* that would be my favorite way. I can't recall as it's ever happened, and I suspect I'd remember it.

Being kicked out of a sound sleep by one of Lord Toshtai's guards wasn't nearly as nice.

Half awake, I thought I had been jumped by Refle again, and I flailed away at him. That turned out to be a mistake; I got my arms caught somewhere in the blankets, and slammed my forehead into the side of his foot, or vice versa.

I didn't try to muffle a scream as I was lifted up by the hair, slammed up against the door, then turned about, grabbed by the short hairs at the back of my neck, and frogmarched, stark naked, down the hall to the stairs, down several flights of stairs to the dungeon, and then kicked into a cell, and the cell locked.

The guard pulled up a stool across from me, and sat down.

"Please. At least, tell me what I did, what they think that I did. I mean, I—"

"No talking. Just sit there, stand there." There was a bucket near his feet, filled with what I hoped was only scummy water; he gestured at it. "Or I douse you."

I wasn't disposed to argue.

Two old woolen blankets lay folded neatly in the corner, neither particularly clean. I wrapped one around my waist and sat down on the other, and leaned back against the wall.

I hurt. My head was pounding, both from the pain of being yanked around by the hair and from being kicked in the head. I thought I'd cracked a rib or two. I was in better shape than the guard—he was slack-bellied, probably from too much time in Den Oroshtai guarding what was safe, and I was an acrobat—but he had handled me with contemptuous ease.

There was a commotion over by the door leading down into the dungeon, and I could barely make out Sala's voice. ". . . must tell me what they think he did? Please ... important ... tell his father."

I wanted to know what I'd done—well, I knew what I *had* done, but not what they *thought* I'd done. There is a difference.

Still, I didn't think that Lord Toshtai really would have me thrown in the dungeon for trying to put pressure on Refle with a bluffed magical spell.

That couldn't be it.

On the other hand, could I have been seen leaving Refle's workshop? Was it possible that Lord Toshtai had let me go long enough to be in last night's performance, and then have me hauled away?

No. That didn't make sense. Even if I had been seen, and even if he had decided to wait out the performance, why let me have most of a night's sleep?

It was hard to think, with my head pounding, and I couldn't seem to concentrate; I didn't even see Narantir walk in until the wizard was standing in front of the bars, his belly almost pressed against the metal.

"Young idiot," he said. "Why did you have to kill him?"

I didn't ask who.

"No, no," I said. "I didn't do it. But the false magical spell we were preparing—maybe he killed himself."

That could be it! Rumors always spread

quickly, and perhaps Refle was more nervous than he had appeared; he might have committed suicide rather than face exposure as a murderer.

"Oh, really." Narantir's eyes rolled up. "You'd better find a better defense than *that*. You'd best have something much better than that to say to Lord Toshtai in a while. I doubt even Arefai would believe that Refle hacked himself to death with one sword while trying to defend himself with the other."

He pursed his mouth. "Lord Toshtai will see you at the hour of the horse. Think of something, or be prepared to be about this much shorter," he said, holding his hands about a headslength apart.

I heard more commotion at the door to the dungeon a few times over the next hour, and vague traces of voices I could follow.

Sala came back again, and Fhilt, and I could every once in a while hear Gray Khuzud's quiet, patient rasp, but that was all. Nobody was allowed in for the longest time, until the door swung open.

It was Gray Khuzud. The dark shadows under his eyes proclaimed that he had been crying instead of sleeping, but even in his grief, he held himself like an acrobat, always in balance.

He looked at the guard, his eyes pleading.

The guard stood silently for a long moment. "Very well, Gray Khuzud. You can speak to him. But don't come close enough to him to pass anything to him. You keep your hands on the wall at all times, and you leave when I tell you to. Understood?"

"Yes." My father was never one for wasted words.

The guard walked down the corridor, perhaps just out of earshot, definitely not out of view.

"Tell me about it," Gray Khuzud said. "And quickly."

"What is the—"

"Don't argue with me, not now!" He lowered his voice. "I will tell them that I did it. But Lord Toshtai is very clever; he will want to know what I did, how I did it, and nobody is saying anything more than that somebody killed Refle in his armory, with a sword. How did you get into the armory?"

"I didn't. Well, I didn't last night. I don't know how the killer got in."

I knew how *I* had gotten in, when I had searched the armory for proof that Refle had beaten me, but I couldn't have done that last night—the branches would have been treacherously slippery in the rain; given that I couldn't make it across terribly well when they were dry, I could hardly have done it last night.

"I really didn't do it, Gray Khuzud," I said.

His mouth tightened. "We don't have time for that now, Kami Khuzud. Please, you must do it my way, you must do it my way, just this once." He took a step forward, then caught himself and stepped back, slapping his hands back against the wall. "I'm too old to continue the line, the family; I need you to do it for me. Tell me. —What *are* you smiling about?"

We sometimes have to live on what is unsaid, my father and I. And he had just left it unsaid.

It didn't matter whether or not Lord Toshtai believed me, or even if Gray Khuzud did—what mattered was that he believed that I hadn't failed to check the equipment. He wouldn't have made the offer if he thought I was responsible for Enki Duzun's death.

I held up a hand. "I can't tell you, Father, because I didn't do it. Just be patient; I have an idea."

"Tell me."

"No. I can't. Leave it to me, Gray Khuzud. I will handle it all." I could start by pleading my innocence, but that was only a start—most people accused of committing crimes claim to be innocent. But it was a start. "Go—and don't worry about me. I'll be fine."

For just a moment, he smiled. I could tell that he didn't believe me, but that didn't matter, not for the moment. He knew that I hadn't murdered Enki Duzun, and that was all that mattered.

"Balance," Gray Khuzud said, his voice hoarse. "Remember balance."

"Always."

My guard popped to his feet.

Arefai, dressed in maroon and mauve, stalked

down the hallway, one hand on the hilt of his sword, as though that would frighten me into telling the truth. I was already quite thoroughly frightened, and when you wet a river, all you can do is cause a flood.

He looked at me for the longest time; I lowered my eyes and didn't meet his gaze. Sometimes members of our beloved ruling class don't like being stared at, and habits are hard to break.

"This has hardly been of help in my courtship, Kami Khuzud," he said, casually, but quite seriously. "It has probably delayed it for several months, at the very least. Quite irritating, don't you know."

In one sense, I really shouldn't have smiled at him, but it was all I could do not to laugh in his face. I mean, Enki Duzun had been murdered, and Refle had apparently been chopped to bits, and there *I* was in Toshtai's dungeon awaiting either death or torture and death, and Arefai, a member of our beloved ruling class, was, as usual, expecting me to share his irritation because all this probably meant he was going to have to continue to prong away only at peasant, middle class, and bourgeois girls for an extra couple of months.

Fair enough, I guess; after all, members of our beloved ruling class are taught only to care about themselves.

Still, this was a bit much. I didn't point that out to him, though.

"Did you do it, Kami Khuzud?" he asked.

"No, Lord," I said.

"I believe you," he said, somberly. "And do you know why I believe you?"

"No, Lord, I don't."

"Because you *smiled*," he said, reaching through the bars to pat my hand, like I was one of his dogs. Nice Kami Khuzud, I knew you didn't bite. "Because of the way you smiled. Only someone who was both innocent and had perfect faith in the ultimate justice of the ruler of Den Oroshtai could smile so easily, so . . . innocently, eh? Yes, innocently, I like that.

"You may count on my support, Kami Khuzud. And while I'm not heir, I do have some influence around here. It is at the disposal of your innocence, Kami Khuzud."

"Thank you, Lord." I bowed at his retreating back. At least there was one person of some authority in the castle who thought that I was innocent.

Even though he was an idiot.

14
Raising Kazuh

THE NICE THING about being brought in front of Lord Toshtai was that they let me—made me, actually—wash and get dressed.

You learn something new every day: that day I learned that fear isn't any antidote for boredom and irritation. I had been getting both more bored and more irritated as the morning dragged on.

He was waiting for me in the hall, the great hall in which we had been received at our arrival in Den Oroshtai, just a few days, a few ages before. I had been so much younger then.

Lord Toshtai didn't look any different than usual.

Today, the fat man was arrayed in many-folded robes of a lustrous yellow silk, his hair combed back flat against his skull. The folds of his neck had been freshly powdered; his hands, scrubbed to that pink, almost a glow, that's a proud possession of members of our beloved ruling class, lay folded neatly on his lap.

At my approach, he sat back on his throne, watching my entrance with eyes that were neither cruel nor kind.

The musicians played, and the guards sang as we walked:

"The acrobat, Kami Khuzud, is brought be-fore Lord Toshtai;

"Our Lord to dispense jus-tice and truth.

"Fearless is the innocent," (the guards tried for too tight a harmony on "innocent," and it kept breaking),

"Fearful the guilty,

"Fearful the guilty,

"Fearful the guilty."

I could have done without the last refrain, punctuated as it was by a heavy thrumming of the drum and low, almost surreptitiously threatening notes from the bassskin, the silverhorns oozing out a morose, cloudy melody, a listless arpeggio on the zivver allowing no trace of lightness to peek through.

They were all waiting for me, across dunams of polished oak floor, the nobles spread out over the dais, the rest of the troupe to the right of it. Some of the juggling gear lay near Gray Khuzud's feet; I gathered that the troupe had been honored by being allowed to entertain Toshtai and Orazhi while they waited for me to be hauled in front of them.

Edelfaule was standing, Orazhi having taken his seat. I didn't recognize one of the nobles on the platform, a younger man in a loose-cut tunic cut open across a naked chest almost to his waist, but from the cast of his shoulders and the way his eyes never fixed on one thing it seemed to me that he was likely Orazhi's chief guard.

But it was hard to concentrate on others when Toshtai sat there, even half the length of the room across from me. The sword lying across his lap wasn't a miniature, not today.

I didn't know him well enough, I didn't *want* to know him well enough to know if he felt that honor required that he dispatch a murderer himself. It would be hard to tell; what nobles consider honor can cause them to act in all sorts of unpredictable ways, and I've never wanted to bet anything on which way that pushes them.

A horrible thought occurred to me. What if it was Toshtai himself who had killed Refle? He was a large man, and a fat man, but that didn't mean he wasn't capable of killing Refle. All he would have to do would be to walk into Refle's armory, and hack him to death, ordering any who saw him not to have seen him.

I hadn't thought I could be more scared, but I was wrong. By the Powers, if Toshtai had killed Refle, and was trying to have me blamed for it, I was a walking dead man.

And not walking for long.

The guards stopped me easily half the hall away from the dais, and from Lord Toshtai.

The music lurched to a halting stop.

"Kami Khuzud," Lord Toshtai said, "it appears that the noble you blamed for your sister's death has been murdered." He waited for a long moment; I decided that he wanted a response.

"Lord," I said—and then grunted, as one of my guards elbowed me quite hard in the stomach.

"Your response, peasant, is not required unless asked," he hissed.

"And what have you to say to that, Kami Khuzud?" Toshtai asked, as though he hadn't seen anything.

"I only have to say that I don't know anything about it. I didn't kill Refle, err, Lord Refle, and I don't know who did." I started to gesture, but thought better of it. "I don't know what else to tell you, Lord, except that whoever did it, however they did it, it wasn't me. I . . . understand that Lord Refle was killed with a sword, and I've never held a sword in my hands."

That wasn't quite true. I had held a sword in my hands when I was prowling through Refle's workshop, and I had borrowed Crosta Natthan's for a moment, but this wasn't the time to be a stickler for details.

"That would be hard to prove," Toshtai said.

Dun Lidjun grunted.

"Dun Lidjun?"

"May I stand, Lord? If it please you? I think better on my feet."

"Very well."

Dun Lidjun rose slowly, and took a few steps

toward me. "It may possible to see how good he is with a sword, Lord. Have the challenge sword fetched, and let him try to use it on me. I'll be able to tell if he's good enough. He wouldn't have to be terribly good to have beaten Refle; Refle was largely a warrior of convenience." Dun Lidjun half-drew his own sword and considered the edge. "Let us test this acrobat."

Leaning against the back wall, his arms crossed over his belly, Narantir snorted. "The trouble with that brilliant idea is that it doesn't prove anything. The only way Lord Dun Lidjun could force somebody to defend himself properly would be to try to cut him, and what if Kami Khuzud is innocent?"

Dun Lidjun started to say something, but Lord Toshtai cut him off. "Then, at least, he might have the honor of a warrior's death. Bring the challenge sword."

Only twice before had I held a sword in my hands; I still didn't much like the feel of it. The hilt was thinner than juggling knives are, less round than the bar of a trapeze—it just didn't feel right. For one thing, it felt too light.

Three of the guards, their swords drawn, stood between me and Lord Toshtai's throne. That didn't make any sense. Did they think I'd get past Dun Lidjun?

I couldn't think straight. None of this made sense. This wasn't how an acrobat was supposed to die: a challenge sword in his hands, cut down by a kazuh swordsman. Ridiculous. Of old age, perhaps, or killed by a jealous husband or father, or by a fall from a trapeze, or a broken neck when doing a high dive-and-roll wrong.

Over by the side of the room, Gray Khuzud picked up three juggling balls. He threw one in the air, and then another, working the three in a shower, and then a circle. Under the suspicious eyes of Toshtai's guards, Fhilt took another three out of his pouch and joined him, the two of them working theirs independently, not trying exchanges.

By the Powers, Gray Khuzud was good, even on a simple juggle. The balls seemed to dance around his fingers, moving smoothly, only occasionally nudged back into their swirl by his gentle fingers.

I shrugged. When you don't know what else to do, go back to basics, Gray Khuzud would say, and that's what he was doing. But I doubt that he would find any wisdom or any help for me in a two-person juggle.

Still, he was good, and Fhilt was almost as good.

The lead silverhorn player took up a light melody, and the second horner followed soon, the bassskin and drummer joining in, the zivver finally chiming in, light on the scratchbox.

Dun Lidjun and I squared off, him circling first to the right, then the left, me just holding the challenge sword out in front of me, hoping to block him.

It was a situation that didn't admit of a victory, not for me. Assuming—and it was an unlikely assumption, purely for the sake of argument— that I could defeat a kazuh swordsman, that would be evidence that I had lied about not being able to have killed Refle, and would be enough evidence for Toshtai to be comfortable in having me executed.

So, assume that I didn't try to beat Dun Lidjun: he surely would see that I wasn't trying, and would take that as a confession.

As he circled to my left, I tried to follow him.

My eyes fastened on Dun Lidjun's, and wouldn't release. The old warrior's eyes were slate gray, every bit as hostile and cold as the Open Sea in winter.

He moved in and slashed, tentatively, at my neck. I got my sword in the way, somehow. Steel ringing on steel, I pushed his sword away as I retreated, Dun Lidjun in pursuit.

The music picked up, the silverhorns dueling in staccato thrills that climbed up toward the limits of their range, the zivver player running through an arpeggio that was punctuated by a hard wrist on the scratchbox, the power of his music growing.

Suddenly, almost in unison, they all raised kazuh.

It started with my father, and then passed from

him to Fhilt, Gray Khuzud's kazuh touching off. Fhilt's, a lit torch touching off another one, sparks from both of their talents, their skills, their kazuh flaring brightly, raising the musicians' kazuh perhaps involuntarily.

The music was something alive now, writhing and hammering in the air, filling my ears and my head like strong drink, but clarifying, not clouding my thought. Raised and lifted by the blare of the silverhorns, supported and held by thrumming of the drum, the bright arpeggio and gutsy rattle of the zivver, my nerves steadied by ringing of the chimes and the deep, solid notes of the bassskin, I suddenly knew what to do, and how to do it.

It was so simple:

I shouted and lunged for Dun Lidjun, slashing at him hard, ever so swiftly, my sword twisting and moving like a striking snake.

He didn't seem to move much; perhaps he just twitched his shoulders and moved one foot back, but metal slid smoothly along my sword, and the challenge sword rang like a bell as it neatly lifted itself out of my hands, tumbling through the air and landing butt-first on the floor.

Dun Lidjun stood, his sword held easily in front of him, its tip barely a handsbreadth from my throat. He was steady as a statue, the sword, even extended, unwavering in his hands.

I had been afraid, and a distant part of me could

feel my body still reacting to that fear: the pounding of my heart, the cold sweat that bathed my face and chest, the churning in the belly and bowels. But all of that was distant, unimportant: by the Powers I knew exactly what he would do before he did it. It was all as clear in front of me as a fine woodcarving: Dun Lidjun would lower his sword, and drop kazuh, and then he would smile.

Dun Lidjun lowered his sword, and dropped kazuh, and the intense blankness left his face, replaced by a dim smile.

The music swelled and rose around us. I could feel the musicians' kazuh burn brightly, illuminating the room. I've always been sensitive to the fire of others' kazuh.

"He *tried*, Lord Toshtai," the old man shouted, over the blare of the silverhorns. He sheathed his sword with an absentminded gesture. "I could see that he was trying as hard as he could. But he couldn't have defeated any kind of trained swordsman; he's just too clumsy at this."

"So? If he didn't, then who did?"

"A pretty puzzle, Father," Arefai put in. "If you don't think that Kami Khuzud did it, then why not get him to solve it for you? He is good at puzzles, I understand."

I deliberately didn't look at Arefai, as I didn't know whether I wanted to hide a glare or a smile of gratitude. Was this his idea of helping me? Yes, it was better than being hacked to death, but . . .

Lord Orazhi considered his fingernails. "Or perhaps you should simply be done with it now, one way or another. I understand that the troupe is to leave shortly for Glen Derenai, among other places."

"True, Lord," Toshtai said. "But since all of the troupe are suspected, they will have to stay here until the matter is disposed of." Idly mirroring Orazhi, he examined his own fingernails for a moment, as though he had forgotten that he enjoyed acrobats. "We shall give Kami Khuzud three days to solve this puzzle."

"Naturally," Narantir said, "the troupe will continue to perform for the three days."

Arefai eyed Narantir as though he had just loosened the drawstrings of his trousers, passed wind, left his eating sticks on his plate, or committed some other equally distasteful solecism.

Narantir smiled at me. It would cost Toshtai nothing in particular to keep us here an extra two days.

Toshtai caught the smile. "Since it amuses you so much, Nailed Weasel User of Magic, you shall assist Kami Khuzud in discovering who murdered my armorer."

"Of course." Narantir bowed deeply. "I am delighted to be of help, Lord. May this one ask where your wisdom suggests we begin?"

"That is up to the two of you, is it not? Were I you, I would begin with Refle's armory, but it is your decision." Lord Toshtai turned to me. "And, of course, it is your decision, as well, Kami

Khuzud. You may feel free to pursue this . . . inquiry wherever it leads. As long as the troupe performs on time each night."

I bowed. "Of course."

"You are dismissed, Kami Khuzud."

All of the troupe was passing the balls back and forth in a freeform juggle. I wished I could have stayed and watched, but I had been dismissed.

I left the great hall to a fanfare of silverhorns, and a low mocking snarl from the bassskin.

15
Sword Talk

I STARTED WITH the armory, and the body.

Crosta Natthan insisted on accompanying us, which didn't bother me; I really wasn't looking forward to pushing my way past the guards.

On the way over he was able to tell me about his discovery of the body, which he insisted on doing in a tone of voice that made it perfectly clear that he thought I was asking purely for effect.

The warrior guarding the door moved aside at Crosta Natthan's scowl, and we slid in through the narrow opening.

Refle's body hadn't been removed. A carpet of flies lay thick on the corpse, leaving only for moments as we fanned at them. The room stank, even though the windows were open and two censers sent clouds of thick patchouli and pungent meryhm into the air.

I raised an eyebrow. "Is there any reason that thing is still here?"

Crosta Natthan sniffed into his handkerchief. "I didn't know whether or not Lord Toshtai wanted to see it, or have it seen."

I couldn't look away, even though I tried. Refle had been cut dozens of times, a sword slashing across his face and torso, some cuts opening his shoulder and hip to white bone. Any ten of the cuts would have killed him instantly.

I tried to turn to the wizard, but the body drew my eyes. "Can you determine which sword made all the cuts?"

"Magically?" he asked.

"Yes, magically. Can you?"

"Easily, given the sword," Narantir said.

Given the sword. That was the problem. It couldn't be that easy, could it? All I would have to do was line up all the swordsmen in the castle, and have Narantir test their swords against—

"Relevance or Pathos?" he asked.

"Eh?"

"I can apply either. Or Contagion, for that matter."

"I don't understand."

"Contagion: things that interact intimately still interact at a distance. A sword killing somebody is about as intimate as there is. Turn around."

I forced myself to look away from the corpse, at the fat magician's outstretched hand, pointing quite directly at a bloody sword in the corner of the room, flies thick on its surface.

"Relevance, Pathos, Contagion—any of the

three is going to tell me that that's the sword that killed him." He walked over to the sword and squatted over it. I joined him. I didn't want to look at Refle again.

So much for the easy way. Unless . . . "Is there any way to know whose sword that was?"

"Quite easily," Crosta Natthan said, kneeling next to us. "Look at the tang."

"Ah." Narantir nodded. He produced a small knife—from his sleeve? by magic? I don't know—and slashed at the silk bands covering the hilt. "One only need look at the tang," he said, pulling at the hilt, and grunting. "But we'll need a tool to take it apart."

I took the hilt in my hands and pulled. It stuck, but an acrobat, even a clumsy one, has strong hands; I pulled harder, and the two wooden halves parted easily. "Or perhaps not," I said.

There was one marking on the tang, a blocky Old Shai pictogram.

"Yes, you are very strong." Crosta Natthan shrugged. "But it is of no use. That is Refle's mark; all it means is that he made the blade. There's no testing marks, no attestations, no indication of who he made it for." The old servitor indicated a rack of swords on the wall. "It was probably one of those."

Narantir took the sword from me and wrapped it in a blanket.

Well, as Gray Khuzud would say, albeit in a

different context, when you don't know exactly how to do something, go back to first principles.

What did I want? I wanted to know who killed Refle.

Well, what would it take to kill him? It appeared to have taken a sword. I had the sword. So, it was somebody who was good with a sword—the dozens of cuts all over him indicated that whoever it was had been very good with a sword.

Inside of me, something relaxed.

It had to be somebody good with a sword, and that left out Gray Khuzud. Unless, of course, there was something tricky. What if whoever it was had, say, hit Refle across the back of the head with a truncheon, knocking him unconscious, and then hacked at him with a sword?

I knelt and examined the sword that Refle still clutched in death. The fingers of his right hand were tight around it; I tried to pry them loose, but it felt too strange: they were colder than fingers had any business being.

"What do you think you're doing, Kami Khuzud?" Crosta Natthan more accused than asked.

I thought a tough response was called for. "Refle won't mind. Not now. Help me with this, Narantir."

Between the two of us, we were able to pry Refle's fingers open. I rose, his blade in my hand. It was bloody, like the other, but not spattered all over—it had lain in a pool of Refle's blood, that was all.

It was quite thoroughly nicked and scratched, none of the nicks or scratches rusty. It was not credible that the castle's armorer had left his own personal weapon in this state of repair; it had been bashed up in the fight, by a swordsman good enough to kill Refle without suffering a wound himself, but who hadn't been able to dispatch him with a single blow.

"Do you still want me to examine the other sword?" Narantir asked. "To find out if it cut him?"

"Find out whatever you can—can you do Pathos?" I admit it—I'd seen little magic, and had never seen an application of the Law of Pathos. More important, though, I wanted to know just how tricky things were here.

Narantir shrugged. "Possibly. But Relevance will tell you easily if this caused those cuts—"

"Did those cuts kill him, though?"

The wizard scowled. "Yes, they did," he said. "At least, he was alive when he started getting cut—see how much he bled? See how far that gout of blood must have splashed? If you cut into a dead body, it doesn't bleed much, because the heart doesn't pump. The blood just oozes out." The wizard smiled idly. "I have cut into more than a few dead bodies in my time."

"Then you won't mind doing another one. See

if this sword killed him, and see if there's any other damage."

The wizard rolled his eyes up. "Diagnostic tests on a dead body are a waste of time, Kami Khuzud. He is *dead*. What does it matter what else is wrong with him?"

"Do it anyways."

"No."

Crosta Natthan cleared his throat.

I looked his way inquiringly; he shook his head. He was toying with the bolt and lock. It was good D'Shaian lockwork: brass and bronze, hand-pounded, handworked, smooth-working. We D'Shai have our flaws, but we are the best crafts-men that there are.

There was too much to it all.

"The door was locked?" I asked.

Crosta Natthan nodded, tapping at his chest. "I had to use my master key to get in."

"How many keys are there that fit this lock?"

"Four," he said. "Lord Refle's key, Arigan the locksmith's duplicate and Lord Toshtai's and my master keys." He tapped at his breast. "Lord Toshtai's and my keys are always with us; the locksmith's copies are stored in Lord Toshtai's quarters, under guard."

While some locks have a handle on the inside, it is done other ways; most locks have keyholes on both sides, enabling the key to work from both sides. That is, not only is somebody with a key the only person who can lock the door, but he can lock it from either side, or lock it open. Assuming Refle had his own key on his person, nobody could have come through the door without using one of the other three.

Refle still had a knife in a sheath on his belt. I knelt beside the gory mess, pulled it from the sheath, and considered the blade. I'd been expecting it to be scratched; knives weren't intended to be shoved into mounting brackets. But it wasn't. He had, of course, repaired any damage to his knife.

Narantir shook his head. "Most of you think magic can do anything—if he did kill your sister, I'm sure he got rid of it."

Refle's pouch was at his waist. That would be next. I reached for it, and—

"What are you *doing*?"

"Investigating, Lord Crosta Natthan."

"You may not do that."

"Lord Toshtai disagrees, Lord Crosta Natthan."

I'd had enough of looking at the body, though. I took two blankets from the wardrobe and covered the body with one, before spreading the others and dumping the pouch onto the soft wool. Members of our beloved ruling class are generally buried with some of their valuables, some dried food and the like, supposedly to prepare them for their next life. Peasants are just reborn from the dust and dirt; they claim that we will come back pure and re-refined. Personally, I'm doubtful.

And how did you know that there were blankets in the wardrobe, Kami Khuzud?

I looked from Crosta Natthan to Narantir. They were both too busy eying the scattered possessions, but I'd have to be more careful.

There wasn't much in his pouch: a few coins, a few gems: a piece of cerulean tourmaline, a lovely malachite marble, two dimong-cut pieces of chrysoberyl with the fire of the sun in their hearts—

"For decorative hilts," Narantir said, joining me, "I would suppose."

—a small, wedge-shaped piece of metal—

"And what's this?" he asked.

I shrugged. "My guess is that's a slice of a sword—see how the edge had been filed here? I'm not sure why an armorer would want a cross-section of a sword, but I guess that's what it is."

—a bone fingering-piece, polished by fingertips and hand-oils to a dull yellowy sheen—

"That is quite a nice piece," Crosta Natthan said, getting interested, despite himself.

—and a single key, brass, with a wooden bow.

I tested the key in the lock. It fit perfectly: the half-moon bolt slid out with a quiet *snick*.

"You said that the door was locked, Lord Crosta Natthan?"

"Yes, that's what I said, and that's what it was. And I also said that there are only four keys that will fit the lock: Lord Toshtai's lord's key, mine, and the two keys that were made for the lock."

Then how did the killer get out? Through the window.

No. The killer wasn't Gray Khuzud, not because it couldn't be Gray Khuzud, but because it mustn't be Gray Khuzud.

But the branch wasn't the only way one could get out of the armory, even if the door was locked. It was possible, I knew from experience, to slip a rope around a beam and lower oneself down, and then to draw the rope back.

I went to the place where I had done just that, and looked at the beam. There were light scratches on the surface of the polished wood, but they could have been here from the time when I had snuck in.

Narantir tapped at them. "Yes. A rope, perhaps?"

"Perhaps." My rope at least.

Still, it would be worthwhile checking the ground below the window.

"What are you all doing in here? This is my brother's—" Felkoi stood in the doorway. "And with him lying here, dead? Get *out*." His hand was on the hilt of his sword, but I knew he wouldn't draw it.

Narantir nodded, not in agreement, but more in greeting. "Lord Felkoi," he said. "Lord Toshtai—"

"We were just leaving," I said. "Lord Crosta Natthan, if you would, please have the body and that sword brought down to Narantir's workshop."

"The dungeon is the traditional place," he said, with something of a sniff.

"I won't have Refle lie in the same place as my sister," I said.

Felkoi stared at me for the longest time, but then he bowed his head.

He knew.

"Interestingly enough," Narantir said, "one of Lord Orazhi's guards reports having heard an argument floating up from these rooms last night. He seems to think it was you and Refle."

Felkoi snorted. "Then why is my head not rolling about the floor, murderer that I am?"

"Because he saw you leaving after, heading out into the rain, and he later saw Refle alive," Narantir said, "when Refle returned to the armory."

I guess I must have looked surprised; the wizard grinned at me, and then shrugged. "This asking questions you have been doing is addictive; while you were relaxing in the cells, I did some of it."

Felkoi had been a devotee of the troupe's performances; I guess that was why I didn't suspect him of having collaborated with his brother. You could see it in his face, as he watched the show. He could have killed him, although over what, it would be hard to guess.

Because of Enki Duzun? One noble killing another over the murder of a peasant girl?

Hardly.

I watched his face very carefully, though, as I said to Narantir, "Let us go take a look at the ground beneath the window."

All I saw was puzzlement. There was more than enough of that to go around.

Below the window, the mossy floor of the flowerbeds was not merely wet, but oozed water at a touch. If I looked very closely, very carefully, I thought I could make out where my own feet had depressed the dry beds days before. Anybody stepping down into the moss since the rain would have gone in to their ankles. Of course, down wasn't the only way out. A kazuh acrobat—only a kazuh acrobat—could have leaped from the windowsill and caught a branch that was treacherous when dry and would be almost impossible when slick with rain.

Almost impossible.

Absolutely impossible for any lesser human. Balance is the Way of the Acrobat; nobody but a kazuh acrobat could have that kind of balance, to land safely on that branch.

Fhilt perhaps. Fhilt couldn't raise kazuh easily, and he was every bit as unfamiliar with a sword as I was, as Gray Khuzud was. It couldn't have been Gray Khuzud, it couldn't have been Fhilt, it couldn't have been Sala or Large Egda or any of us.

Nothing made sense.

Fine. Forget for the moment how the killer had gotten in—how had he gotten out? Refle locked the door behind him, it seemed, and I didn't see any way that the killer could have locked the door behind him and snuck the key into Refle's pouch.

No, it still didn't make sense. How did the key come back to the armory?

"Kami Khuzud?"

I turned. Narantir had the sword tucked under his arm. He gestured at the two servitors who were grunting with the weight of the planks supporting Refle's body. "You wanted to see the Pathos?"

"Yes."

Narantir's preparations took us through the end of the hour of the ox, and well into the octopus; I managed to grab a quick meal—but well outside of his workshop in the former dungeon of the old donjon. I had caught a glimpse of some of his work in progress, and insisted that he throw a cover over it before I came back in.

Finally, though, he called me back in. Over by one wall, Refle's body lay under a sheet.

"The body is covered, and I will be ready to start momentarily," he said. He waved me to the side of the room, while he busied himself at his desk. He moved quickly, efficiently, and he bound the sword, still hiltless, to a manheight stand in the center of the room, lit only by a single, shrouded lamp. A large cone, suspended by almost invisible wires from the overhead beams, hung near the tang, the small end of it near the sword, the large end near me.

I didn't like looking at it, so I turned to examine the fist-sized models on the desk near me: horse, ox, octopus, bear, lion, and tiny bellows.

The lion looked like it had been whittled with an axe. "Is it safe to touch these things?"

Narantir's back was to me, as he worked with some piece of apparatus. He didn't turn around.

"My models? Well, yes and no." He grunted as he shoved something into place. "Yes, it's safe, as long as I don't rig up the lens set and take the model from its case, because there's no power in them. No, it's not safe, because I've gone to a lot of trouble with the lot of them, and if you damage them, I'll be very unhappy with you."

"Lens set and models?"

"Yes, yes, Kami Khuzud, lens set and models. It's how I do the lights above the castle, the show for arriving troupes. I have a model of Folesly Hill in a case, carved from rock from Folesly Hill."

He grunted again. "This grommet is giving me more trouble than—ah, got it. As I was saying, I have a model of the mountain, made from rock from inside the hill. I use a lens to project a very small image of the models against the wall, and apply a simple animation spell to the image. Then, by the Law of Proportion—the greater is to the lesser as the greater is to the lesser, eh?—I have images that are as much larger than the little ones as the hill is larger than the model. Simple, no?"

He turned. The wizard's face was sweat-slick and ashen, and small plasters covered his hands. He took a long pull from a mottled-glass mug as he leaned up against the wall. "I'm almost ready. I just need a human subject. You'll do, I suppose." He tugged at my sleeve. "Out of those clothes, if you please."

I shook my head. While I had appreciated Narantir fixing my broken bones, I hadn't enjoyed his needling, and had no intentions of putting myself in his hands. "I don't think that I—"

"Oh, don't be so silly, Kami Khuzud. Pathos is just a variation of a basic similarity spell. Like functions as like, eh? It won't hurt. Have you ever heard a sword say ouch?"

I shrugged. "Well, no."

"See? Off with the clothes, then." He made a hurry-up gesture. "Let me help."

Over my vague protestations, he pulled the tunic over my head, and tossed it in the corner, while I doffed my pantaloons and shoes.

He picked up a small paintbrush and scribbled a few runes across my chest, the paint—I hoped it was paint; it was the color and consistency of pus—cold and foul-smelling. With a smaller paintbrush he scribbled some of the same ones on the sword, over the blood.

That took a lot more time than it looked like it should have. He kept moving more and more slowly, but not like he was lazy. I had the feeling that the paintbrush was growing heavier, and heavier, or that maybe time itself was pulling down on his arm.

But finally he stood back, and uttered a few triumphant syllables, and the paint on my chest flashed into a cold flame—

—the paint across my blade, across my self, flashed into a cold flame. I couldn't move, although for a moment I felt softer, from point to tang. My back straightened painfully, my bloodied edge went all crooked and weak, while my arms jammed themselves down by my side, locking themselves into place, right along my break. My knees locked and tried to bend themselves backwards, and my diaphragm froze.

But, it didn't hurt. I didn't need air. Air carried water, and water would rust me.

I needed to be stroked with a nice coat of oil, and then slip into a warm, dry sheath, and wait, to be grasped by firm, clever, knowing hands, to be released into the bright sunlight or the dark of the night, to cut and bite, to part skin and muscle, to cleave through bone, to drink warm, warm blood, living blood.

Can you hear me?

Of course I could hear the soft one. Clean me, soft one. There is cold blood on me, and it wishes to rust me. I don't wish to rust.

Did you kill him?

Yes, of course I had killed, and it felt good.

I was *supposed* to cut, to kill, I had been made to kill, to cut, that was what I was for. Killing is the way of a sword, it is a last third of the way of the sword. The second third is to block, to frustrate the others of my kind, and the first third is to wait for the killing, dry and warm and pleasantly oily in a sheath.

I am waiting for you. To clean me, soft one. To put me in a sheath. To drink of your blood.

But first, foremost, to clean me.

Who wielded you?

Strong, knowing hands, stronger and more knowing than those of him who had made me, but other than that I didn't know, because I didn't care. Hands that knew enough to use me, and not one of the lesser swords by my side.

Who wielded you?

A sword cares about the strength of the hands, about the cleverness of the hands, not about the name of the wielder. Soft fools, all.

Do you care that you killed your maker?

Oh, of course I care. How could I not care? He bled warmly, he struggled vainly, he raised his own sword, but I batted it aside, and then I parted his skin and muscle, parted them to the bone over and over again. I drank his blood.

He was wonderful.

Who wielded you? That idiot, Kami Khuzud, wants to know.

Idiot indeed. Soft fool. To move, to be still, soft

one—it is all the same to me. I don't care; I don't know whose strong hands, except that I want more strong hands wielding me.

Soon. Or soon enough.

Dress my tang in good wood and taut silk, clean me and oil me and put me away, soft one. I need to wait, and then to block and to strike and then to drink again.

It's no use asking you, is it?

Silly, silly soft one. Clean me, or let me drink.

Something foul occupied my head and my nose, expelling the clouds, but only partway.

My eyes sagged open. Narantir loomed over me, his beard-rimmed face creased with either concern or a reasonable simulation.

"I thought," I said, but the words only came out as grunts. I tried again: "I thought you said it wouldn't hurt."

"I did, at that." He shrugged. "Aren't you a bit old to believe what a wizard tells you?"

I got up, wobbly, and dressed, then staggered out through the door, into the daylight.

Sun filled the courtyard, the grasses and mosses and leaves of the trees taking on that full, darker green they sometimes have after a heavy rain. From the limb of a tree high above, a redbird looked down at me and tootled an unflattering opinion.

I shook my head. All that trouble to have Narantir run a magic spell and all I knew was something I'd already known: Refle had been killed by a swordsman, and no acrobat was a swordsman; only an acrobat could have entered the building from that window.

That didn't leave many possibilities.

Toshtai and Crosta Natthan were the first two. They had the keys.

Forget them. If it was either of them, I was a dead man. Besides, that just didn't *feel* right. Perhaps Toshtai was a real warrior, and not just a fat ruler, but I couldn't see him sneaking through the night to hack apart his armorer. Why bother? If he had decided that he wanted Refle dead, why not just have him killed?

And Crosta Natthan? That was just plain silly. He was really just a bourgeois servant, elevated to our beloved ruling class as a convenience to Toshtai; there was no reason whatsoever to believe that the clumsy old man had taken up the sword.

Dun Lidjun? Certainly, Dun Lidjun could have hacked Refle to death, if he'd wanted to. I would have bet on Dun Lidjun if faced by a hundred of the likes of Refle. But he didn't have a way in or out of the locked room. Not without going through Lord Orazhi's people on the third floor.

A cold chill washed across my neck. If nothing else was possible, then somebody had come down from Lord Orazhi's floor, coming in on a rope through the window.

But the only people who could have gotten past Orazhi were him and his men.

Why would Orazhi want the armorer dead? The ways of the members of our beloved ruling class are complicated. This whole mess might affect the alliance negotiations or the marriage negotiations in some subtle way that could redound to Orazhi's benefit—it certainly couldn't do Lord Toshtai any good. But maybe—

No. I didn't need to know why, if I could show *how*, if I could show *that*.

I had eliminated everyone else; it had to be one of Orazhi's people. And how could I prove it?

The evidence might be there, for somebody who had eyes to see it. I had to get into the quarters, and these were well guarded, never abandoned the way Refle's armory was. Of course, if there was going to be a performance in Orazhi's quarters . . .

I had to talk to Gray Khuzud before the next show.

"But *why*, Kami Khuzud?" he asked, checking the rigging around the trapeze platform for the thousandth time. "Why do you want me to ask this of them?"

"Because," I started, then stopped. "Because you trust me, Gray Khuzud," I said.

He looked at me a long, long time.

We take what victories we can, Sala had said, not too long ago. Like much of what Sala said, it didn't apply to the then-and-there, but maybe it did apply to the here and the now. Maybe she had been talking about the moment that Gray Khuzud's head nodded, once.

"Of course," he said.

After the performance, Lord Toshtai didn't leave when he dismissed the crowd; he sat in his chair under the darkening sky, perhaps admiring the sunset, and certainly talking with Lord Orazhi while Gray Khuzud and I finished cleaning up the props.

No retainers, no advisers, no guards—just the two of them.

Just as I cleaned the final juggling stick and slid it away into the canvas bag with the others, Toshtai beckoned at me. I trotted over. A bottle of Amber Breath and two tourmaline warming-flasks stood on the table between them; Toshtai filled the flasks, then politely tasted from both before letting Orazhi choose.

"So, Kami Khuzud," Toshtai asked, "how goes your investigation?"

Orazhi, leaning to one side as he sipped, watched me through eyes that were in no way a window to his mind or heart.

"Well, Lord," I said, more confidently than I felt, "I hope to have an answer for you sometime tomorrow, perhaps, or perhaps the day after."

Toshtai raised an eyebrow at that. "It would be best if you do, it would seem."

Orazhi didn't seem affected one way or another. I had been hoping he would be—if he had started, and Lord Toshtai had seen it, that would have brought me a step closer.

Maybe.

Gray Khuzud had been loitering a polite distance away; at Toshtai's nod of permission, he approached. "You enjoyed today's performance, Lord Toshtai?"

"Very much so."

"As did I," Orazhi put in. "I wish you would play extra days for me when your travels take you through Glen Derenai."

Gray Khuzud smiled at that, smiled as though his heart wasn't broken. "That can be arranged, Lord Orazhi, and soon, if you'd like. Our travels might take us to Glen Derenai for our performance tomorrow."

Orazhi smiled at that. "Are you runners as well as acrobats, Gray Khuzud?" he asked. "Even if you are, I am not."

"It is but a short walk to Glen Derenai," Lord Toshtai said, smiling thinly. Toshtai had already figured it out. "Glen Derenai is, in a sense, here, Lord Orazhi. That was your intent, Gray Khuzud?"

"Yes. It would be convenient if tomorrow's performance could begin in your quarters. In fact, that is where the best view might be," Gray Khuzud said.

Lord Orazhi seemed more amused than anything else as he nodded. "It would be my pleasure to host Lord Toshtai there," he said, turning to Toshtai. "I never thought I'd play host to you within the confines of Den Oroshtai, Lord Toshtai."

The corners of Toshtai's mouth turned down microscopically. "As well you should not, perhaps."

16
Investigation

BEING A PEASANT and an acrobat is no particular help when you're investigating something; it would be handier to be a swordsman.

I spent the rest of the evening trying to find out about Orazhi, and his daughter, and Arefai, with no success. The servants either didn't know or wouldn't answer directly, and the soldiers wouldn't answer at all. Even old Crosta Natthan was close-mouthed on the subject.

Finally I presented myself at the entrance to the living quarters.

I guess I had been accorded some status; the servitor on duty—a warrior this time—didn't argue with me: he simply nodded, then took a brush and ink and quickly painted a note in the elegant hand that all of Toshtai's warriors had, and sent for an attendant to take the note to Arefai.

Only a few minutes later an ancient old woman in an equally ancient silk robe came up to the entrance. She scowled at me for a long moment.

"He will see you," she said, turning around. The back of her robes was decorated with a bear-and-snake design, very fine, very old needlework, the fiery colors long having faded to delicate pastels.

One of the guards stepped forward to search me, but she hissed at him, and he subsided.

"Yes, Lady Estrer," he said.

I started out walking the traditional three steps behind her, but she quickly brought me to her side with an impatient, imperious gesture.

"You are that Kami Khuzud who has been making all this trouble of late," she said.

I didn't think I was the one making trouble, but—"Yes, Lady. I'm very sorry."—it doesn't pay to argue with members of our beloved ruling class.

"You don't have the slightest idea who I am, do you?"

"Well, no, Lady. I apologize for my ignorance—"

"Enough." She held up a bony hand. "Enough, enough. I'm an old woman, and I don't have time for formality or silliness; I'll likely be dead before you stop apologizing. I am Lady Estrer, sister to Lord Arefai's mother—*late* mother, may she be reborn with fewer problems, poor girl."

She had been setting a brisk pace, but it seemed to disagree with her; she slowed down and gripped my arm, leaning heavily on me. But she wasn't interested in saving her wind: she kept up a monologue as we walked.

"Now, now, I used to be even prettier than that

294

NaRee of yours. Truly I was—all of the young lords would call on me, they would, even after I was married.

"If the little bourgeois packet lives long enough, she'll be even more of a fright than I am, eventually. How would you fancy waking up next to such as I?" Her grin was almost infectious. "I would wager against your NaRee surviving that long, mind—preferring the attentions of a muscular young acrobat to those of a solid armorer? Brainless little chit—she'll douche herself with lye some day, and rot her insides out."

Despite the insult to my beloved, I was beginning to like this old woman.

"Even without that," she went on, "from what Toshtai tells me, she's much prettier than she is bright. Ah, you're surprised that Toshtai takes notice of the comings and goings of the likes of you and her? Never be surprised, Kami Khuzud—he sees half of everything, and infers the rest.

"Here we are." She knocked twice on a sliding door, then slid it aside. "In-in-in, we don't have time to wait on ceremony; I'm getting old."

"Ah, Kami Khuzud," Arefai said. "You wished to see me—sit."

I lowered myself to a sitting pillow.

The room surprised me. I had been expecting Arefai's quarters to be rich and lavish, with ankle-deep rugs and soft, over-carved furniture. But Arefai's was a single room and plain, albeit richly so.

The floor was highly polished wood, larken-built like Refle's wardrobe—tiled by thousands and thousands of pieces of different woods that had been glued into place, no two pieces alike, none larger than a thumbnail. Simple textured paper covered the walls, and the polished beams of the ceiling were bare and uncarved, unornamented. A neatly folded sleeping mat occupied one side of the room; sitting pillows lay scattered around the brass brazier that dominated the other side of the room. The brazier sat in a large but empty fireplace, at the moment heating a battered iron pot where a fist-sized ceramic flask rested in the simmering water.

Arefai was dressed simply, perhaps to match the room; he wore a long black robe over black leggings. His hair was combed back without oil, and bound back with a silver headband.

I started to speak, but Arefai raised a preemptive finger.

"A moment," he said, lifting the flask out with a wire loop and setting it down on the floor before him. Protecting his hands with a linen cloth, he squealed the top off and poured some of the white liquid into two fist-sized cups, presenting one to his aunt, and taking the other one for himself.

"Yes," he said after a quick sip. "Quite good."

His aunt drained her mug in one motion and beckoned for more.

He clearly didn't think to offer me any, but I was curious.

"Snow Blood?" I asked.

"Eh?"

"In the flask." I've only had Snow Blood once, and it was served at room temperature, not heated.

"Snow Blood?" He frowned for a moment, then smiled. "Ah. No. It's hot milk."

"We often drink hot milk together in the evening," she said. "We have, ever since he was a baby."

"And we often will, Aunt Estrer," Arefai said, fondly. "Now, Kami Khuzud, you wanted to talk to me about this murder?"

I nodded. "We talked about the politics, Lord, the other day—"

"Before Refle's death. Yes." He frowned, again. "This has complicated all of that. I wonder if Father and Lord Orazhi are going to be—"

"Be still, Arefai, be still," his aunt interrupted. "Your mouth is too much a mirror to your mind."

"But he—"

She silenced him by raising a gnarled finger. "Just because he asked a question doesn't mean you have to answer it. What business is it of a peasant's whether or not you will marry Lady ViKay, eh?"

"Because," he said, his expression one of infinite patience, "I had asked him to put his inquiry into the murder of his sister aside until Lord Orazhi and Father concluded their business. If not, he might have shown that Refle had killed his sister, and then Refle might be dead differently, no?"

"Hmpf. So it's *your* fault, then." She turned to me. "What do you really want to know?"

I took a moment to phrase it correctly, or at least try to. "Is it possible that there might be somebody in Lord Orazhi's party who might want to interfere with the negotiations between the two lords—enough to commit a murder?"

"Silly acrobat." She laughed. "Of the thirty or so in his party, I can think of five nobles who are or might be Lady ViKay's suitors, three with ties to Patrice and Lord Demick, and twelve—certainly including Lord Orazhi—who could be devious enough to want to stall the negotiation simply to see how eager Lord Toshtai is to conclude it. And I am only an ignorant old woman—there are probably a dozen others, each with a score of other reasons. Does that help you any?"

"More than I can say, Lady Estrer," I said. Far more than I needed.

I thought about it as I walked down the twisting road toward town. The jimsum trees lined the road like so many crooked soldiers; they whispered to me on the evening breeze, their still-damp silken threads clinging to my face and chest as I walked.

It had taken a warrior—*strong, knowing hands,*

*stronger and more knowing than those of him
who had made me*—to kill Refle.

It would have taken a kazuh acrobat to enter
Refle's workshop in the way I had. But none of
the troupe were warriors; you don't get to be good
with a sword without practice, long and hard
practice.

So: the killer hadn't entered the way I had.

That left two ways in: through the lock or
down through the window. The keys were spo-
ken for; the killer had, therefore, entered down
through the window. It was one of Orazhi's party,
perhaps under the orders of Orazhi himself. Some
warrior had lowered himself from a window on
the third floor, and had surprised and killed Refle,
using one of Refle's own swords as a diversion.

I had the explanation, but one I couldn't use.
Not directly.

It all depended on Lord Toshtai. I would have
to get him to do the hard part for me. That was
the way you had to deal with nobility: show them
the facts and let them work out the truth. Waving an uncomfortable fact, an awkward truth, in
Toshtai's and Orazhi's faces would only get me
killed. It would be like waving a green pennant
in front of a mad ox.

Somewhere near the window above Refle's, the
Powers willing, there was evidence that somebody had climbed out of it and into Refle's. There
had to be. I would have to find it, and show it to

Toshtai, and carefully coax him down the path, letting him see that it led to Orazhi.

But what if there was no evidence there? What if they hadn't let the rope rub against the edge of the window, or run it over a beam and split the wood just a bit?

Or worse, what if Lord Orazhi and his people were innocent? Never mind that, I decided. I didn't give a bean for their innocence, but what if there wasn't any evidence?

That might be fixable . . .

When I got back down into town, NaRee was waiting for me in the sitting room at Madame Rupon's.

Madame Rupon, mildly scandalized, left us alone; "what is not seen is not," after all.

NaRee's face was pale under her already white makeup; her hair was pulled back in a severe bun that looked like it hurt her ears. Her robes, green as spring grass, were gathered tightly at waist, neck and knees, and she was wearing boots instead of sandals.

She came into my arms, trembling. "My father has given Felkoi permission to marry me.—No, Kami Khuzud, don't look like that."

Anger pulled the words from my mouth. "It was Felkoi who did it. He killed Refle. He wanted you, and he eliminated both of his rivals with one stroke. But how?"

That was the trouble. How? He couldn't have

come in over the branch; he could have gone out through the door, but not have locked it behind him; he couldn't have come down from the window above without the collaboration of Orazhi.

It was all getting too complicated. "No, he couldn't have done it."

"Not for me." She shook her head. "I've got a . . . feeling for such things."

"Are you saying that he doesn't want you?"

She laughed, her voice silver bells, and kissed me.

"Oh, Kami Khuzud, you are so foolish. Of course he does, but only a little. It's not the same kind of hunger that you have for me, or the kind that Refle had. Trust me, please. I understand men, and it wouldn't make sense. You think that my father wouldn't prefer I be courted by a warrior like Felkoi rather than a barely noble armorer?"

She was right. That didn't make sense. Assuming that he was willing to murder for her, it still didn't get him into the room, or out of it.

Besides, if he'd wanted her, why not just court her?

"What are you thinking of, Kami Khuzud?"

I shrugged. "I'm just hoping that there are scratch marks on the right places."

17
Kami Dan'Shir

THE ERESTHAIS HAD set up the high wire to run from building to building, but the rest of us hadn't been allowed on the third floor of the old donjon.

I looked across the wire at the old donjon, and wondered. The thumb-thick cable ran from building to building, now singing-taut. I tapped on it; it gave a deep but tight basso rumble.

I looked at the others, but mostly at Gray Khuzud, his face still a mirror to his pain. He tossed his head, his pigtail flopping limply.

"It will be fine, Kami Khuzud," Eno said, giving a turnbuckle another minuscule twist, then stroking a fingernail along the wire. "Josei is watching the other side, and it all will be fine."

Sala smiled at me. "You seem, I don't know, different somehow." She patted my arm. "But you're still the same Kami Khuzud I've always loved. You know, we have a window only to our own heart, if that."

I chuckled, more out of tension than anything else.

"What is so funny, Kami Khuzud?"

I slipped an arm around her waist. "You've never doubted for a moment that I love you, Sala."

She was indignant. "Well, of *course* not."

"But you just said that—" I waved it away. "Never mind, Sala." It would be pointless to try to keep Sala's mind on the here and now. Besides, would I want to change her? Really? Or any of the rest? Evrem's sliminess, perhaps. But Large Egda's trustworthiness, or even Fhilt's sarcasm, that revealed as much as concealed his caring?

Not for a moment. You don't change the people you love.

"Better pay attention to the here, Kami Khuzud," Sala said. "To the now."

"True enough." I'd have to lead Toshtai to it, somehow. But how? "Nothing to worry about. All the juggling equipment is over on the other side?"

"Yes, yes, yes," she said, irritated. "And the musicians, as well."

After a snake-quick snatch into his snakebin, Evrem stuck a viper in a bag, and hung the bag from his belt.

"Then I am off," he said, unaffected.

Fhilt was eying me curiously. "There's something different about you today, at that. Can you still keep two wands in the air?"

"Don't you worry about me. I'll do my part. Just let me get into the room across the way."

I'd find the evidence, and set it in front of Lord Toshtai in a way that he could choose to act on or ignore, and then . . .

And then I didn't know what. But with a bit of luck, I would be out of Den Oroshtai, and back on the road again, where an acrobat belonged.

Gray Khuzud stood. "Then we begin."

The act began plainly, with Gray Khuzud and Large Egda on the ground below, introducing first Evrem, and then Sala. Gray Khuzud picked up a theme from the drunk act: he did tumbling runs almost through their performances, seemingly not noticing Evrem's snakes or Sala's rings, but barely missing them as he cartwheeled idly about the sand, then turned the cartwheel into a series of handsprings and a final jump that brought him to Large Egda's shoulders.

Then it was Fhilt's turn to bring the attention up to the wires, and he did, with a brilliant, weaving, barefoot wirewalk that had my fist in my mouth. Fhilt was playing above himself: it looked, time and time again, that he was going to lose his balance and fall, but he always pulled back from the brink of disaster.

Finally, he made it to the center of the wire, and reached up to where the rope and pulley hung from the rigging. Below, Gray Khuzud seized the other end of the rope, just as Fhilt stepped off,

Fhilt's greater mass and downward motion neatly pulling Gray Khuzud up to the wire while depositing Fhilt safely on the ground below.

Gray Khuzud quickly made his way from the middle of the wire to my end, and stepped out into the room.

He pulled a pair of thick leather gloves from his belt and donned them. "Ready?"

I nodded, and stepped up to the window.

I hate wirewalking, but I'd spent enough years learning it.

This time, I guess I stopped worrying about how bad I was at it, and just did it: slowly, working a trio of juggling sticks, I made my way across the wire.

Behind me, Gray Khuzud had again stepped out on the wire—I could feel it, but I was supposed to not notice it—and walked quickly toward me, as though he wanted to pass me. But I, the buffoon of this act, didn't notice him, as he kept catching up with me, and then standing, his arms irritatedly crossed over his chest, waiting for me to hurry up.

And then I stopped in the middle of the wire, simply juggling as though there was nothing else of interest in the world.

Below, the crowd laughed, perhaps a bit nervously; across, through the open window, I could see Lord Toshtai, sitting on a massive chair.

Finally, unable to get my attention, Gray Khuzud shrugged, squatted and lowered himself to the wire, and then began to make his way, hand over hand, beneath the wire, while I continued at my same pace.

It looked practiced, but it wasn't—it all depended on Gray Khuzud raising kazuh enough to keep his hands out of the way of my feet.

He passed underneath me to loud applause and shouts of approval, and then pulled himself up and into the far window, me coming in behind.

With a bow in the direction of the two lords, I tossed the juggling wands to Josei, and moved away, toward the window at the far end of the large room, the one above the armory's window. All I had to do was find evidence, of something—scratches from a rope over the windowsill, or over the beam.

There was nothing.

The sill was polished and pristine; the beam above was flush with the ceiling overhead. There was no hole in it where a support for a pulley could have been stuck or screwed.

Nothing.

One by one, the others of the troupe made their way up into the third-floor room for the juggling finale. The musicians picked up the pace, the silverhorns laughed mockingly at me.

Everything was wrong. Not only hadn't there been any evidence that somebody had been lowered from this room or raised to it, but my inspection of the window hadn't drawn any attention, as it easily could have even if all of them were innocent, and as it surely would have if the guilty one were there.

Nobody cared what I was doing, because nobody felt endangered by what I was doing.

I was trying to sort it out when I felt Gray Khuzud raise kazuh.

His talent flared brightly in my mind, but I didn't need to have that feel for kazuh: all I needed was a pair of eyes. He was working with three juggling knives, heading toward the finale, and his juggling had suddenly become keener, clearer, each of his moves as sharp as the edges of one of the knives.

It burned as brightly as I ever had seen. That was the answer, of course: kazuh. It had always been the answer.

Fhilt's face creased in puzzlement. "What's going on, Kami Khuzud?" he whispered. "This isn't—"

"Fhilt," I said, knowing that he was my brother of the spirit, even though we were of different kinds, "by all that you love me, juggle."

I didn't have to turn to Sala; she was smiling as she picked up the rings she had put away, and flung half a dozen into the air, reaching up and pulling them into a complex shower.

The silverhorns roared, and the bassskin rasped.

Toshtai's brow furrowed microscopically for a moment; he'd felt the kazuh tugging at his own.

As I had at mine, at whatever it was. It wasn't the kazuh of the acrobat.

It was something else, I knew. *I* was something else, I knew, as I stood there juggling, my own kazuh flaring bright in my mind.

And then brighter, as the musicians caught fire; as it had before, their kazuh all flared at once: the cry of the silverhorns solidified in the air, becoming a glass snake that writhed and coiled in my ears and mind. The rapid notes of the chimer were a peppery rain, supported by the deep red rumble of the bassskin, the fast-picked zivver and pounding drum weaving golden notes into a net that supported the whole structure.

Off in the distance, old Dun Lidjun's nostrils flared, and while the old warrior didn't move, I could feel that he too had raised kazuh, involuntarily, unwillingly, as the spark passed to him.

I picked up my own juggling wands and tossed them into a simple shower, my eyes closed. I am a good juggler, although not a kazuh one, never a kazuh juggler, but a something else.

In my mind, the flare of kazuh marked all of those who could practice zuhrir, all those who could raise kazuh, far further than my fleshy eyes could ever have seen:

A cook stood in his kitchen slicing onions, his kazuh flaring, his slicing knife beating out an impossibly rapid staccato against the oak cutting board, he never for a moment slowing in his banter.

A dozen warriors' talents flashed into motionlessness, not blurring motion, their hands not nearing their blades, because a true warrior didn't have to wave his sword around to raise kazuh.

Somewhere in the village, a painter, his brush wet with ink, his mind filled with sky and grass and bird, and his soul now illuminated with his kazuh, set brush to paper with swift, sure strokes. A runner, dispatches bound to his skinny thighs, rose from his now-unnecessary meditations and blurred into movement, his kazuh cleaving him through the thick nectar that the air had become. A peasant stopped staggering through the paddies behind the plow; he steadied it with simple graceful movements as he became one with the ox and the plow and the earth.

Others, more distant and indistinct, burned brightly in my brain.

They and I shared something; I could feel more than see another kazuh flare into brightness, as well.

My own.

I could see it all now, all clear in my mind. There was no secret to be discovered. It was simple, logical, and it had always been in front of me, waiting for me to see.

Written in stone, and sand, and kazuh.

In mine, and in the killer's.

We had the crowd there, we *owned* the crowd as Fhilt, his kazuh fully upon him, began to exchange wands with me. We began to add the phantom wands, as we had before: instead of picking up my fourth wand, I pretended to, and substituted the phantom wand, and then another, and another, as Fhilt and I juggled wands real and phantom between us.

The wands flew through the air, slapping into moving palms, as we moved through crisp throws and precise catches.

All eyes were on us, and both Toshtai's and Felkoi's were glowing as I tossed a real wand to Sala and a phantom one to Gray Khuzud, and what the four of us were doing became a free-form weave of phantom juggling wands and real ones, Sala's bright brassy rings and Gray Khuzud's sharp knives all passing among and between us.

Anyone could see in Sala's and Fhilt's and Gray Khuzud's faces that they had raised kazuh, as we all had, and anybody could have heard the musicians catch the fire as the wail of the silverhorns cut through the room, followed momentarily by a firm, imposing run on the zivver, a raindrop spatter of sound from the drums, a heartbreakingly precise arpeggio all up and down the chimes, and a deep thrum of pleasure and power from the bassskin.

It was all a matter of kazuh, after all.

Imagine, if you would, that you were meant to be a warrior, but that you had been born wrongly, as a peasant. It was only right that you would, someday, be driven to prove that, even though you knew that picking up the challenge sword endangered your life. What did life matter next to your kazuh?

Or me. Imagine that you were meant to be, ought to be, needed to be something that did not yet have a name, but were trapped in the life of an acrobat, knowing that no matter how good you became, you were misplaced.

Start over again.

Now, imagine that you knew, deep within you, that you really were an acrobat, that if you had only been born within the right womb, you would have spent your days with the juggling wands and the ropes, and the trapeze and highwire, moving through beauty, creating joy and laughter in motion.

Imagine that you knew, deep within you, that you were a brother of spirit to the likes of Enki Duzun, a talented acrobat, one destined perhaps for the greatness of her father.

Imagine, again, that you had finally allowed yourself to know that there was somebody who had murdered that acrobat, that particularly promising acrobat.

It wasn't a tribal loyalty, it wasn't a personal matter—imagine that you knew that somebody had murdered not just the *person* of Enki Duzun, but all of the juggling and highwire and tumbling and beauty that she would have created.

Could anything be more foul?

Could you stand the stench of that in your nostrils?

And imagine that you found yourself standing outside your brother's armory in the rain, having fought with him, having argued with him, perhaps having gotten him to admit to you that he had tried to kill that useless acrobat, Kami Khuzud, only to murder his sister.

Feel yourself looking up at the window into his shop as the rain spattered down upon you, as the lightning flashed and the thunder roared.

Your anger would have grown, Felkoi, as you stood there, and then climbed up and into the tree, your fury at the desecration of that murder growing and flaring.

A warrior couldn't have walked across the branch, but a kazuh acrobat would take the first step, the body's inertia resisting the motion as you pushed hard with calf and thigh, your balance on the slippery branch impeccable as you moved into the second step, your arms out to the side as lightning and thunder flashed and crashed all around the castle, your arms out to your side for balance, your speed increasing, the step becoming a bound, the bound becoming a spring, and your kazuh flaring into fury as you flung yourself outward through the window, into a flat somersault over the sill and into the room.

And then you seized a sword and killed the slime that had foully murdered one who was my sister; one who was, soul to soul, your sister as well.

I had touched on a truth as we buried Enki Duzun, Felkoi: we can't do what we want to, but we do what we can.

As you had, Felkoi.

Nothing you could have done would have touched on the core of the matter, that Enki Duzun lay cold and dead in the ground, but you would do what you could, and you would do that with all the force of body and of will at your command.

And then, as you stood over the bloody body, a sword in your hand, you lost it. The anger, not the kazuh. Its fire had long been lit within you. But the anger had turned to fear, and you wouldn't overcome that fear to admit to a crime when the suspect was clumsy Kami Khuzud, who would never be a kazuh acrobat. You might have traded your life for that of an Enki Duzun, or a Gray Khuzud, for a Fhilt or a Sala, but never for Kami Khuzud.

I looked over at Felkoi.

His tensed shoulders slumped in resignation. He knew that I knew, and he didn't have the strength of will to deny it.

Just a few moments of life left, eh, Felkoi?
Idiot.

No. Felkoi was, in his heart, in his soul, a kazuh acrobat, and not what I was, what I always had been: something that did not have a name, not yet. Somebody whose kazuh it was to see the last piece, the missing piece of a puzzle, to fit it all together neatly in a box.

Let me show you the rest of the puzzle, Felkoi, I thought. Let the last of the pieces fall neatly, elegantly, exquisitely into place.

Out of the jumble of flying wands, real and phantom, rings and knives, I reached in and grabbed a knife, and sent it tumbling through the air toward wide-eyed Felkoi.

There was a relaxed smile on his face as he did what only a kazuh acrobat could have done: he reached out into the air and threw it back.

I could see awareness dawn on Fhilt's face first, and then Sala's and finally Gray Khuzud's, as they included him in the juggling. Knives flickered through the air in a freestyle pattern that only years of training and complete concentration could let me follow.

But Felkoi was beautiful, his movements unpracticed, but precise, relaxed. He was *there*, kazuh taking him to a grace and ease to which work and skill could never have propelled me.

It was beautiful.

Somehow I stepped back out of the juggling, and let my hands drop down to my side, and watched them until Lord Toshtai caught my eye.

A knowing smile barely moving across his broad face, a flipper of a hand beckoned to me, his eyes never leaving the flashing knives and rings, the real and phantom wands.

All the pieces of the puzzle were in place, spread out before anyone with eyes to see. Toshtai smiled at me as he beckoned to me, the same way he had smiled when I had assembled the squares in the box.

"It is a pity that the murder will never be solved, isn't it?" he asked, his eyes glowing, never leaving the flashing knives. "And that poor Felkoi, have disgraced himself as a warrior, will have to be stripped of his nobility and banished. Felkoi Khuzud will leave with the troupe tomorrow."

"Never to return, Lord?" Sharp-eyed Lord Orazhi asked with a smile that said he, too, knew the answer. You can't be a competent ruler and not have some feel for this sort of puzzle.

"Oh, perhaps," Lord Toshtai said, as though considering the matter idly, "perhaps never to return without a troupe about him, eh?"

Typical D'Shaian hypocrisy. He wouldn't have hesitated a moment to have had clumsy Kami Khuzud executed for murder, but it was so much simpler to turn his face from the truth than it would be to forgo the annual visit of a kazuh acrobat such as Felkoi the Acrobat, Felkoi Khuzud.

Lord Orazhi chuckled. "A great pity," he said, pouring a flask of Crimson Tears, and handing it to me with a slight, perhaps mocking bow of the head. "Don't you think so, Eldest Son, err, Who Isn't An Acrobat?"

"A great pity, Lord," I said. I curled my fingers about the flask, warming them.

"Felkoi Khuzud will be leaving with the troupe tomorrow," Toshtai said, again. "It would please me, perhaps more than a little," he said, his voice taking on a formal lilt, "if you would remain behind, Discoverer-of-Truths." His livery lips pursed for a moment. "I will have use for one such as you."

There was only one answer. "I am at your service, Lord. Perhaps as *Eldest Son* Discoverer-of-Truths."

Whatever I am, Lord Toshtai, I am still son of Gray Khuzud, brother to Enki Duzun, and I will not forget that.

"Kami Daniray Shiragen? Hmm . . ." He thought it over for a long moment. "That is too long: Kami Dan'Shir," he said. The fat man gestured at my flask. "Drink, Kami Dan'Shir."

18
Many Farewells

THE WHILE BEFORE bedtime was our time, it was in some ways a quiet time as we all sat on Madame Rupon's porch, looking out at the town, and at the flickering lights in the castle above the town, and at the stars above.

All of us: the Eresthais, Large Egda, Fhilt, Sala, Evrem, Gray Khuzud, and even Felkoi.

A last time, for me. A time of little talk, if not as quiet as usual. The musicians were practicing loud and hard tonight; I could hear and feel the lead silverhorn player slip in and out of kazuh. We sat alone, under the flickering lanterns.

High above, the stars watched us, cold and uncaring.

Evrem was the first to leave; he gave a quick nod of goodbye, then headed off to have a few moments alone with his snakes before bedtime.

"There's a last time for everything," Sala said.

"You'll take care of yourself?" She stretched and yawned.

I nodded. Actually, I was expecting NaRee to do much of the taking care. A Dan'Shir clearly wasn't a peasant; I was going to be at least a middle-class, most likely a bourgeois, possibly even a noble. Let Ezren Smith close his door to Lord Kami Dan'Shir. Once.

"Better go to bed, Sala," I said. "You've got to be on the road tomorrow."

She kissed me on the cheek, and then left.

Fhilt snickered. "I don't know why we're getting all soft and sniffy about it. We'll see you next time the troupe is here, eh?" He gripped my hand for a moment, then turned to leave.

"I don't understand," Large Egda rumbled. "If you don't know why, Fhilt," he asked, as he rose to accompany Fhilt, "then why are tears running down your face?"

"Egda, you *are* an idiot," Fhilt said, as the two of them walked away.

I clasped hands briefly with Eno and with Josei, then turned to Felkoi.

He opened his mouth, then closed it, then shrugged and turned away. I sympathized. We really didn't have anything to say to each other.

Gray Khuzud and I were left alone. I thought that we'd talk, if it had turned out that way, but there was nothing to say.

Finally, I rose. "I'd better go, Father. There's somebody I have to see."

He was silent for a long time.

"Be well, my son," Gray Khuzud said. My father was never much for wasted words.

Gray Khuzud gripped my shoulder for a moment, and then he was gone.

INTERLUDE

Way of the Ruler

THE GREAT HALL was empty, as it always was when the hour of the bear gave way to the lion.

Lord Toshtai sat alone, the room lit, to the extent it was lit, only by a single flickering candle.

He was tired, and he had overeaten yet again, and had swallowed too much of that deceptively smooth Crimson Tears; it had his head swimming. He really ought to keep better control of his appetite. That was his one unconsidered indulgence. Everything else he did, was—had to be—calculated cautiously, each decision weighed with care.

He knew that he really ought to be getting to bed, but these moments at the end of the day were precious to him, too dear to abandon, to toss away into the Great Nothing.

An apple lay on the table at his elbow. Unblemished and red, polished to a high gloss, its crispy sweetness waiting for him.

Well, nobody was watching; he drew his miniature dress sword—more of a knife, really—and quartered it.

It had been a useful day, all things considered, Toshtai decided, as he picked up the first quarter of the apple. He cut out the sliver of core and slipped the quarter into his mouth.

Orazhi had been impressed, once again, with Toshtai's insight, and that boded well for their delicate alliance, and perhaps for the future of Arefai and all of Den Oroshtai as well. The loss of Felkoi as a warrior and armorer left Den Oroshtai weaker by an almost infinitesimal trifle, but that was well outweighed by the gain in the strength of the alliance.

Everything must balance, after all.

He ate the next quarter quite quickly.

Best of all, it seemed that Kami Khuzud—no, Kami Dan'Shir—had discovered a new form of kazuh. That was a rarity.

Hmmm . . . would it breed true? Could others be trained in it?

Toshtai would have to find out, although that might be tricky. It was not the simple matter it was with a stud horse. Humans were much harder creatures to master. He could ask Narantir; but no, he wouldn't be able to trust the answer. Wizards were suspicious of anything they didn't control, and they clearly didn't control zuhrir, and kazuh.

He balanced his knife in the palm of his hand.

The balances would be difficult for that. Best to let things proceed at their own pace.

But, in the interim, it would be pleasant to have someone about who could solve puzzles even better than Toshtai himself could.

That was a rare treat, indeed. A great treat, but a deserved treat, also indeed.

He cored another quarter, and ate it slowly. A small puzzle: What was the ranking of a Dan'Shir? The simple solution would be to make the boy a noble. Lord Kami Dan'Shir, carrying a sword—perhaps trained in the sword by Dun Lidjun himself—would not have to worry about losing his head for an idle comment. More importantly, Toshtai would not have to worry about losing his Dan'Shir. Hmmm . . .

No, he didn't like the feel of that. That would make everything too easy in some ways, too difficult in others.

Arguably, a Dan'Shir could be a bourgeois position, instead of a middle-class one. That would be best, all things considered, all balances taken into account.

Yes. Kami Dan'Shir would be a bourgeois. That could work out nicely.

Perhaps that could be changed, later, if convenient, but there was no need to rush into making the boy a noble. He could spread his seed far enough, wide enough, without that, and for now, a burgeoning friendship with Arefai would provide enough protection. Toshtai could weave another web of protection about Kami Dan'Shir later, if necessary.

Lord Toshtai tossed the last quarter into his mouth, carefully cleaning his knife on his tunic before putting it back in its sheath.

Besides, if Toshtai did want to make Kami Dan'Shir a noble, that would be best done at a time when the boy would be happy. Being raised to nobility should be a pristinely pleasant occasion. That didn't describe Kami Dan'Shir's immediate future.

Poor Kami Dan'Shir was going to be unhappy for the first while. He didn't see what was coming, how things would balance out. Kami Dan'Shir was only a discoverer of truth, and would miss some of the symmetries that Toshtai couldn't help but see.

Because an eye for symmetry was merely a form of balance. And balance, of course . . .

Toshtai sat in the great hall, laughing, long and hard.

19
One Last Farewell

THE LAST WORDS NaRee said to me, as we sat in her father's garden under the uncaring, unblinking stars, were, of course:

"But you know that I need to see the world, Kami Khuzud, or Kami Dan'Shir, or whoever you are. And you are staying here.

"Which is why I'm leaving with Felkoi."

STEVEN BRUST ===============

__JHEREG 0-441-38554-0/$3.95

There are many ways for a young man with quick wits and a quick
sword to advance in the world. Vlad Taltos chose the route of the
assassin and the constant companionship of a young jhereg.

__YENDI   0-441-94460-4/$3.50

Vlad Taltos and his jhereg companion learn how the love of a good
woman can turn a cold-blooded killer into a _real_ mean S.O.B...

__TECKLA   0-441-79977-9/$3.50

The Teckla were revolting. Vlad Taltos always knew they were lazy,
stupid, cowardly peasants...revolting. But now they were revolting
against the empire. No joke.

__TALTOS 0-441-18200/$3.50

Journey to the land of the dead. All expenses paid! Not Vlad Taltos'
idea of an ideal vacation, but this was work. After all, even an
assassin has to earn a living.

__COWBOY FENG'S SPACE BAR AND GRILLE
0-441-11816-X/$3.95

Cowboy Feng's is a great place to visit, but it tends to move around
a bit—from Earth to the Moon to Mars to another solar system—
and always just one step ahead of whatever mysterious conspiracy is
reducing whole worlds to radioactive ash.